GRAVE IS THE DAY

Michael Drakich

Copyright © Michael Drakich
ISBN-13: 9780987770615
Amazon Edition

Cover Jennifer Brooks
Editor Kate Richards

CHAPTER 1

"Startling, isn't it." Leaning over his officer's shoulder, Commander Kraanox stared mesmerized at the console, viewing the intercepted high frequency analog transmissions. The people of this planet referred to it as 'television'.

His communications officer looked up. "What, Commander?"

"The similarity. All this time we've been orbiting in space, the question has plagued me so. The people of this world are roughly the same as those of our home world, Traanu. A little larger, and with hair all over their bodies and a most noticeable thick mass coated on top of their heads, but other than that, at a quick glance they could pass as related. Two arms, two legs, upright posture, ten fingers and ten toes—though they lack the second opposable thumb on each hand we enjoy."

His officer laughed and held his hands up, flexing his second thumbs into a finger position. "It must be hard for them to properly grip things.

"Perhaps, but the variance is minimal. Facially, they're almost identical—more prominent noses, and ears that stick out from their heads, but everything in the right place." He ran his hand over his right ear to push it forward in mock representation. "When the high frequency electromagnetic waves led us here, we knew we would find intelligent life, but I bore little expectation they would appear so similar to us. Nature must have a standard plan when evolving intelligent life."

The officer grimaced. "Still, there are many differences. Outside of the fact these creatures are mammalian versus the amphibian of our people, there appears to be a huge cultural difference as well. Although areas of the planet are predominated by certain types of humans, they seem willing to intermix. And, most shockingly, interbreed. Such integration of societies is unheard of back home, and interbreeding, heresy!"

Kraanox clapped a hand down on the officer's shoulder. "Yes, but they are a lot alike, these people. Aggressive, yes, combative even, as attested to by the current wars they are engaged in across the globe. The world appears dominated by what seems like a large multitude of different countries and religions, each vying for more than they have. Two of these countries seem to dictate the politics of this world, with different philosophies on government. What are they again?"

"Communism and democracy, sir."

"Yes, that's them. Personally, I can see little difference. In each case, power rests in the control of a select few, no different than the governments of Traanu, back home. Our ideologies are not as fractured, there being only eight different countries and the same number of religions and people."

Commander Kraanox pondered these things as he roamed the bridge of his ship, the Flower, visiting with his officers. Not as roomy as some of the others in the fleet, with barely enough room for him to pass between the different stations. But this was his first command. He took pride in each and every part of it, from the polished obsidian floors, to the illuminated ceiling with light to match that of his home world sun. And each crew member, despite his presence, was diligent in their duties; from navigation to tactical, communications to science.

The main focus of his mission from his homeland of Braannoo involved the search for alien technology. And, after all this time in space circling this planet, he found the people of this world lacked the necessary scientific advancements to help his people, with only one exception.

He grew angry as he stood there, considering the first alien civilization they discovered. Yes, their journeys indeed found life elsewhere, but no intelligence. The goal here should be one of first contact. But orders were orders. The war at home continued to go badly, and money could not be spared for purely scientific missions. Nowadays, everything required a military application or it received no funding.

The only discoveries suited to their needs were the atomic weapons these aliens possessed. But the technology to build such devices was useless, since Traanu was all but devoid of the metals uranium and plutonium.

Nevertheless, they worked tirelessly to obtain the knowledge. In his heart, he knew himself a patriot, and with military training as well, but the scientist in him wanted to discover, to explore, and to delve into the unknown. Sneaking to the surface in an effort to purloin technology ran contrary to his mindset. Why not just set down in the middle of all those people and openly trade with them?

Besides, with nothing of real value militarily, perhaps it might be right to break with protocol. The number of times they'd been spotted in their late-night sorties showed reason enough to admit they existed to these people. He chuckled to himself at the antics some of the locals went through upon seeing his ship cruise through their area.

Yes, these people had much to offer in the way of trade, metal for one. Only recently did Traanusians bore deeply enough into their planet to recover reasonable quantities of the stuff. The cost of mining proved to be so high the value made using it in day-to-day life unrealistic. Unlike the people below, where every day common items were made from products like steel or nickel and discarded easily.

Commander Kraanox sighed. As much as his heart told him what to do, the reasoned objectivity of his mission took precedence. If he made first contact, he would be in breach of orders and face a court martial back home. The mines in the penal system were not the kind of retirement he planned for. Though, given his family heritage, such a penalty would be unlikely for him. More likely, he would lose his post and be consigned to a desk in the royal offices.

He made his way to the captain's chair, elevated in the center of the bridge. It allowed him to rotate and see each station with ease. Microgravity gave the impression of more hopping than walking, but as their tenure in orbit approached three months, he proved an old hand at it. He took comfort in the daily regimen that kept him fit. It allowed him the ease of mobility where his actions bespoke of fluidity versus awkwardness. When he took his station, his helmsman, the first officer, acknowledged his presence with a nod.

He acknowledged the nod with one of his own. "Anything to report?"

The first officer turned to face him. The man was a standard example of his people. Deep blue eyes set in a clear, almond-toned face. Smooth skinned, with no markings. His ears lay very flat against the sides of his head. His nose also lay very flat across his face. His eyebrows featured darker-toned ridges of skin stretched across a slight protrusion in the bone structure of his skull. They were designed to channel water away from eyes that, every now and then, would blink an inner set of transparent eyelids, maintaining the level of moisture his eyes required. "Nothing we haven't heard before, Commander. Those coded transmissions offer little for us to learn."

Raising his hand to scratch at the side of his head, he applied pressure from both thumbs in a gentle massaging of his scalp. Stretching his other hand across his jaw in musing, he allowed the webbing between his fingers to pull against his chin as he contemplated the mission to date. A decision needed to be made—whether to remain here or set out for home. "It's time to wrap up this mission everyone. Complete whatever you're working on. When I get a status that all reports are in, I am going to take the Flower home."

Feeling melancholy, he set off for the shower unit. His skin felt dry, and he needed to moisturize—the heavens knew he missed a good swim. Working his way through the narrow corridors of the ship, he found himself among the crew's quarters when the sirens began. *"Alert! Alert! Commander Kraanox to the bridge!"*

Turning around, he made his way as quickly as possible back to the bridge. With a few precision micro-gravity leaps, he covered the distance in less than half the time it would normally take to pull himself forward. "What's happening?"

His tactical officer spun in his chair to face him. "Commander, another ship just entered orbit. We picked up its signature and scanned it. We aren't positive, but we believe it to be a Muurgu ship! And it is twice our size and heavily armored. How did they find us?"

Kraanox leaned over the console to examine the readouts for himself. There could be no doubt. The configuration exactly matched reports of Muurgu spacecraft. This cruiser class attack ship would make short work of the Flower, his own frigate. "Heaven's curse! Of all things to encounter, a spaceship from the very country we're currently at war with. Quick, plot an immediate withdrawal from here. Let's get going home before they spot us."

The helmsman pointed to the tactical display on his screen. "I don't think that's possible, Commander. They appear headed straight for us, and with their current speed we will never be able to accelerate quickly enough to elude them."

Kraanox examined the trajectory plotting on the monitor showing the route planned. With the acceleration factored in by the helmsman, he knew it would not be quick enough to escape the incoming enemy ship. He recognized there could be no option left but to fight. His ship was poorly armored, with limited fighting capability. There would be no contest.

Commander Kraanox stood as tall as he could and faced his staff. Bravado was what was needed. "Break out the weapons, everyone. I doubt they intend to board us, but if they do, we'll give them a taste of Braannoo courage."

The men began to hustle around in preparation for the coming battle. The crewmembers donned space suits in case the ship lost compression. It all seemed so meaningless. Should they survive this battle but their ship be breached, they would die anyway.

He did not believe in coincidence. Someone back home was a traitor, and he did not believe he would live to find out whom.

CHAPTER 2

Seven-year-old Justin Spencer knew it was way past his bedtime. After he went to bed and his parents gone downstairs, he climbed out on the roof of the porch that stood immediately below his bedroom window. Staring up at the night sky, Justin scanned the heavens. He remembered how his teacher at school told the class the Russians launched a satellite called Sputnik, and you could see it when it passed overhead. The other kids were saying the Russians were spying on them, but Justin didn't care. Let the Russians look. He didn't have anything to hide, and he *was* wearing his pajamas.

They couldn't see through those, could they?

He just wanted to see the satellite when it passed by.

Downstairs, his parents were watching President Eisenhower on television, talking about the Sputnik satellite. The windows were open and Justin could hear bits and pieces as he stared at the sky.

"...no additional threat to the United States...from what the Soviets say, they have put one small ball in the air...no one ever suggested to me . . . a race except, of course, more than once we would say, well, there is going to be a great psychological advantage in world politics to putting the thing up, but . . . in view of the real scientific character of our development, there didn't seem to be a reason for just trying to grow hysterical about it...to the limit of my ability . . . and that is all I can do."

He heard his father ranting about the President being incompetent and a few other things he didn't understand.

Having brought his pillow with him, Justin settled down to lie on his back, looking up. The clear night sky filled his vision, not a cloud in sight. The moon shone brilliantly and the stars glittered like so many Christmas tree lights. It appeared to be a perfect night to spot the Sputnik satellite when it passed overhead. Folding his arms behind his head, he settled himself to wait.

Justin strained his eyes. Maybe he just needed to look a little harder. Almost two hours passed, and Justin began to nod. "Gee, maybe I better get back in bed."

As he rose, he gave one last quick, sweeping gaze across the heavens, and noticed a red flicker in the sky.

Justin stopped to rub his eyes. Looking again, he momentarily lost where he'd marked the spot in the sky, and panicked.

Where was it? There!

The red glimmer caught his eye again. He watched intently as it seemed to swell and change to a teardrop. It appeared to be headed directly toward him as it grew in size.

The Sputnik was on fire and about to crash into his house!

Mesmerized, he couldn't move as he watched the red tear flame its way down. But rather than hit his house, it fell into the woods a short distance away, just past the city limits. He jumped at the loud boom it made as it crashed. Forgetting he was supposed to be in bed, he scrambled back into the house and raced down to the living room, where his parents were still arguing. With the television blaring in the background and voices raised, Justin figured they didn't hear the noise. "Mom! Dad! Ya gotta come see! The Sputnik just went down in the woods outside of town!"

Justin raced up to his parents and tugged at their hands. "Come on, come on! Ya gotta see it now, while it's still burning!"

His parents stood and followed, although it seemed he needed to tug really hard. His father was complaining about the disturbance, but Justin wasn't really listening. They all stepped out onto the porch, and he pointed in the direction of the forest. Their home was the closest one to it, so no other homes blocked their line of sight. "Over there! It fell over there! I saw it fall, right into the forest. It was all on fire!"

The three of them peered into the night, but there was no fire burning, nothing at all appeared visible, save the outline of the woods in the dark. His father bent down to turn him around and look him straight in the eyes. "Justin, what are you doing up? You must have been dreaming, boy. You probably heard your mother and me talking about the Sputnik when we were in the living room. You need to get back in bed, young man."

Justin twisted in his father's grip. "No, Dad! I saw it. I did! I was out on the veranda roof, looking for it in the sky, and I saw it fall!"

His father stood up. "And what, pray tell, were you doing out on the veranda roof when you were supposed to be in bed?"

Justin realized his secret was out. He kept his voice quieter as he stared down at the floor. "The kids at school told me that the Sputnik would fly overhead, and I wanted to see it, that's all."

His mother knelt down to pick him up. "Justin, you know that you are not supposed to climb out on that roof, and in your pajamas, no less! You could have fallen and killed yourself. Then what would you do!" She fussed about to see if there were any rips or stains. "What probably happened was you fell asleep out there and dreamed it. Now let's get my little man back to bed."

Justin put a pout on his small face. "But I did see it, Mom, I did."

Smiling now, his mom continued on into the house and up the stairs. "Yes honey, I believe you think you did. Now let's get you to bed and no more talk tonight of Sputniks."

His mother gently laid him on his bed and pulled the covers up over him. She bent down and kissed him on the forehead. "Now, go to sleep, and be a good little dear."

Justin gave one last protest and finally resigned himself to his fate. As his parents left the room, he said quietly, one last time, "I did see it," then snuggled down into his pillow.

CHAPTER 3

Managing to pull himself up to a tree, Commander Kraanox examined his bleeding. All the cuts were superficial, but there could be no doubt, there were other injuries his eyes could not detect. His insides hurt tremendously, probably from a cracked rib or two. He only hoped none of his internal organs suffered any serious damage.

Scant yards away, the wreckage of his ship lay steaming in a mangled heap. The plummet through the atmosphere had super-heated the exterior, and he could still feel the heat radiating from it. At rest, it was cooling quickly. Landing in a forest pond helped. How he managed to survive, he still did not know. A stroke of luck, he guessed.

After blowing a hole through his ship, the attackers attempted to board the Flower. Once they managed to attach their trans-variant outer space bridge to his ship, Kraanox played his last card. Though his interstellar drive was disabled, he still retained his positioning thrusters, and fired his engines to kick the Flower into a death spiral toward the planet, dragging the enemy ship with him. Unfortunately, the ploy failed, the Muurgu were able to disengage, and Kraanox descended with a severely damaged ship.

Taking the controls, he angled the craft back and forth to prevent as much drag on the ship as possible since the hole punched by the enemy ship compromised the integrity of the hull. He couldn't prevent the onrushing air at the steep angle from trying to shake the ship apart. The intense atmospheric friction engulfed the ship in flames, the surrounding gases igniting upon contact. Blinded, and with little control available, he held on, belted to his chair, as the ship plummeted to its doom.

11

The hull breach saved him in the end. Spiraling, the onrushing air caught at the damage and ripped the ship in half only moments before impact. As if on a hinge, the forward cabin flapped backward and bounced off the tail of the vessel. The bounce took tremendous velocity off the cabin, and sensing a chance, he fired all the steering jets, and those that yet remained were enough to redirect him into a somewhat horizontal trajectory with the ground. It was sheer chance he didn't follow the rest of the ship as it smashed into the ground below. The cabin careened through dense vegetation that further slowed the ship's speed. For over a quarter mile, branches banged away at the hull, until at last, what remained of the ship, hit a massive tree, somersaulted in the air, and landed hard in the pond.

The decision to don space suits made a big difference. Giving them the ability to breathe through the descent, they withstood the superheating as well, and, as a last measure, provided some protection on final impact. Regardless of this, Kraanox suffered from severe injuries, including the possibility of some broken bones. Three other crewmates survived, though none in any better shape than him, and one remained unconscious.

The first order of business is always survival. Yes, the Flower is gone, we are marooned on a distant world, and we are without food, water or shelter. But we have our lives. Something the Muurgu did their best to deprive us of.

The initial effects of the crash wore off, and Kraanox began to regain his equilibrium. Sadly, the hurts upon his body became more acutely evident as he made an attempt to stand up straight. A moment of nausea passed, and his vision cleared. He stood in a thicket of trees, small and coarse compared to those of his home planet, but shelter nevertheless, for now anyway. Doing a quick perimeter search, he noted the forest spread in all directions, but appeared to thin quickly to his right. From beyond the edge of the tree line, he could make out lights, indicating civilization.

Once his surviving crew was gathered, he huddled near them. "Stay here until I get back. Don't touch the water in that pond. It appears to be so choked with algae as to be undrinkable. I saw lights some distance away, and I'm guessing there are human homes nearby. Maybe I can get some fresh water there."

He got up and moved through the forest. When he reached the edge, he found his suspicions confirmed as human houses stretched in a line away from him.

Stealing into the yard of the nearest home, he spied a garden hose on the ground. Having seen these in use in the television broadcasts they intercepted, he immediately went to the end to get a drink of water. He held it up, but nothing came out. Disappointed, he followed the hose to where it connected to the dwelling. There, a spigot protruded from the wall. He turned the spigot until water emerged from the end of the hose. After taking a drink, he doused himself with water then looked about the yard. He needed to find a receptacle to carry water back to his shipmates. He came across a square of sand surrounded by a wooden framework. Lying about in the sand were plastic pails of various sizes. Finding the largest two, he filled them with water and set off back to the woods to rejoin his crew.

Kraanox entered the woods in what he believed to be the proper bearing, but he became momentarily disoriented because lights were visible in that direction. Proceeding with caution, he neared the crash site and observed much activity through the trees.

Humans.

They were walking all about, holding flashlights. One set up some type of generator and illuminated a much larger area. By its light, he could see his fellow Traanusians being carried away on stretchers, their hands bound.

13

Human voices were barking away at each other as they scoured through the remains of his ship.

Kraanox did not know the language, but he recognized a certain word from the intercepted transmissions. "Troops." It was obvious these were military personnel who worked for the government, and his first intuition told him to avoid capture. Staying in the darkness of the woods, he watched as the men went back and forth. More soldiers arrived, bringing some heavy equipment as well. They packed up the remains of the spaceship and hauled it away, perhaps to be studied elsewhere. Kraanox smiled inwardly. The humans would find little; the engine now totally obliterated, and the onboard computers, with their crystalline memory cores, would never have survived the crash. Nothing would remain except for wires and scraps.

He watched for a very long time, all the while contemplating what he should do next. He could not stay there forever, but no other idea formed on what else to do. Surrender always remained an option, but seeing his comrades in shackles, despite the severity of their wounds, made him doubt whether his captors would be lenient. But choices needed to be made. There appeared a hint of morning coming, and the exclusivity of his position now endangered. His daytime eyelids flicked closed, and he knew it time to go.

Commander Kraanox could hardly move. After the trauma of the crash and having crouched for so long, he could feel his muscles tightening tremendously. It felt as if they were in knots. He barely cleared the forest when he heard shouting behind him. He needed somewhere to hide.

***

Justin got up early, despite little rest the night before. On any school day, his mother would have to drag

14

him out of bed. But it was Saturday, and that meant no school! It was a day to play, and he raced outside to enjoy the morning. He thought he might go across the street and see if Suzie Derkins wanted to come out and play.

His mother followed him out to hang the laundry. On her way, her foot entangled in a loop of the garden hose and she nearly tripped and fell, which would have spilled all her clean laundry on the ground. "Justin! How many times have I told you not to play with the hose? And look, you left the water running. Wasting water is a bad thing! And my slippers are soaked." She turned to retreat into the house, probably to put on some proper shoes.

Startled by his mother's accusations, Justin felt at first frozen where he stood. As she headed back in, he made a weak protest. "I didn't do it." But she was already behind the screen door and didn't answer. Pouting, he made his way to the sandbox. Dropping heavily into the sand, he puttered for a bit, feeling out of sorts at being blamed for something he didn't do.

After a few moments, he decided to forget about being upset and began to play in earnest. His mother came back out and began to hang the clothes on the line. After several minutes, he realized a couple of his sand pails were missing, including the blue one with the yellow starfish on the side, his favorite. Justin looked around a bit, then finally at his mother. "Have you seen my blue pail?"

Looking exasperated at him for a moment, she continued hanging clothes. "Where did you put it last, Justin? It must be around somewhere."

Rising from the sand, he dusted himself off and began to search all around the yard. His mother finished her chore and went back inside. After a few moments, he gave up his search and returned to the sandbox to play.

***

15

In the forest, the military nearly completed its removal of the remains of the spaceship and were conducting a wider sweep to make sure they didn't miss anything that might have been flung from the craft. First Lieutenant Wayne Bucknell, as commander in charge, liked being thorough, and would leave no stone unturned. While standing next to the last truck about to depart with debris, one of his men yelled from a thicket about fifty yards away, "Lieutenant! You'd better come see this!"

Wayne looked up to locate the direction of the yelling soldier, excusing himself from his current conversation, and headed off into the woods. By the time he made it to the spot, a couple of other men showed up as well. The four men formed a semi-circle around what lay on the ground. By their feet were two plastic pails filled with water; one was blue with a starfish on the side. Deep impressions in the Earth showed where someone must have squatted for some time. Based on the angle, that someone must have been watching him and his men.

Wayne immediately summed up the situation. Another alien must still be on the loose. Looking quickly in all directions, he didn't see anything, but daylight showed the forest ended not far to the west.

Good God, there are houses over there.

Quick action was needed. "You, Private, chase down some dogs to smell out this creature. And you two, gather all the men to the edge of the forest. If he's still there, I want to keep him contained until more troops arrive. Grave is the day to have some Martian wandering down the middle of Main Street!"

The men set off at a run, while he worked his way back to his jeep. He thought about how those boys in Washington were going to want an update, and he wanted to make sure he followed orders on this one.

Damnedest thing, aliens crashing here. There was nothing in any manual for something like this.

16

***

Justin headed into the house to get some juice. His mother gave him a slice of carrot cake, left over from dinner the night before, to have with his drink. "Don't let your father know about this. He'll say I'm spoiling you."

Justin said thanks and headed back out the door. When he returned to the yard, one of his mother's sheets had fallen off the line into his sandbox.

Now I'm going to get it. Mom would never believe I didn't pull it down. Maybe I could hang it back up before she comes out and sees.

He set his juice and carrot cake down and reached to pull the sheet from the sandbox.

***

Kraanox's muscles had seized. Stumbling, he had grasped at the clothesline for support, but only managed a handful of linen, which fell with him. His wounds still unattended, he continued to weaken, until the last of his strength left him. He had crawled into the partial cover of the sandbox and pulled the white linen over himself in an attempt to hide. Footsteps neared. He waited for the soldiers to nab him. There remained nothing else he could do but wait. He needed medical attention, and surrender appeared the only option left.

The sheet moved back and Kraanox saw a small human standing over him. Wide-eyed, the youth stood open-mouthed. Kraanox tried to smile, but only managed to have both sets of eyelids blink in rapid succession at the sudden light. Sitting up, ever so slowly, he once again felt dizzy and nauseous, and he reached his arms out to the side boards of the sandbox to steady himself.

Justin didn't know what to do. He just found a really strange looking man in his sandbox. He appeared to be hurt and was bleeding.

Maybe he's a Russian from the Sputnik! Wait until I tell my friends at school! They will never believe me!

He should be afraid, but the old man looked really sick. His skin was kind of gray and it looked like he was turning green. His mother told him if he ate bad food, he would turn green, but he'd never believed her.

Now he knew it was true. Justin looked at his carrot cake and orange juice. They were healthy foods, and maybe they would make the stranger better. He picked up the plate and glass and leaned forward to offer them to the old man. "Hey mister, you don't look so good. Want me to get my mom?"

Reaching slowly, the man lifted the slice of carrot cake from the plate and took a bite. Justin watched for a reaction. The odd man smiled and drank some of the juice. Then he looked at Justin and said, "Traak doo."

That must be Russian talk!

Justin crouched down to watch the old man eat and drink.

I did a real good deed today. Maybe Mom will give me a special treat.

Standing back up to go get her, he could hear some shouting and footsteps coming from his left. He turned and saw a whole bunch of soldiers running his way. The men raced into his yard and grabbed the old man in the sandbox. Justin grew afraid at what was happening. He must really be a commie! He turned and ran into his house. "Mom! Mom! Ya gotta come quick. The army men just caught a Russian in our backyard!"

His mother breathed out a heavy sigh. "Army men? Russian? What are you saying, Justin?"

Justin reached up to pull at his mother's arm. "Come on, Mom, ya gotta' hurry!"

"All right, Justin, show me the army men and the Russian."

Justin dragged his mother outside, but when they got there, everyone was gone. He looked up at his mother in utter dismay. The only thing she saw was the now dirty white sheet.

She's never going to believe me.

CHAPTER 4

Commander Kraanox awoke in a white room, with very bright lights that kept his inner lids shut. They did not impair his vision. Clear and yet protective, they offered solace from ultraviolet and infrared light, and shielded his eyes when underwater. He was unaware of how long his state of unconsciousness had lasted, but the intensity of his hunger pangs and thirst were a testament to an extended period of time.

He noted his wounds were bandaged, with his mid-torso fully wrapped. Moving was painful. He must have cracked a couple of ribs in the crash. Kraanox strained to turn his head and look around. Even that hurt! Everything in the room flashed brightly white, the lights, the walls, the single door, even the floor tiles. The room contained much strange equipment, and a number of chairs. Seated in the room were a couple of humans. Kraanox surmised they were military personnel, probably there to keep an eye on him. So, he could look forward to life as a prisoner.

He was lying on a bed that angled to elevate his upper body. A reasonably soft pillow cushioned his head, and a sheet pulled up just past his midriff. Like the room, all the linen was white. Kraanox decided to get up out of the bed, but as he attempted to rise, he discovered his ankle was chained to the metal rail at his feet.

The jingle of the chain alerted the two men seated there, who jumped at the noise. They spoke to one another, and one of them promptly left the room. Kraanox smiled weakly at the remaining guard, who hoisted a long, metal tube, probably a weapon of some sort.

Suddenly the door opened and a number of humans entered the room, some in uniform, and others in white clothes. What's with all this white? Back home on Traanu, decor was dominated by bold, loud colors.

The men in uniform just watched, although Kraanox noticed some held their hands to what looked like more weapons at their hips. The others must be doctors, since they held his wrist, looked in his eyes, checked his pulse and generally poked and prodded their way around his body. After a few moments, one of the men in white gave some type of head shake in the direction of the soldiers, and after an exchange of words, they retreated from the bed, and the man wearing the most insignia on his uniform stepped forward.

***

First Lieutenant Wayne Bucknell approached the extraterrestrial with trepidation. Rumors about the alien's abilities were rampant throughout the compound. He did not believe any of them, but regardless, his approach was cautionary. The boys in Washington were on their way. Until then, Lieutenant Bucknell's task involved asking the standard questions—who, what, where, when and why. He began deliberately and slowly, but with few expectations. The others they'd captured showed no signs of understanding. He doubted this one would either.

"Where are you from? How many of you are there? What are your intentions? Why are you here?"

The Martian simply stared back and tilted his head a little in each direction as Wayne asked away.

Wayne held up a map of the solar system and pointed toward the Earth on the picture. "We are here." Making sure the prisoner was following along, Wayne next pointed to Mars. "Is this where you are from?"

At first, the alien stared with a perplexed expression. Then, as if he began to understand, he gestured for Wayne to bring the map closer. The lieutenant placed

21

the map on the bed in front of him. The alien placed a finger on the picture of the sun, then, using his free hand, he pointed to the ceiling. It could only mean one thing. The prisoner came from another star, another solar system than this one. "Well, at least we can quit calling him a Martian."

After several more attempts at questioning, Wayne turned and faced his associates. "I am afraid, gentlemen, that we will get nothing else here today."

Resigned, he was preparing to leave when he heard a noise from behind him. "Fend!"

Turning slowly to once again face the alien, he watched as the alien gestured at his chest and repeated the statement. "Fend!"

A commotion broke out in the room as people suddenly became much more alert and crowded in to hear.

Wayne smiled at the sudden animation of the alien who looked around and repeated, "fend" once more.

Wayne knew instantly that 'fend' was meant to be friend, but was he really? Stories of alien encounters were out there. If this alien was behind those encounters, then why weren't they more forthright? Well, no matter, there was a team of men on route to take charge of things. He was merely to report and maintain security until then. Still, it never hurt to make a new friend rather than an enemy, especially one with such unknown aspects. First Lieutenant Bucknell smiled and reached out his right hand toward the spaceman. "Friend."

The alien tilted his head and stared at the proffered hand. It seemed he was trying to make sense of what Wayne was doing. Obviously, not a practice wherever he came from. Wayne waited to see what would happen. When the prisoner lifted both hands, Wayne took the initiative and reached out to take the alien's right. Grasping it firmly, he shook it vigorously. Smiling to portray his friendship offer, Wayne watched as what appeared to be an inner set of eyelids flutter. The alien at first offered a limp

22

grip, but following Wayne's example, began to return the pressure. My God, he was strong! Wayne tilted his hand just a little and was awed as he spied the second thumb. No wonder the grip was powerful. Wayne let go and the spaceman followed suit.

The alien seemed to relax, and it appeared that he was smiling. Wayne decided to take things a step further. "Are you hungry? Would you like something to eat?" Gesturing as if to put food in his mouth, he smiled back to see his motions mirrored.

Turning to the guard, Wayne ordered food brought. Returning momentarily, the guard wheeled in a veritable buffet. On the cart were fresh vegetables and fruit, as well as an assortment of meats, fish, and poultry. The fellow must have cleaned out the commissary. Watching carefully, Wayne placed the array within reach of the spaceman, took an apple from the cart and bit into it, then gestured for him to do the same.

The alien put his hand over the fruit bowl and wavered over the other apple. Wayne could see his eyes darting back and forth between all the items on the tray. He finally picked up the plate with the smoked fish instead. Wayne became fascinated as the alien looked about the tray for something else, gave up, and dug into the fish with his hands.

"Soldier, do we not have any utensils?"

The private looked sheepish. "Sorry, Lieutenant, right away." He darted out and returned with a plastic knife and fork. When he placed them on the tray, the prisoner reached, grabbed the utensils, then offered a nod in the direction of the soldier.

"Well, at least we know he has table manners."

A few of the men chuckled, easing the tension in the room. Only after finishing off the entire plate of fish did he examine the tray again. It wasn't until then that Wayne saw something he hadn't noticed. "Beer. Private? What were you thinking?"

The man shrugged. "I don't know. It's just that, when I'm really thirsty, nothing goes down better than a cold beer."

Their guest seemed in agreement with the private as he drained the glass.

Lieutenant Bucknell analyzed the spaceman's dietary choices. First, he was a meat eater—well, fish anyway, which made him a predator, like man. He drank the beer, indicating that alcohol was not unknown to him. The doctors in the room were all clucking away like a flock of chickens, which made Wayne chuckle under his breath.

Eventually, it appeared the alien ate his fill, and Wayne moved to take the cart away, but at the last moment, the alien grabbed the water pitcher and dumped its contents over his head. A doctor leaned in and whispered something about amphibians, and an understanding came to him. Yes, the hairless body, no pores—this creature needed wetness applied externally at regular intervals. Enough dissected frogs in science class as a kid definitely imbued this memory in him.

"Well, I'm glad you're fed, and...all wet. The boys from Washington will arrive soon, so you will no longer be my problem. Between now and then, if there is anything you need, or wish to tell me, ask for First Lieutenant Wayne Bucknell—that's me, Wayne Bucknell."

He nodded to the men on either side of him and turned to go. Behind him, he heard the raspy voice as it said, "Traak doo, Buukeel." Turning back, he saw the alien smiling at him and the stunned looks on his men's faces, which more than likely mirrored his own appearance. He broke out laughing. "It's Bucknell, not Buuckeel, First Lieutenant Wayne Bucknell"

The alien pointed at himself. "Kraanox."

Wayne smiled back. "Well, pleased to make your acquaintance, Mr. Kraanox."

Wayne left the room. His visits with the other aliens proved far less productive, most likely because of their injuries. One had yet to achieve consciousness. Each of the four was being held in a separate room. He worried that they would all die on him, making his tenure as their caretaker one of dubious success. First things first. He immediately ordered sponge baths for all the aliens. He didn't need any dying from lack of moisture. As he strode down the hall, a private ran up with a message. "Sir, you are needed in the officers' mess. The men from Washington have arrived. Be advised, Lieutenant General Kelsey McTague is here."

He picked up his pace. "Thank you, Private. I'm on my way."

Upon entering the lounge, he noticed the senior officer right away and saluted. "First Lieutenant Wayne Bucknell reporting sir!"

The general, busy pouring himself a drink, turned and smiled, "Relax Wayne. It is Wayne, isn't it? This is the officers' lounge, pro forma is not required here, and as a captain, you should know that."

About to reply, he stood stunned for a second. "Captain?"

The others in the room laughed as Lieutenant General McTague approached him and pulled the single bars from Wayne's shoulders to replace them with double bars. "That's right Bucknell, Captain. It gives me a privilege to pin these on you for the job you've done these last couple days. Now, brief me, boy. I want to get up to speed on what's happening here."

Wayne smiled broadly, as he detailed all that occurred to that point, all the while running three words through his mind, Captain Wayne Bucknell.

CHAPTER 5

"It's true, I tell you!"

"You're a liar!"

"No, I'm not!"

"Liar, liar, pants on fire, sitting on top of a telephone wire!"

The other kids in the schoolyard gathered around to join in the chant, but Justin was prepared to stand his ground. He wasn't making it up. He saw the Sputnik crash and met a Russian! The schoolyard was abuzz with talk of the army men all over town, looking through people's yards, but none of the other children believed Justin's story.

The bell rang and the children lined up and headed into class. Once inside, the teacher waited until they were seated at their desks before making an announcement. "Children, today we have a special guest, First Lieutenant Wayne Bucknell from the army base outside of town."

Wayne stepped forward. "Thank you, Miss Grainger, but it is Captain Wayne Bucknell now." He turned to face the children and found a stool to perch upon in front of them. "Good morning, kids. Your teacher has been asking me for some time to stop by and pay you a visit. So, I decided I could spare the time today to come by to tell you about our wonderful country and the armed forces that defend it."

Wayne launched into a long list of what kind of forces defended them, describing the navy, air force, marines, coast guard, and finally the army. The kids were rapt and asked a lot of questions. "Did you fight in any wars?" "Do you know my dad? He fought in World War II." "Are we fighting anyone right now?" "Do you know the president?"

Justin finally piped up, "Did you just catch a Russian?"

Wayne turned to meet Justin's gaze. "A Russian? There are no Russians around to catch." Then he paused, leaned back, and smiled. "You must be the one who encountered the troops in their war games. We were practicing a search and capture, and one of our men pretended to be an enemy of the state for us to nab. I guess it must have been your backyard he was hiding in."

The other children giggled, and one said," See, I told you so!"

Justin fidgeted, and then looked back at Wayne. "I thought it was a Russian from the Sputnik that crashed the night before."

Captain Bucknell eyed him carefully. "What is your name, son?"

The teacher supplied the information. "Justin Spencer."

Wayne swiveled back and forth from between the teacher and Justin. "All right then, Justin, let me explain things to you. We did not shoot down the Sputnik. That would be the wrong thing to do, and it would make the Russians angry. No, the Sputnik is still in the sky, circling the planet right now. Besides, the Sputnik satellite is quite small, no bigger than a beach ball. There is no one on board, just equipment, and I don't think a Russian could fit into a spacecraft the size of a beach ball, do you?"

Justin puzzled over the question and let his head dipped to his chin. "I… I guess not." He then looked up directly into Wayne's gaze. "He looked like he was sick. Is he okay? I gave him some juice and carrot cake."

Captain Wayne Bucknell smiled and reached down to tousle Justin's hair. "And that was a real kind thing of you to do too. In fact, I think somewhere I have a gift for you from the fellow. He pulled a pin from his pocket and bent down to fasten it to the boy's shirt. There now, Justin, you are now an Honorary Warrant Officer with the specific duty of providing healthy nourishment to men in the field."

Justin's grinned wide, and beamed at all of those who teased him and called him a liar. "See! I told you so! Maybe it wasn't a Russian, but the man taken from my sandbox by the soldiers was real! Wait until my mom and dad see this!"

After a few more questions, Wayne excused himself from the class. A few others remained to visit, but with the true mission of the day now done, he intended to keep the other visits shorter so, that he might return back to the base as soon as possible.

***

Kraanox felt much better. The food they were bringing was agreeing with him. He'd feared their alien micro bacteria would kill him, but so far, no problem. Apparently, any microorganisms were not compatible with his physiology, and hence, no sickness.

The guard on duty watched him as he continued to eat. From time to time, he would stop and tilt his head when one of the doctors in the room spoke. When the tray was cleared away, the alien reached down and pulled lightly on the chain locked to his ankle. Kraanox maintained the gaze of the guard, who gripped his weapon tighter and paled, then gestured toward the door. "Feerst Luuteenaant Waan Buuckeel." The private appeared startled, but made for the door and disappeared from the room.

***

Wayne returned to base to discover that Lieutenant General McTague would be leaving, and a Colonel Steven Smeeton had arrived to take command. Wayne reported in to him, but unlike McTague, with his cavalier attitude, this man was all about protocol and authority. He brought the colonel up to speed and reported that he just returned from the school where he discussed the alien landing with the kids. Smeeton looked up in surprise. "Just what the hell were you thinking, man?"

Startled, he stepped back and straightened up. "Sir?"

Colonel Smeeton grimaced at him. "This is a damned covert operation, Captain. Surely, your instructions from Washington made that clear. Informing the general public is an absolute no-no. And school children, no less. Are you out of your cotton-picking mind? Do you realize what kind of panic could be created from all of this?"

Wayne tried hard to stop from smirking. Obviously, the colonel was ill informed. "Begging your pardon, sir, it was only last night that my men were fully debriefed, and that I learned how a child observed our capture of the last alien. There was no telling how many of his friends he may have informed, and I did not wish to panic the parents by visiting the home, so I used the cover of a school visit to mitigate the situation. Once I discovered the child's identity, I was able to convey to him a plausible misdirection, which he and his friends accepted in total."

Colonel Smeeton paused as if absorbing Wayne's report. "Yes, I guess that was the proper course of action."

Just then, a private entered the room. "Excuse me, sirs. Captain, the prisoner is asking for you."

The colonel spun on the man. "What the hell did he say?"

The fellow saluted again. "He asked for First Lieutenant Wayne Bucknell, sir."

Colonel Smeeton turned again on Captain Bucknell. "You gave this goddamned alien your name? These Martians are to know nothing about us. Nothing! Do you understand?"

"He's not a Martian sir. He's an…extraterrestrial."

"Martian, moon man, extra… whatever. He's not human, and he sure as hell is not from planet Earth!"

Wayne saluted and dipped his head. "My apologies, sir. He gave me his name, and I felt the least I could do was reply in kind."

Colonel Steven Smeeton grimaced at no one or nothing in particular, as he seemed to look all around the room. "All right then, let's go and see what in tarnation this thing wants."

The three men filed out of the lounge and headed down the hall. Wayne was the first to enter the prisoner's room. Kraanox smiled when he saw the captain, but his smile disappeared when Colonel Smeeton entered next. "Hello Feerst Luuteenaant Waan Buukeel!"

Wayne couldn't resist smiling. The improper way in which his name was pronounced, combined with the friendly demeanor of the alien made him like the fellow. "Good day, Kraanox. I trust you are feeling better. But it is Captain Wayne Bucknell now, not First Lieutenant. Captain Wayne Bucknell. I understand you have called for me. Is there something I can do for you?"

Wayne pointed to the bars indicating his new title, and it appeared comprehension came quickly.

Kraanox gestured to himself. "Kraanox, Traanu, Traanu man. More Traanu man, hello Kraanox."

There was no doubt the alien wanted to see the others they'd captured. Before he could reply, Wayne felt a tug on his arm and turned to see Colonel Smeeton indicating with his head that they should step outside. Wayne started for the door, but looked back to Kraanox as he went. "Back in a minute."

Once the door was closed, Colonel Smeeton exploded. "Just what in hell is going on here, Captain? You have this man a total of three days and he already has a grasp of the English language. What, pray tell, are you doing? Teaching him?"

Wayne swallowed the quip on his tongue. It looked like life was going to be a bit more difficult from now on. "No, sir. He must be picking it up from the men when they are working in the room."

Colonel Smeeton frowned. "Don't always try to be right with me, Captain. Starting now, all verbal communication will cease in front of the Mar...extraterrestrial. We don't even know a single damned word of his language, but we are giving him ours willy-nilly. I do not want you replying to him, do you understand? Now, see that my order is carried out."

Colonel Steven Smeeton spun and marched away, leaving him standing there like an idiot. With a sharp salute to Smeeton's retreating behind, Wayne got to the task he was now assigned.

Wayne re-entered the room and ordered that all verbal communication in front of the alien was to cease. Spinning on his heel, he opened the door once more to exit. Behind him, he could hear Kraanox question one more time, "Hello Traanu man?"

CHAPTER 6

The following morning, Captain Wayne Bucknell reported to Colonel Smeeton. "All men have been notified of the new rule, sir, including those off duty."

Smeeton ignored him for a moment, then looked up. "Fine, Captain, bloody well fine. Now what is needed here is a plan to get these aliens to tell us what they know. I'm leaving that up to you, Bucknell. Make it happen. I am going to spend my time monitoring the operations dealing with the wreckage. I suspect we will learn a lot more from that scrap heap you brought here than from interrogating a bunch of dumb aliens."

Wayne checked in on all of the prisoners. Kraanox appeared to be recuperating quickly. The two other males also were on the mend, though they'd suffered greater injuries. The female was still unconscious and appeared to be weakening. The doctors did not have high hopes.

Wayne began a monitoring plan that involved recording everything said and done by the aliens. The process proved to be extremely painstaking, but slowly he began to assemble a word for word list of the alien dialect. Helping in this process were some linguistic specialists sent by Washington.

The new detail presented a challenge. To house the aliens, they converted the officers' building and moved the men in with the regular enlisted. Wayne himself now bunked in one of the barracks, something he hadn't done since boot camp. After a couple of days, some trailers were brought in to temporarily house the officers. Definitely lacking the comforts of the officers building, but at least it got them out of the barracks.

The mess Sergeant showed up one day at the door to Wayne's office. "Sorry for the intrusion, sir. I just thought you'd like to know. I went into town today to pick up supplies and the people there were asking a lot of questions. There are plenty of rumors floating out there, and some of them not so good. People are talking of secret goings on here at the base."

"Thanks, Sergeant. I'll discuss it with the colonel." He stopped writing his reports to reflect on things. It was amazing, that they were able to maintain the secrecy of their operation so far. He already knew a lot of people heard the crash, and the official excuse was late night maneuvers. But stories get out. No doubt, men on leave would have loose lips. Especially once they got drinking.

It wasn't too long before a reporter showed up at the base. Wayne was sent to handle things. Colonel Smeeton didn't want anyone to know that he was there. For once, the old codger was right. How would you explain a colonel at such a small post? The journalist was Sam, from the local paper, a rag he printed in his garage once a week. "Morning Sam, what's up?"

Sam looked at him, glanced over Wayne's shoulder at the busy camp, and scratched his head. "Hi, Wayne. Sorry to bother you, but there seem to be a lot of strange stories circulating lately, and I thought I'd run down here and take a peek. What in blazes is going on?"

Wayne looked over his own shoulder at the base and the obvious new things like the row of trailers parked along the main road. Perhaps it was best to step away from the entrance. He turned sideways and pointed to his left. "Walk with me for a bit, will you?"

Sam nodded. "Sure thing, Wayne. Just as long as I get the scoop."

As they circled the camp, Wayne gave the reporter a sideways glance. "Now Sam, what do you think is going on? Just your federal government doing what they do best-- spending money. They brought in a whole bunch of *specialists* to give us *special* training and make us all *special* soldiers in the *Special* Forces, it's their *specialty*. A couple of months and they'll be gone, and we'll all go back to being the local yokels we once were."

He chuckled, and Sam laughed with him. "I knew I could get a straight answer from you, Wayne, but what about these rumors of Martian prisoners."

Wayne smirked at Sam. "Oh yeah, those. Well to tell you the truth, Sam, I was up there just last month, on vacation, and brought a few of the boys home with me."

Sam stopped walking along with him and gave his head a small shake. "Up there Wayne? Up where?"

Wayne reached out to keep pulling Sam along. "Why, Mars of course, didn't I tell you? I have a cottage there."

Sam shook his arm free. "Now Wayne, you're foolin' with me."

Wayne reached out and pulled Sam with him once again. "Of course, I'm foolin' with you. You ask me about Martian prisoners and expect me to take things seriously? Now, Sam, I want you to go home, print whatever you like, but ask yourself, if you print that we have Martian prisoners here, who will be the bigger fool—the people who believe it, or you for writing it?"

Sam stopped once again, and this time Wayne let him go freely. "Yeah, I guess you're right, Wayne, it did seem kinda stupid, but ol' Bobby there, he says it's all true."

Now it was his turn to stop cold. "Bobby? As in Bobby Vance?"

Sam looked worried. "Now Wayne, I don't want to get Bobby in any trouble now. Take it easy on the kid. He was drinking down at Stanley's and tellin' everybody this cock and bull story."

Wayne allowed a smile back onto his face and put a warm hand on Sam's shoulder. "I know Bobby, and I know what he's like when he's drunk, so here's the deal. I won't punish him for talking, but if you write that story, I won't have any choice."

Sam looked relieved. "Okay, Wayne. I never believed it anyhow. I have to get going. I need to pick up the specials list from the market so's I can get it in for Saturday. Hey, you can tell your specialists about them market specials." And with that, Sam went off, chuckling at his own poor joke.

Wayne went back inside to report to Colonel Smeeton. "I bought us a couple of months, sir, but I suspect we will need to relocate if we want to keep things under wraps any longer than that."

"I'll take your suggestion under advisement. Though I think moving would bring even more attention to our activities. As time passes, these townsfolk will forget everything, and we can go on about our business. Now what brought this reporter out in the first place? Were you able to find out his source? Whoever it was, I intend to court martial the bastard to the fullest extent. The security of this information is paramount."

He was not about to surrender his man to the colonel. "I am working on that, sir. Leave it to me. I assure you there will be no more leaks."

"You understand that should there be another, I will hold you personally responsible. Now, what is the status of the prisoners? Have you made any headway in cracking their language?"

Wayne maintained his composure. "Yes, sir, we have been monitoring their conversations at lunch."

Colonel Smeeton went bug-eyed. "You let them talk together? Don't you realize the inherent danger in that? They could be plotting our annihilation!"

Wayne couldn't stop a small smile from creasing his lips. "No, sir, they are unaware that we are secretly taping them. So far, the most common expression we have picked up is pass the salt—they seem to need a lot of it."

Colonel Smeeton leapt up from his seat and faced him straight on. "This meeting of the aliens will end right now. Do you hear me? The original orders were to keep them apart, and I have had no countermanding orders since. Have you?"

Wayne took a step back. "Sir, you asked me to learn their language. I cannot learn what I cannot hear. Giving them dining privileges together has boosted their morale. They seem healthier and less frightened. As a result, they talk more. I am personally learning their language and can handle a number of mundane phrases, including pass the salt. It is my hope to be able to hold a conversation with them in their own language within a few months. Perhaps then they will feel comfortable enough to tell us why they are here. I have filed my reports. Have you not read them?"

Colonel Smeeton purpled. "Your reports are forwarded to Washington. I do not have the time to read everyone's reports, but from now on, with yours, I will make the time! Now get the hell out of here and find that informant. Lieutenant General Kelsey McTague will be here on the morrow, and I intend to bring up any misconduct with him then."

***

That afternoon he chased down Bobby Vance. After a thorough tongue lashing, Wayne felt that he extracted the necessary pound of flesh, and Bobby would trouble him no more.

He decided to drive into town and pay Sam a visit, just to make sure their deal was still on. Driving down the main street he spied the little boy whom he spoke with at the school. Stopping his car, he got out to say hi, and saw the child still wore his honorary badge. "Hi, Justin. It is Justin, isn't it? What'cha doing?"

Justin looked up from his toy soldiers. "Hi, Mr. Captain sir. Nothing, just playing."

Wayne looked down at the array of miniature men. They were spread out in some type of battle plan. "So, which one are you?"

Justin beamed. "I'm the commander. See? You appointed me." He bent back down to move a few of the pieces around, then looked up at Wayne. "How is that soldier doing, Mr. Captain? Is he still sick? I gave him some orange juice and carrot cake, remember? I hope that made him feel better."

Wayne squatted down to be nearer the boy. "He's doing fine, thank you. That was a good thing you did. It's too bad he can't thank you himself."

Justin stopped playing to give him a big grin. "Oh, he did, he said thank you. At least, that's what I think he said. I'm glad he's better; he was a nice man. My mommy always says you can tell whether someone is a nice man by their eyes, and when I saw his eyes, I knew what mommy was talking about, and that he was a nice man."

Wayne reached over to tousle the boy's hair and stood up. "Yes, he is a nice man. I have to go now. You be a good boy, too. Bye, Justin."

As Justin said goodbye and resumed his play with the toy soldiers, Wayne climbed back into his car and gave him one last look. He reflected that innocent children saw the world in black and white, and it was an observation by a seven-year-old boy that solidified his resolve to face the general in the morning.

***

Wayne squinted at the early morning sun while he and Colonel Smeeton stood on the grounds waiting for the general's car to pull into the yard.

Pulling out a pair of sunglasses, he slipped them on and breathed a sigh of relief.

"Take those off!"

He turned to see the colonel glaring at him. "Sir?"

Smeeton pointed toward his eyewear. "You heard me. The general will be here shortly and the last thing he needs is to be met by a disrespectful officer. Now take those things off."

Sighing again, he pulled them off and folded them into his shirt pocket. As he did, the general's car pulled into the yard.

Lieutenant General Kelsey McTague climbed out, smiling broadly and wearing a large pair of sunglasses. "Good morning, gentlemen. Awfully bright out this morning. Bad for the eyes. Don't you fellas have any shades to wear?"

Wayne smiled briefly in the colonel's direction, then, as he pulled out his pair once more, returned his focus to the general. "Right here, sir."

"Good thing. Get them on, Bucknell. No sense damaging your corneas on my behalf. How about you, Smeeton?

"None sir."

The general jerked his head, giving Smeeton a sideways glance. "Too bad. Gotta be prepared, Colonel."

The general looked Wayne's way. "Show me around the base Bucknell, give me the low down on what's been happening. Let's let old SS get out of the sun."

The general waved a hand at the colonel. "I'll see you in a minute, Smeeton. I hope that officer's lounge you're set up in still has some of the old stock left in it.".

Colonel Smeeton saluted McTague. "I'll make sure of it, General."

Surviving a scowl from Colonel Smeeton, Wayne nodded toward the general. "Right this way, sir."

After the tour, Wayne showed the general to Colonel Smeeton's office.

Colonel Smeeton stopped Wayne at the door with a hand to his chest. "I wish to speak to the general alone, Captain. We will call you when we need you." The door to the lounge closed in his face.

Wayne stared at the closed door. He did not know whether to storm in or leave, or stay and wait. Unexpectedly, the decision was made for him. A young medic came running.

"Captain, come quick. It's one of the prisoners. She's died."

Wayne spun and chased the young man down the hall. The only female, she'd never come out of the coma since the crash. When he arrived at the room, he found a large group of people milling about the hall outside. The senior medical officer spotted him coming and intercepted him.

"I'm sorry, Captain, we did all we could. The IV fluids sustained her until now, but her organs failed and she lost the struggle. My team would like to do an autopsy now that she is deceased."

Wayne hesitated. This wasn't science class, and they weren't dissecting a frog. It was an alien, true, but too much like a human. The thought made him squeamish. Behind him, a soldier approached, informing him that the general and colonel would like to see him.

He turned back to the doctor. "All right, I know you need to do this, but keep it clean, and put her back together when you're done." Then he addressed the soldier who came to fetch him. "Tell the general and the colonel I will be along shortly. I have something I need to do first.

Wayne then went down the hall to the area where the others were being kept.

Wayne walked into the room at the end of the hall to find Kraanox sitting all alone watching the door. He tried to smile at the alien, but only managed a half smirk, and then it was gone. This was not pleasant business. Kraanox moved to stand, but Wayne motioned for him to remain seated. He pulled up another chair and sat directly in front of Kraanox. "Grave is the day, Kraanox."

Kraanox tilted his head at him. More than likely, he did not understand what Wayne said. "Gravity?"

Wayne recognized the perplexed look upon Kraanox's face. "No Kraanox, not gravity, grave is the day, although the gravity of the situation is a heavy one. I need to inform you that one of your crewmen has died. The woman who was injured. She was in a coma all this time. I guess her body just gave up the fight and she's gone." Wayne watched Kraanox to see if comprehension was there and if he could tell whether Kraanox understood the main message, that one of his people was gone. As he gave no immediate reaction, Wayne tried again. "Traanu woman...hurt...sleep...die."

Upon Kraanox's face, a flurry of eyelid flutters occurred and, yes, tears. So, these spacemen cried just like we do. He decided he would give his poor Traanusian tongue an attempt. It seemed like the proper time. Before he could, the door opened behind him and the colonel and the general entered the room with Colonel Smeeton making an accusatory "There you are!"

Wayne, rather than standing and saluting, leaned over to repeat a phrase he heard the Martians use time and again to console one another, though not truly sure of its meaning, only its intent. "Laapitoo dooraad aallissuu Kraanox."

Kraanox stopped his eyelid flutter to look at Wayne. He rose, and Wayne rose with him. He grabbed Wayne in a hug. "Thaank Yoou, Caaptaan Buu…..Bucknell."

Wayne returned the hug and then excused himself to address the general. "Sir!"

The look on the face of Lieutenant General Kelsey McTague read as one thing, compassion. Without a word, the general turned and left the room with an apparently stunned Colonel Smeeton hot in pursuit.

The next day Wayne received a note from the senior medical officer. The autopsy was complete, and he wanted the captain's instruction on the disposition of the remains.

He entered the mess where the aliens were having breakfast and sat down at the table with the three of them. Their expressions told him all he needed to know. "Good morning, Kraanox. I have come to ask you what rites your race performs for the dead. Here, we bury our dead in the ground, but you may have a different practice." Then, after a pause, he simplified. "Traanu woman…what do now?"

Kraanox seemed to understand enough. Wayne watched as he turned to the others and engaged in a short discussion in their native language. Almost in unison, the others responded, and Kraanox turned and faced him. "The sea, she go sea."

Wayne got up and nodded toward the three aliens. "I will make the arrangements." He headed down to the room where they held the body to give instructions to the medical staff.

***

Later in the day, Wayne headed down to check that everything was done, and found the dead alien being loaded onto a truck. As he signed the shipping orders, he noticed the destination changed. "What gives?"

The doctor overseeing the loading was sheepish as he faced him. "Sorry, sir, your orders were countermanded by Colonel Smeeton."

Wayne stormed off in the direction of Smeeton's office. Rather than knock, he charged right in. "All right. What is going on with the dead prisoner?"

Wayne had not spoken with the colonel since the general left and was expecting the usual blow-up from him, only to find Smeeton calm and in control. "I countermanded your orders, Captain, because I am locking this facility down. Deceased aliens are to be held in a freezer for future study. You need to vacate the main office for the new general in charge, so get to work clearing out. That will be all, Captain."

Dismissed, Wayne returned to his office and began packing his belongings. He was left with the hard decision of whether to inform Kraanox of the change in plans.

***

The next morning a package arrived by courier for Captain Wayne Bucknell from Lieutenant General Kelsey McTague. When he opened it, he was incredulous to find enclosed a set of pins for the rank of major. Attached was a note from the General.

Sorry for the lack of formality on your new appointment as major. I would return and handle this personally, but after deep thought, I have surrendered my commission and am retiring. I hope you continue on with the good work you are doing. Don't let Smeeton bother you too much. Steven is a good soldier who follows rules to the letter. He is such a stickler that we nicknamed him SS, and as such, can be a hard man at times, but when you are in the right, he is a good man to have in your corner. Work with him, not against him. Your increase in rank will make

42

it harder for him to bully you, and you will need an ally when your new superior officer arrives. Brigadier General Francis Johnson is as tough as they get, and he is the new man in charge. God bless you, son. Kelsey McTague

Wayne took off his captain's bars and clipped on the major's pins. In a few short weeks he'd been promoted twice. Why wasn't he happy?

CHAPTER 7

Justin ran for the nearest tree. Hiding behind it, he couldn't resist giggling. About ten paces away, his mother searched for him.

"Come out, come out, wherever you are. I'm going to find you!"

It was very thick around, and he remembered his mother telling him it was a black oak. It didn't look black. But under any circumstances, it was a great place to hide.

Justin could hear his mother on the other side of the oak. "Now I wonder where he went. Maybe now is my chance to get away."

He charged out from behind his hiding place. "Mom! Don't go!"

His mother scooped him up and nuzzled him closely. "Now I got you!"

Justin squealed in delight. After a moment she put him down. "Now, come on, Justin, no more time for play. Help me find some wild mushrooms to bring home. The best place to look is around fallen limbs and branches."

At first, he fidgeted a toe into the ground. "Aww, Mom, I was just playing." But after a stern look from his mother, he picked up the small basket. "Okay, I'll look."

The forest always made him feel like playing. The trees were everywhere—some real big ones, some not so big but neat anyway. There were trees that he could climb on, or could hide under, and even some he could pretend were playmates. As he walked, the light from the sky glinted on and off as it peeked through the branches. He dodged from spot to spot in a game of avoid the sunbeam, dropping his basket on the way.

"Justin, are you looking?"

So much for the game.

"I'm looking, I'm looking!"

Justin picked up the small basket again and strayed off through the woods. Fallen trees, Mom said. As he walked, she yelled out. "Don't go too far, Justin. I don't want you getting lost."

He stopped in his tracks. She wasn't going to let him have any fun at all. "I'm just looking for some fallen trees, Mom."

Another dozen paces and he could see a small clearing ahead. Maybe he would find a whole mess of mushrooms over there and make his mom happy.

As he reached the clearing, he could see lots of branches lying on the ground, and a bunch of them busted apart. They seemed to run in a line through the woods. He glanced around and could see big tire-tracks all about. Something happened here. He wondered if maybe some lumberjacks knocked them down and would be coming back for the wood. Or maybe they were planning on putting a road through the area. He began climbing through the fallen trees looking for mushrooms.

While crawling through the fallen trees, he paused underneath a number of branches. He thought to himself this would make a cool fort. He would definitely come back here with his buddies. The limbs were parallel with the ground but because of the angles they stuck out at, the main trunk hung about three feet off the ground. The branches above were so thick it looked almost dark underneath.

Justin couldn't resist, and got down on his knees to climb into the area under the big tree. Once below, it wasn't quite as dark as it looked from outside. Light was getting in, and he could see just fine. The space was about the size of his bedroom, although a lot lower-ceilinged. The ground was damp, and only then did he see the knees of his pants all black with mud.

He figured, it was a fallen tree, so there should be some mushrooms around. He looked from one end to another. Glancing around him, he spied a grayish object sticking out of the mud.

Wow, did that ever look like a big mushroom!

He scrambled over to pick it and put it in his basket. Once he reached it, he discovered it wasn't a mushroom after all. Pulling at it, he found it was half embedded in the ground. Using both hands, he gave a mighty tug, the object popped free, and he landed on his rear in the soft mud.

He was going to get it from his mom. He was covered in mud. Justin lifted up his prize. It was oval, shaped like a football and almost the same size. But it was heavy, like a rock. It felt a little like stone, but very smooth, as if someone polished it. Justin remembered his trip to the museum. He was infatuated with dinosaurs. Maybe this was a dinosaur egg! There were a couple on display at the museum, and this was the right size and color.

As he was putting the thing into his basket, he heard his mother call for him.

He scrambled out from under the branches. "Here I am, Mom."

She walked over and helped him stand up. "Look at you! What a mess! Justin, what am I ever to do with you? Come on then, let's get you home and into the tub. I picked enough mushrooms for now, anyway."

He looked down at the mud caked on him, front and back. He tried to wipe off the sludge, but with little success. Then he remembered his prize. "Mom, look what I found! A dinosaur egg!"

His mother peered into the basket he was carrying. "Hmm, looks like just a big stone to me. If you want to bring it along, don't expect me to carry it. So, if it gets too heavy you just drop it here now."

It was heavy, but he wasn't about to give up his find. "No, Mom, I can carry it. Don't worry."

His mother sighed. "All right then, let's get going. It's going to take a one heck of a scrubbing to get that much grime off of you."

Using both arms to carry his basket, he began to trudge his way home.

CHAPTER 8

Wayne set up his desk in a small barracks with Colonel Smeeton. The main offices were now vacant and awaiting their new arrivals. As well, a host of new technicians were being transferred in. As a result, there were a lot of new bodies floating around and it was going to take him some time to get to know them. First, though, was the briefing with the new commander, Brigadier General Francis Johnson, or Frank, as he liked to be called. Both Wayne and Colonel Smeeton reported in, and the general eyed the two men up and down before beginning.

"Gentlemen, this operation is now under my complete command, and, as such, I am expecting results. Colonel, you will continue to oversee the examination of the spacecraft and its contents. Captain, sorry, I mean Major, I see old McTague gave you a parting gift. Major, you will learn from the prisoners all they know. I expect those results yesterday, gentlemen, so if I were you, I'd be getting back to work, pronto. That is all for now."

The general returned to his desk. Wayne and Steven looked at each other and headed out the door. There was no doubt this was a different kind of man than McTague and he figured they both knew it now.

Wayne rounded up his team so he could meet all the new people and let everyone get acquainted. From the twenty-two who originally served under him, the numbers suddenly swelled to over forty. A hefty medical staff, linguists, psychologists, biologists, and anthropologists. It was obvious that Wayne was going to be on a large learning curve. The general also assigned a squad of soldiers for security, although, so far, Kraanox and his men showed no signs of challenging their internment.

A major expansion of the base facilities began. The rooms for the aliens were modified to include steel doors and cameras so their every move could be monitored.

When Wayne headed down to check on Kraanox and the others, they appeared to be handling the renovations without duress, and he hoped the new routine would come easy.

***

Weeks passed and stretched into months. Wayne and a couple of his men were now able to hold limited conversations with the aliens. Kraanox, in the meantime, seemed to have mastered the English language, while his crewmates were slower, with one in particular making little effort to learn. It was frustrating because the slow learner also was becoming more resistant toward responding, even when spoken to in his native Braannoo.

Wayne's questions were becoming more detailed. Information as to the methods of propulsion for their ship and any other technological questions were often answered with an "I don't know." These men were soldiers, not technicians, and the General was clearly disappointed with the replies. "What these Traanusians need, Major, is some motivation."

One morning, when Wayne went down to talk with Kraanox and the others, he discovered that one of the rooms was empty. And the uncooperative Traanusian was missing. He chased down the second lieutenant in charge of security to discover the whereabouts of the missing alien.

"I'm sorry, sir; the general ordered him transferred to quarters on the opposite side of the base last night."

Following instructions from the lieutenant, Wayne made his way over to find out what was going on. On his way to the building, he thought he heard a scream. Breaking into a run, he came face to face with a pair of

49

soldiers guarding the entrance. "I'm sorry sir. General's order, no one is to enter."

Wayne was livid. After shouting a few expletives at the men, he charged off in the direction of the general's headquarters. When he got there, a shaken Colonel Smeeton was coming out. Smeeton, upon seeing him, straightened up and headed off in the direction of his quarters. Seeing the Colonel looking so upset, some of Wayne's resolve melted. The aide ushered him into the general's office. "Brigadier General Johnson sir, I am here to inquire what has happened to my third prisoner."

The general was standing facing out his window. "Things have changed, Major. Last night an attempt was made to purloin a significant amount of Uranium 135. Somewhere in the neighborhood of half a ton. We believe that it is the compatriots of these fellows. I told you before, Major, I expect results. You still have two men, and I intend to get my results with this third fellow. Let's see who finds the answers first, shall we? You're dismissed."

The aide held the door as Wayne slowly saluted and spun to leave. Rather than head back to his own area, he sought out Colonel Smeeton. He found Steven embroiled in some paperwork at his desk and muttering to himself.

"Colonel, what's going on? The General has sequestered one of my prisoners away, and I fear that he is torturing him."

Colonel Smeeton looked up at him. His eyes were smoldering. "That is a serious goddamned allegation, one that will get your sorry ass kicked out of the army if you can't prove it. Now get the hell out of here before I cite you." Then, surprisingly, cursing, Colonel Smeeton threw a book at him, so he beat a hasty retreat from the room.

***

The soldiers escorted Kraanox to the mess to eat with his fellow crewmen. When only one greeted him, he inquired of his guard as to the whereabouts of the other. All he received was silence. This did not sit well with him. Until now, the humans remained civil toward them, even kind. Major Bucknell was friendly and showed concern about their well-being. But the previous night, the new general in charge visited him. It was still an unrefined skill, but Kraanox was becoming a good judge of character with these humans, and this one worried him. There was something merciless about this man, and with his associate missing, he feared the worst.

Major Bucknell entered the room and Kraanox immediately motioned for Wayne to come sit with him. Even after all this time, he still walked with ankle irons. "Major, one of my men is missing. What has happened to him?"

The major waited until he was comfortably seated. "The general has sequestered him for private interrogations. There is nothing more I can tell you."

Kraanox looked carefully at his new friend, trying to read his face. No, Major Bucknell was not lying. He truly did not know the status of his crewman, though there was something else he was holding back, which could only mean that things around there were changing. And he needed to adapt to this new reality. "Tell me, Major, what is it the general wants so badly?"

Major Bucknell ordered something to eat, and the mess chief put it in front of him. He pushed a forkful of food into his mouth before responding, in an apparent effort to downplay the seriousness of the situation. "Why, Kraanox, he only wants what I have been trying to get from you all along, information about your intentions, your scientific knowledge, what brought you to Earth in the first place."

Before Major Bucknell could put another bite into his mouth, Kraanox reached over and restrained his hand. "So, it is the intention of this general to force the information from my countryman?"

Major Bucknell leaned back and dropped the fork with a clang onto his plate. "I do not know for sure, Kraanox. But if you want to get him back, then give me what I need. As I understand it, your people tried to heist a shipment of uranium. Now what would you need that for, hmm?"

Kraanox considered his juxtaposition. Until now, he and his men resisted telling the humans anything of value. He'd reached a time for choices. "Major, me and my men are but soldiers, so when it comes to technology, there is so little for us to tell. The scientists back home build the spaceships. We only fly them. I can no more tell you how to build one, than you can tell me. But as to why we are here, that much, at least, I can answer.

Before I truly answer, I must give you a brief picture of my home world. Mine is a planet much like yours, continents, vast oceans separating them, and a variety of cultures dividing them. It is not important what cultures or governments exist. It is only important that these differences are stark enough that we are constantly at war with one another. I am from Braannoo. Our just and honorable king is a Traanusian of great nobility. We are an advanced country in the scheme of things, and are currently at war with the Muurgu Empire, the largest of them all, and looking to expand. Defending our homeland is our first priority, and one that is most costly, not just in wealth, but in the lives of our people.

"We were the first to create the technology for interstellar space flight. In recent years, it appears the Muurgu have managed to copy our systems, though some doubt they managed to develop it themselves. Espionage is more likely. No other nations on Traanu possess the knowledge. You are the first intelligent life that we discovered. Until then, space flight only found worlds with environments hostile to us, and no sapient beings. Coming here was a costly mission with a single, military purpose. To recover new technologies that would aid us in our struggle against the Muurgu. Needless to say, it was with great disappointment that we found your people have yet to discover space flight, let alone anything that may serve us in our quest. We have studied your atomic weaponry, but uranium is almost nonexistent on our home world, so that technology is useless. If an attempt was made to steal this uranium you speak of, I can only assume it was the Muurgu."

"We remained in orbit around your planet for several months, until a Muurgu ship appeared and shot us out of the sky. As a result, they are the only Traanusians remaining in your space. It was with only the greatest fortune that any of us survived, and now that there are only three of us left, I must do what I can to protect the last two men in my charge. You, as a commander of men, must appreciate what I am saying. We crash landed, you captured us; there is no more to tell."

"The Braannoo your general now holds is a simple soldier, nothing more, the other, the same. I am the commander, an opportunity given to me by birthright as a cousin of the royal family, but which I still worked to earn. I am several times removed from the king. The royal family numbers in the hundreds. As captain, I needed to know all functions of the ship, but if you asked me to build it, I wouldn't know where to begin."

***

Wayne absorbed what Kraanox told him. He thought of his own limited knowledge in the making of such a simple device as a car, in comparison to a spaceship, and recognized the truth in what Kraanox was telling him. Thanking Kraanox for his honesty, he headed out the door to find General Johnson. When he arrived at the general's office, things were in upheaval. The staff was relocating to a larger building on the grounds connected to where the spacecraft wreckage was situated. Stopping an aide, he discovered Colonel Smeeton reassigned and relieved of command. The general was taking a hands-on approach to the analysis of the debris, with Smeeton reassigned to security. Now Wayne knew what upset Steven so.

When he located General Johnson and informed him of what Kraanox told him, the general was unimpressed. "Listen, Major, you and the colonel spent half a year trying to learn something from these aliens, and outside of a few words of their language, you have nothing to report. There has been even less on the technological side, which is why old SS has been reassigned. I would do the same to you if my information didn't include that you have gained the leader's trust. Golden boys like you are usually a disappointment. Promoted to major at your age, it's a joke. But the boys in Washington know of you, and so I can't just go dismissing you as well without good cause. But give me one good reason, Major, and you can join Smeeton walking night patrol."

Wayne saluted and requested the release of the third Traanusian back to him, although it seemed like a futile effort, and the general denied his request immediately. The only thing to do was return to his desk and continue with the job assigned to him. Perhaps, in time, he would unravel this problem and get the answers he needed.

Over the next few days, he made side trips to visit the building where the third Traanusian was being held. Each time, his request to visit the prisoner was denied. On the sixth day after the relocation of the alien, Wayne was surprised to discover that the guard was gone. Wayne walked into the facility to see that it was empty. No bed, no bathroom facilities, only a cement floor, a couple of chairs and a plywood table. In one corner stood a generator for emergency backup and a tool cabinet. The building would better serve as a garage than as a domicile.

It was only moments later when a number of security personnel entered, dragging the other Braannoo between them. "What is going on here? Why have you brought this Traanusian here? Where is the one that was here before?"

The lead soldier, a large fellow, saluted lazily. "Orders, sir. The General has asked me to bring this second alien here. I'm sorry, sir, you aren't allowed to be here, and I am going to have to ask you to leave the building."

Wayne could hear one of the other soldiers snicker in the background at his repudiation. He thought about admonishing him, but time was of essence. He needed to do something quick. He feared the worst for whatever happened to the first Braannoo.

Wayne dashed across the courtyard to Colonel Smeeton's office. Steven was on the telephone when he entered. "My God, man, don't you ever knock?"

With no time to waste, Wayne stepped over and placed his fingers on the telephone, disconnecting the colonel.

"What the hell are you doing, Major! That was a personal call. Is there no goddamned limit to your insubordination?"

Wayne gently took the receiver out of the Colonel's hand and placed it in the cradle. "Steven, I know you aren't fond of me, and I know you would love to cite me right now for anything you can. But if there is one thing I have learned about you is that you are a man who takes the rules seriously—all the rules. And if regulations are to be enforced, the job falls on you in your new position as security chief."

Colonel Smeeton turned away momentarily, as if hiding his shame. "What the hell do you want, Wayne?"

He moved around the desk to face the Colonel again. Smeeton never called him Wayne before. "You told me that if I wanted to state that the General is torturing the prisoners I needed proof, and I don't have it. Well, I want you to know that I managed to get into that building today, and the prisoner was nowhere to be seen. I think he's dead, Colonel. If you think that suggesting torture was bad, how about murder? Does that seem worse to you? Now, you can arrest me for these accusations, or you can investigate. All I know is one Traanusian is gone, another one taken, and when he disappears, there will be only one left."

Colonel Steven Smeeton seemed to galvanize. Grabbing his jacket and hat, he headed out the door. As he left, he pulled Wayne along, and shoved him in the opposite direction from his trajectory. "Major, you did not see me, you did not talk to me, you have no goddamned idea what is going on. Do you understand?"

Wayne, surprised by the ferocity exhibited by Steven, nodded his head, and with that the colonel was gone.

He returned to the facility that housed the Traanusians. Kraanox sat alone in the commissary, with two guards standing nearby. "Major, would you please explain to me where my crewmen are?"

He was not prepared to lie to Kraanox, nor was he prepared to tell the truth. "Grave is the day, Kraanox."

Kraanox tilted his head. "Once again this phrase comes from you. This time I know it for what it is. And gravity is the situation, not the force. Are they dead, Major?"

Wayne paused to place his lunch order. When the quartermaster strode away, he pivoted in his chair to face Kraanox directly. "I don't know, Kraanox, I don't know. It is possible, or they may just be incarcerated within the general's part of the camp. Colonel Smeeton has gone to find out."

Kraanox straightened in his chair. "Colonel Smeeton. I do not feel so reassured when having to rely on this man."

Wayne reached out and placed his hand over one of Kraanox's. "Normally, I would agree with you. But something tells me that, this time, we can trust him."

When his lunch arrived, he shoved the plate away. "Perhaps he has answers now. Kraanox, excuse me while I go and find out."

***

Colonel Steven Smeeton strode across the yard with a renewed sense of purpose. Having served in the army for over twenty-two years and fought in two wars, he took great pride in his sense of duty and patriotism. Always a good soldier, he followed orders to the letter and never disobeyed a command. But as he aged, he also came to learn his shortcomings, and one of them was that he was not a particularly bright fellow. Promotions were difficult and often long overdue. He learned the hard way that he wasn't overly admired, but no one challenged his loyalty to the cause.

It was his one ace in the hole. His record was impeccable, and if this General Johnson was going to stain that record, it was something that Colonel Smeeton could not stomach. He didn't care for Major Bucknell, a brash upstart. Steven couldn't see the big difference between himself and this young man, who in a few short months elevated as many ranks as it took him in ten years to accomplish. A man is just a man. What makes one better than another? All men should be treated the same.

This brought Steven to the problem that now faced him. These aliens…were they men? Should they be treated

57

as such? The turmoil of that question bothered Steven since his arrival. It was only his own demotion in recent days that galvanized that thought in Steven's mind to one of acceptance. It was one thing for him to be removed from his responsibilities, another for a man to be tortured. His humiliating position as head of security suddenly provided him a way to redemption.

Steven rounded up his entire team of security personnel and, after a quick briefing, headed for where the general was holding the aliens. At the entrance to the compound was a single soldier who stood in front of him as he approached. "Sorry, sir, no one is admitted entrance without the general's permission."

Steven came nose to nose with the private. "Stand down, soldier. I am here to investigate a serious charge of war crimes. You will either stand aside or be considered an accessory to such a crime, if it exists." At this moment, Major Bucknell arrived. Startled at the arrival of the major, the private turned his head to look behind him, and in doing so, stepped sideways. Steven seized the momentary lax and strode past the surprised soldier, his team in close pursuit.

Steven knew General Johnson to be a man of results. He learned from the best in World War II and was known to believe that casualties were the cost of success.

When he entered the building, Steven saw the general and two other soldiers huddled around the alien who was bound in a chair. The Traanusian appeared slumped and unconscious. Based on the wires connected to his limbs, they must be applying electric shocks in an attempt to coerce information.

A guard posted inside the door tried to halt his progress, but Steven and the security detail brushed past. "Brigadier General Francis Johnson, I hereby place you under arrest for a breach of the Geneva Convention and crimes against humanity."

Johnson spun to face him eye to eye. "Humanity? Humanity! Tell me, Colonel, what humans do you see here? We are at war with aliens from outer space, and you want to preach the Geneva Convention to me! For all I know, they may be intending to wipe out the entire human race, and you want to practice politics. I am ordering you and everyone with you to stand down right now."

Steven slowly, methodically, and without any regard for Johnson's tirade, reached out, took the general's hand and placed a cuff on it. It took all his willpower not to smirk. "You are under arrest, General. You can save your speeches for the tribunal at your court martial."

General Johnson stood there, agape, as Steven completed the task of cuffing his second hand, and his squad performed the same on the rest of the men there. Steven directed two men to help Major Bucknell take the Traanusian back to his quarters. "Come along, General, we have a plane to catch."

CHAPTER 9

The ignominy of it all.

Captain Pruutoc of the Muurgu battle cruiser, Emperor, could not believe his troops lost their first encounter with these...humans. It was an affront to the Muurgu creed, *victory above all else*. The officer in charge of the debacle stood before him. "This is your complete report? Utter failure?"

"My apologies, Captain. I already lost four men. I wasn't prepared to lose them all."

"Your apology is not accepted. Starting immediately, you are demoted two ranks. Have your previous second report to me immediately."

He spun his chair around, but none of his officers returned his glare, all avoiding eye contact. He studied the bridge of his ship as he contemplated what he should do next. His helmsman and navigator sat at their bay stations in front of him, facing the forward window. Behind him, his communications, tactical, science and weapons officers sat in their own station bays, lined up in twos and also facing forward. Each man had decorated his own bay with the emblems of their family crests. As such, the bays were adorned with fangs, claws, knives and swords. Above his own chair hung the giant head of a faarnoo, the terror of the skies of his home province.

After vanquishing their enemy, the Braannoo, his ship stayed in orbit. Pruutoc remained to conduct his own survey of the aliens. After all, the Braannoo were probably here for months. There must be some reason of interest. He found it unlikely these creatures could offer anything of value to the Muurgu Empire, but staying for an investigation seemed the militarily correct thing to do. Pruutoc reasoned, if not for something of immediate value, then perhaps as an advance scouting for interstellar expansion of the Muurgu Empire. Once all of Traanu was under Muurgu control, space would be the only option for further expansion.

Although these aliens seemed years behind in military or scientific developments, a number of surprises led Pruutoc to look closer. The first and most startling thing was the extensive use of metals—iron, copper, nickel. Materials in such vast quantities that these people did not even bother with the development of silicate products. Only in the last few years did the Muurgu dig deep enough to extract metal ores from within the planet. The entire crust of Traanu was buried two miles deep in basalt, with no real metals to speak of. It was no wonder his people developed silicate products first, whereas these humans could avail themselves of easily attainable metals.

What followed next was his astonishment when he discovered the development of nuclear weapons among these humans. After examining one of the devices, they discovered the key ingredient was a little-known mineral called uranium. This substance was practically nonexistent on their home world, but apparently in enough abundance here that it could be mined successfully.

This led to the now aborted mission. As Captain Pruutoc sat waiting for the second officer, his anger continued to grow. They discovered a store of uranium and learned the simple technology required to make the atomic weapons the humans developed. The raid should have been a simple one. Yes, the metal was well protected and locked away, but the defenses were arrayed against a ground assault, not an aerial one. Especially not from such as the Emperor. The ship was silent running, able to hover and deploy ground troops in an instant, and armed with particle beam weapons that could slice through human constructs with ease.

The second in command arrived and stood before him. "Here, Captain. I received your order to report."

Pruutoc looked the man over. The Muurgu bloodline ran deep in this one. The green mottling on his olive skin appeared a darker shade than most. And the bright red skull ridges crested higher than usual. "I have already heard the report from your former senior officer; effective immediately, you are in command. I wish to hear your report."

The man at first seemed surprised by his promotion, but then appeared to calm. "Well, sir, after you positioned the Emperor over their facility, we used the cover of darkness to deploy our assault team of ten Muurgu warriors. I took point, with the commander taking the rear."

"All of us were dressed in full combat armor. Chest, arm and leg silicate shielding and helmets equipped with both infra-red and ultra-violet readings. I and most of the men carried our multi-phase laser rifles, while the commander was armed with a pistol and sensors carrying the bio-reader."

Pruutoc interrupted. "So, you were at the point and the commander at the rear. I waited too long to demote him."

"Yes, sir, I was at the point. As I was saying, we landed on the roof, and after making quick work of a rooftop door, gained entry into the building. The sensors indicated some type of material in the walls was shielding his readings while on the roof. But once we were inside, the device began to get proper locales of all enemy positions. Fortunately, there were no humans in close proximity to the roof entry."

"As we proceeded down the stairs, we came across the first humans we encountered. At lead, it was my decision to cut them down quickly so that our mission would not be compromised. I can tell you, Captain, that though they seem a little larger than your average Traanusian, they die just as easily."

Pruutoc waved a hand, urging the man on. "Yes, yes, after all, they are flesh and blood, but please continue."

"Well, sir, we made it down to the main floor area. The building from this perspective seemed quite large. Sensors informed us that the material we were seeking was located halfway across the floor. Thinking that speed was our best course of action, the commander ordered us to charge out and kill any resistance."

"When we broke from the cover of our position, it became apparent that many of the humans working there were unarmed and unshielded. We slew many, and the rest ran from our assault. When we reached the area where the material was contained, we met our first resistance. Waiting for us there were four humans of, I suspect, their military, with weapons raised."

In the ensuing firefight, we killed all four, but two of our own suffered severe injuries. Apparently, the weapons these humans use fire metal projectiles that pierced our silicate shielding easily."

Captain Pruutoc considered the ramifications. Muurgu armor was designed to withstand laser weapons. At least that would explain the losses. "Go on."

"Yes sir, well anyway, we were at the center of the facility and the material we sought was in a large vault. Gaining access to the secured area was easy enough, but once inside, the sensors indicated again that he lost all readings and we didn't know where enemy combatants were located. The plan was to contact you here on the Emperor, blast away the roof and extract the material, but the vault proved to be a difficulty, so the commander decided we should move the canisters out first."

"By the time we managed to move some of the large containers out of the vault, the humans mounted a counter-attack. Two more of my team went down. That was when the commander called for a retreat. We signaled for the roof to be blasted as in the plan, but rather than stow the material, we jumped on the lift and escaped the humans. Since our return, the two wounded soldiers have died in the medical lab from the injuries they sustained. I'm pretty sure the other two died where they stood when the humans attacked."

Pruutoc waited a moment to see if the soldier would add any more. Sensing none, he rose from his seat. "Thank you, Commander, you were only following orders. Return to your station."

Captain Pruutoc moved over to the sensors console. "Now, if I recall, we detected caches of the same material elsewhere on this planet."

The man on duty pulled up readings for the captain to examine. Looking over the details, he noted locations on almost the other side of the globe. Yes, it made sense to shift any future attempts to a different location, as the one they just attempted would no longer be caught by surprise.

CHAPTER 10

"Major Wayne Bucknell, please accompany me. You are next to testify."

Wayne rose from his seat. Nervous was just not good enough to describe how he felt. Preparing to go stand before a military tribunal to give his account of the charges against Brigadier General Francis Johnson terrified him. Pulling his dress uniform tight, Wayne preceded the MP into the courtroom.

As Wayne entered, General Johnson sat at the defendant's table, and glowered at him as he walked by. Wasn't this supposed to be a private interview? There appeared to be no sign of Colonel Smeeton. Wayne stood in front of the sole chair located before the panel. After taking the oath, he sat down. The feeling was oppressive. The panel was raised on a dais and looked down on him from on high. Although only a witness, he felt as though he was the one on trial.

"Major, you have reviewed the submission by Colonel Steven Smeeton in regards to this matter?"

Wayne looked up to the man speaking. The insignia he bore marked him as a general as well. "Yes sir."

"And do you find the details in this account to be totally correct?"

Wayne turned his head so that he could glance at General Johnson. "Sir, I was of the understanding that this tribunal hearing was to be a private session."

"Never mind the General, Major. As chairman, I have given Frank the opportunity to hear his accusers."

"Yes sir, I see, sir. I thought that, begging your pardon, the General would be afforded that opportunity should the matter proceed to trial."

"Damn it man! Am I not making myself clear? The general is a long-serving, high ranking member of the armed forces. His executions of duties for the protection of this country are irrefutable. I am not about to disrespect an old comrade over this matter. Now answer my questions."

"Yes sir. My apologies. I have indeed reviewed the report submitted by Colonel Steven Smeeton and find the record of the account to be exact. Colonel Smeeton is a man of detail."

The general in charge of the proceedings banged a gavel. "That's enough, Major. I am not looking for your opinion. Now, I want you to think carefully. Did you actually see General Johnson commit the acts alleged in this document?"

"Well, not exactly, sir. When we interrupted the general it appeared…"

Bang! The gavel pounded again. "This is a yes or no question, Major."

"Yes sir. No sir, I did not actually see the general commit the alleged acts."

"Thank you, Major. That will be all."

Wayne looked about and then back to the general chairing the tribunal. "That's it?"

"You are dismissed."

Wayne hesitated, and then slowly rose from his seat, but before he could step away, the lieutenant general located at the left end of the panel spoke up. "Before you go, Major, I have one more question."

Bang! "The major has been dismissed!"

"I'm sorry, general, this won't take a minute. If I am to rule properly, I feel it necessary to ask one more question." The judge now again faced Wayne. "Major, in your mind, are you convinced that the general committed the acts alleged?"

Wayne looked from the lieutenant general, to General Johnson, to the chairman and then back to his questioner. "Absolutely."

"Thank you, Major. You are free to go."

Wayne peeked once more at General Johnson and then preceded the MP out the door.

***

Time passed and the second Traanusian appeared to be slowly recovering from his ordeal with General Johnson. It was only after some weeks word arrived the trial never occurred. Apparently, the tribunal remained deadlocked over whether to proceed. Further, charges were now pending against Colonel Smeeton for insubordination. It was a veritable circus. Until they sorted it out, instructions were to take charge and continue on, but make sure the security of the prisoners was paramount.

Taking command of the entire base exposed Wayne to a number of new things that previously weren't in his purview. The remains of the two aliens killed in the uranium raid were delivered to the base. Upon first seeing them, he was shocked to see how dissimilar they were from Kraanox and his men. Although of the same physical size and structure, they were loudly colored and bore bone ridges that ran across their heads and shoulders. It reminded him of war-painted Indians from the old West. He wondered what he would have thought of these aliens should it have been one of these Muurgu he'd captured instead of the harmless looking Braannoo. The sheer ferocity of their appearance gave him pause. Delivered with the remains was the body armor they wore, but it appeared to be made of some glass-like substance that shattered easily when fired upon by the troops.

On the technological side of things, the scientists were at a stalemate. They simply could not fathom much from the remnants of the ship, smashed and battered as it was. The only parts that remained salvageable at all were the position thrusters, which offered little more than what they already knew. What appeared to be the control panels were nothing more than smashed cloudy glass. There were no wires, levers or any type of equipment that seemed to run anything. One of the boys hypothesized that all the electronics worked through the glass, though how, he had no idea.

Glass armor, glass electronics, it was obvious the technology of these Traanusians was far beyond that of his own men. What Wayne needed was some insight.

Wayne found Kraanox playing chess with one of his guards.

"Good afternoon, Major Bucknell. I am just about finished. Care for a game?"

Wayne chortled. "Yeah, and be your latest victim. You sure were quick to master it."

Kraanox moved a piece and spoke to his opponent, the guard. "There, that should just about do it. Checkmate in two moves, I believe." Resigned, the guard turned his king sideways in defeat. Kraanox returned his gaze to Wayne. "If it will help, I will play without the queen. There are only so many days that I can spend idling the hours away reading *Life* magazines. And with all those things missing from them, they aren't very fun to read at all."

Wayne marveled at the speed with which Kraanox mastered the English language. Already fluent, he now was learning to read. Giving him the *Life* magazines showed the human side of Earthlings, but the pages were censored to prevent Kraanox from reading anything that could be deemed dangerous for him to know. "Not today, Kraanox, perhaps another time. Right now, I would like you to accompany me."

Wayne waited for the alien to rise and join him. With Kraanox's movement came the clinking sound of his ankle chains. "Hold on a moment. Guard, give me your keys."

The guard retrieved the keys from his belt and handed them to Wayne. He knelt and unlocked the shackles from Kraanox's ankles. Rising, he tossed the chains to the guard. "Put these away for good. I don't think we need them anymore. It's not like he has anywhere to run."

Kraanox bent to rub at his ankles, stood up and smiled deeply. "And how are you today, Major? You have no idea how I have waited to get rid of those things. Is there something that I can do for you?"

Wayne walked, and Kraanox kept pace, the guards trailing behind. "I need you to explain a few things to me. Your assistance today, may, depending upon how much you help, determine whether you will be allowed a few more freedoms around here. Perhaps, even, a few perks."

Kraanox stopped in his tracks. "Perks? Your offer intrigues me, Major. Lead the way. I will do whatever I can."

Wayne stepped backward to clap Kraanox across the shoulders and get him going again. "I was hoping you would say that."

He led Kraanox into the lab where all the parts of his ship were disassembled. "Seeing it this way and the state of damage that so much of it seems to have suffered, it's amazing that any of you survived at all."

A couple of the men working nearby walked over. "Kraanox, I would like you to meet two of the men who are trying to make heads or tails out of this mess. What I would like you to do for me is answer their questions to the best of your ability."

Wayne introduced the men, and Kraanox shook their hands. Wayne watched and withheld a chuckle as he thought back to that first time when Kraanox used the same pressure from that extra thumb, and true to form, Kraanox gave both men sore hands. Someday, Wayne was going to have to teach Kraanox the appropriate level of pressure to apply.

Kraanox looked over at him. As I told you before, Major, I am just a simple soldier."

"Yes, Kraanox, you've told me. But I am not asking you to build the ship, merely answer some questions. I'm sure you can manage that."

The scientists brought Kraanox over to a table where he could sit down. "I'll try my best, Major. Don't expect a lot."

***

What the scientists found most interesting to note was the actual metal itself, it seemed to have a high silicate content. "What is this stuff made from?"

Kraanox decided a geography lesson of Traanu was needed. "Unlike Earth, with its massive continents, Traanu is a world with thousands of islands spread across its surface. Some of these are of great size, the combination of hundreds of small land masses merging, but islands all the same. All land on Traanu developed from the build-up of lava. At one time, in its beginning, Traanu must have been a total water world, with no dry land. The magma that burst to the surface covered the land in basalt flows. Through the ages these flows layered to the depth of miles and breached the surface of the water. Indeed, the topography is one of lowlands surrounding numerous mountain peaks."

"These volcanic mountains have eroded away over time, creating our most abundant resource, sand. Metals were hard to get. Though deep within the planet they might be abundant, little was near the surface. We simply adapted and learned to manufacture most of what we would use from sand."

He watched as the group chatted among themselves before returning to him with the next question. "If you have no standard metals at home, then no heavy metals either, like uranium?"

"That's correct. Although we know of this substance through very minute quantities, there is nowhere near enough for us to amass any levels of note."

The men furiously scribbled away on notepads "Hmm, then if no uranium, you could not be using nuclear energy to power your space flight. How do you do it?"

Kraanox sighed. It looked like it would be a long day. "I will make an effort to explain how, but I must admit the science is beyond my knowledge. So do not expect me to explain how it works, just that it does."

"I suppose you have heard of black holes. Immense gravitational power, these massive stars have such great magnetic strength that even light cannot escape their gravitational pull, hence, black hole. Yet if the speed of light is truly the fastest thing in the universe, as I've been told has been hypothesized by your Albert Einstein, then how does gravity catch it? Our scientists have discovered how to identify the constant gravitational waves that exist from all things. In space, the larger the astronomical object, such as your sun, the more identifiable the wave. It is there, right now, all around you, as are waves from this planet, my home system... you... me... that pen in your hand. All things have constant gravitational waves and what we have been able to do is latch onto the larger ones."

"The reality is that magnetism is faster than light. How else could it catch the light in a black hole? Once we latch onto a gravitational wave, we ride it to its source."

One of the scientists raised a hand in question. "Science dictates that nothing is faster than light."

Kraanox smiled. The rapt attention of these men felt like telling bedtime stories to children. "Originally, our scientists thought so as well. We have since learned of another type of invisible matter that acts as a mesh, connecting all things. It is through this mesh that these waves are able to travel at almost unlimited speed."

Also, we envelope our ship in a stasis field that wards off all other gravitational waves, so we are only affected by the one. It's a slow start, but grows exponentially as you ride, the farther the faster. Someone once explained to me that it is like a free fall without resistance. We fall all the trillions of miles it takes to get here, and break once we get close. When we arrive in a system like yours, we merely latch onto your planet's wave and draw ourselves in. We can grab onto multiple waves at once and use them to counterbalance each other, allowing us to move in any direction."

Another hand rose. "In the wreckage we found conventional thrusters. If you have this gravitational wave technology, why do you need them?

"Our ship is equipped with conventional thrusters as well, for when a more immediate push is required. Remember, our system starts slow but builds exponentially."

Over the days that followed, each part was displayed before Kraanox to provide a definition and purpose. Many pieces were mangled and burned beyond recognition, and just as many were outside his knowledge. But he was able to identify several components for them, and provide them with a simple explanation of the ships computer system and how the crystalline components were made. In the crash, every single one shattered, leaving nothing working, and Kraanox did not possess the scientific knowhow to replicate them.

In truth, he gave them very little. Most of what he told them were things they already figured out. But if anything, they were grateful for the confirmation of their theories, which would serve greatly in their analysis, so they could try and move on toward the application of their newfound knowledge.

***

Kraanox retreated to his quarters. Over the many days working with the humans, he took a complete inventory of everything scavenged from the wreckage of his ship. He was absolutely sure the part he looked for was not there. This could only mean that it was still at the crash site, in the forest.

His fellow crewman was still having health problems. Kraanox feared the fellow would never recover from the shock treatments inflicted by the general. If ever there was a chance for rescue, he needed that device.

CHAPTER 11

Three long years.

Captain Vreedoo mused on this fact as his Braannoo ship pulled into orbit. As expected, there was no sign of the Flower, captained by Commander Kraanox. The King would not be pleased.

When intelligence learned the Muurgu returned from this system and that its Captain Pruutoc claimed victory over a Braannoo ship, the worst was feared. For a while, the royal family grieved for the loss of one of its own.

Vreedoo recalled the campaign that ensued after the news became public. Commander Kraanox, already dear to the public as the front man of Braannoo's exploration of space, now served as the centerpiece in a fresh drive for troops and money.

The surge proved effective, as the military launched a fresh assault on the Muurgu at a strategic island they controlled, just outside of Braannoo territorial waters. The victory gave cause for great celebration.

Now, with the Muurgu in retreat, licking their wounds, and momentum on the Braannoo's side, the king ordered the current expedition in hopes his nephew was, somehow, still alive.

"Ensign, you're positive that no other ships are in orbit, ours or Muurgu?"

"Yes, Captain. I have been scanning since we began our approach. No sign of either."

"All right then, we have only so many days to conduct a search. With all the radio static emanating from this planet, we will be hard pressed to hone in on the transponder signal of Commander Kraanox's ship. Set up a grid pattern and narrow our search to only the correct frequency."

"Sir, with atmospheric interference and so many other signals, it could take months. For an effective search, we will need the Dragonfly to enter the atmosphere."

"Then I suggest you get started, the sooner the better. In the meantime, let's learn what we can about this planet and its people. There must have been some good reason why Commander Kraanox stayed in orbit so long."

Over the next several days, Captain Vreedoo reviewed reports from his crew. These humans, as they called themselves, were only now beginning to advance technologically. His own estimation, they were at least a hundred years behind Traanusian levels. Considering this fact, surely, there couldn't be anything of military value to the Braannoo.

More days passed, and he was slumped in his command chair when a shout from one of the monitoring stations startled him. Looking over, he saw a crewman waving him over to his monitor. "Captain, you better come and look at this."

"What is it, Ensign?"

"It appears to be a spaceship headed our way from the planet's surface."

"I thought that this world was incapable of space flight!"

"Perhaps the reports were inaccurate. Wait. Something's happening. It's blown up. No, that's not it, it's separated. The main body of the ship has fallen away and only the top section is continuing toward us."

"A warhead! They are trying to take us out! Take evasive maneuvers!"

"No, Captain, wait, it's going to miss us. It will pass below us at a safe distance."

Everyone gathered around the monitor and watched the small capsule pass under them. After only a short period of time, it re-entered the atmosphere and plunged to the planet below.

Already unhappy with the mission, Captain Vreedoo felt apprehension about any contact with these creatures. They'd fired on him without provocation. One option of his mission involved making contact and enlisting the assistance of the government of these... mammals, but they obviously were not to be trusted. He would have to do this on his own, however long it took. He ordered the crew to obtain a higher orbit and restarted the search. While they were here, he was not going to be threatened again. He initiated a secondary search to track any further launches. These humans were not going to catch him by surprise again.

***

The five men stationed at the radar tracking station who followed the flight path of the Little Joe 1B rocket began the job with a sense of optimism. As it continued to rise into the sky, it exceeded the previous Mercury flights in both distance and time aloft. Until now, many of the Little Joe's were considered failures. The lieutenant in charge watched over the shoulder of the radar operator as the rocket reached an apogee of nine point three miles. "Record that soldier; the time, date and distance, longitude and latitude. We'll submit the report to both Washington and NASA as confirmation of flight details."

The lieutenant was walking away from the station when the operator called him back. "Sir, I have an anomaly here. I'm tracking something directly above the flight pattern of the Mercury rocket."

Stepping back quickly the lieutenant peered at the screen. "Could it be a Doppler image?"

"No, sir, its trajectory, altitude and speed do not correlate with that possibility."

The lieutenant picked up the phone. As he dialed the numbers, watching the return of the rotary never felt so slow before in his life. "Hello. Yes, give me the colonel...right away. It's an emergency...Yes, Colonel, Radar Station Five reporting. We were tracking the flight of the Mercury rocket, Little Joe 1B, when we picked up an unidentified flying object directly over the rocket flight path...Yes, sir, a UFO. We are wiring over the coordinates now...We will track it as long as we can."

The lieutenant cupped his hand over the phone and yelled across to the radar operator. "Do we still have a bead on that UFO?"

"No, sir, it just crossed out of range."

The lieutenant turned to the communications officer. "Quickly, notify the other radar posts of the UFO's last known position. See if they can pick it up."

He returned the telephone to his ear. "We lost track of it, sir. We've notified the other stations of the last coordinates in hopes they can pick it up...Yes, sir, I understand, right away, sir."

Hanging up, he faced the men seated around the room, all now looking in his direction. "Gentlemen, what has just happened here today is classified. I am to remind each and every one of you that any relaying of the details of this event will be dealt with most severely. Am I understood?"

A chorus of, "Yes sir's" filled the room.

"Let's get all the details logged and sent off to Washington. It's their problem now."

The lieutenant sat down and began filling in his report. A wry smile crossed his face as he contemplated the flight path of Little Joe 1B directly below the UFO. On board, if only she could talk, the Rhesus monkey Miss Sam would have one story to tell!

CHAPTER 12

Dinner was served.

Pork chops and mashed potatoes. Mmm, just what he loved. And boiled spinach. Bleah! Leave it to Mom to ruin a good meal.

Dinnertime involved a lot of rules. He must be on time. He must have his hands washed. He must eat what was in front of him… there were people starving in China. And most of all, he could only leave the table if he were excused.

This last rule was the toughest of all. Justin's mom would sit down and want to talk. First, she would begin with a lot of questions for him. "How was school today? Do you have any homework? I haven't seen that Derkins girl lately, do you still play with her?"

Then the questions would take a turn from him to his father. "Have you heard anything about the Derkins lately? I heard he lost his job, do you know?" And other boring things to pass the time. Sometimes Dad would call Mom a gossip, and then she would stop asking and Justin could get up from the table.

His dad always brought the paper to the table and read while he ate. Most of the time, he did his best to ignore the questions as well, offering accommodating grunts and until something caught his eye in the paper and that would be the center of all future discussions at the table. When Dad talked, it was almost always about politics. When he began, Justin's mom would just sigh and "Yes, dear," the rest of the meal.

Normally, Justin would ignore this talk as well, but tonight, it caught his attention.

"I see that the Mercury missions have suffered another launch pad failure. What's that make it now, three in a row?"

"Yes, dear."

"It's sabotage, I tell you."

"Yes, dear."

"More than likely the work of communist spies at NASA."

"Yes, dear."

"I tell you, they stopped McCarthy too soon."

"Yes, dear."

Boy, if I could only get my hands on that Russian spy!"

"Yes, dear."

Justin, normally a passive bystander in these conversations, could contain himself no longer. "Then that man in our backyard *was* a Russian!"

Both of his parents stopped to stare at him and ask. "What man?"

"Remember a few of years ago, when those army men came and took that guy out of my sandbox? He was a Russian, I bet." Justin looked up to see the puzzled expressions on the faces of his parents. "Remember when I saw the Sputnik crash from the sky. You said I was dreaming, but I wasn't." His mind raced furiously now. "Maybe it wasn't the Sputnik. Maybe it was a spaceship that the Russian was using, and he crashed here in our forest." Still staring at blank faces, he continued. "Mom, remember when we went mushroom picking and we found that spot where all the trees were knocked down. I bet that's where his ship crashed."

His mother gave his father one of *those* looks. "Justin, it's good to have an active imagination, but you must remember not to use it when your father and I are having a serious discussion."

His father put down his paper and squarely faced him. "Now, Justin, I seem to recall now. You were falling asleep on the porch roof, and my guess is that you saw a shooting star just as you were about to nod off. The

Russians do not have spaceships. The best technology in the world is right here in the good ol' USA. No way can those commies over in Russia outthink us Americans. We're going to beat them into space, just wait and see. As for the forest, more than likely that spot was hit by lightning. Lightning is pretty powerful stuff, son. It can do all kinds of damage in the blink of an eye!"

Having finished this sermon, his father resumed reading the paper. Justin knew his dad was finished and wouldn't discuss things anymore. He recognized this stance from prior talks at the table and decided to retreat to his room. "May I be excused?"

With a sigh, his mother gave him permission to leave the table. As he bolted up the stairs to his room, he could hear her arguing with his father. "You have to be careful how you talk to Justin, dear, you know what Dr. Spock says about bruising the boy's ego."

"You and that kook, Dr. Spock. It's because of that nut ball that you named our son Justin. You said having a unique name would be good for his self-importance. Poppycock! We should have named him after my father, that's what we should have done."

"Really dear, I just don't think Bartholomew would have worked..."

Once inside his room, Justin kicked a few toys around. Why wouldn't his parents believe him when he talked about the strange man in the backyard that day? Although a couple of years passed, and there were a lot of things he couldn't remember, he could still recall the face of the stranger, all yellow-green in color, and the man was bald to boot. He wore a uniform of some kind, nothing like the one that the nice man from the military base wore. In his mind, the man just must be a Russian. He heard later that the Sputnik crashed back to Earth. Maybe that man from the base was wrong. Maybe the Sputnik was larger and could carry a Russian. Maybe that was what crashed in the forest, not some silly lightning.

Justin booted a few more toys around until he came upon the dinosaur egg he found. It was still as it was when he found it. Justin continued hoping it would hatch. He'd put it in his window where it would get lots of light and warmth, but nothing happened. Finally, he gave up and just put it in the corner. His father said that it was probably petrified, whatever that meant. He bent to pick it up and look at it again. Surprisingly, it was nicely warm. He glanced at the window and guessed that it must have been in the sunlight during the day. Putting it away, he quickly decided to forget about it and went back downstairs to watch some television.

***

"Commander, come quick. I believe I have found it."

Captain Vreedoo strode over to peer at the controls. "What is it, Ensign, what have you found?"

The transponder signal. I have linked to it. I'm getting a complete download of the ship's records. It's going to take a little while to get the entire data file, but at least we know it's still working and sending. I will plot the location for you up in navigation. From there you can chart a course to intercept."

"Can you instruct the transponder to give the details of the last day of ship's movements first?"

"Yes, sir. Give me a moment."

Vreedoo drummed his fingers on the arm of his chair waiting for what he suspected he already knew.

"Got it, sir! I am feeding the details to your personal console now."

"Good job, Ensign, an extra dessert for you at dinner tonight." Captain Vreedoo scanned quickly through the myriad of reports. Telemetry readings, ship environmental reports, log entries from the various departments. Finally, reaching the video log of the bridge, he started a playback. The beginning seemed mundane, and so he pushed fast forward. When the first explosion sped by, he stopped the play and ran back to the report of the Muurgu ship in pursuit. Crossing over to the ship's external camera recording, he watched as the Muurgu ship, twice the size of the Flower, fired laser pulse cannons and extend its trans-variant bridge. From the attempted boarding to the tear away by the flower, to its hopeless, careening dive down to the planet's surface.

He switched off the replay. "The Flower is gone. Let's hope the Commander isn't. Helmsman, take us to that transponder now. Where is that linguist, Shookaal? Tell him to be prepared to join the landing party."

***

Justin got back into his room from watching television before bedtime. A new show, *The Flintstones*, was on and his parents let him watch. He crossed the room to pick up his dinosaur egg again. Funny, it was still warm. Hoping it might still hatch, he placed it near the window once more. As he climbed into bed, he propped up his pillow so that when he lay down, the dinosaur egg was completely in his line of sight. Justin nodded off with visions of romping around with Dino.

***

The Braannoo landed in an open forest glade. As they set off toward the signal from the transponder, Vreedoo stopped for a moment to take in his surroundings. "If the entire world is like this, it would not be such a bad place to be marooned." Regaining the urgency of their mission, the men set out toward Justin's home. There were only four of them in this scouting party, and the captain elected to come along. Also were the linguist and the ensign responsible for maintaining the signal lock with the transponder.

They approached the house with care to avoid making any noise. After a few calibrations, the ensign assured the captain that the transponder was inside and that its signal was coming from the second floor, in particular the northwest corner of the domicile. The troupe moved carefully around the house until they faced the correct corner. Looking up, they spotted the open window and decided to try a foray into the darkened room. After some effort, Vreedoo and Shookaal managed to scale the front porch roof. Stopping before entering, they listened carefully to determine whether their ascent was overheard. The same noises emanated from below, and so the duo proceeded to climb through the window.

It took only a moment for their eyes to adjust to the darkened room. Looking about they immediately noticed the young human sleeping in the bed next to them. At the same time, Captain Vreedoo recognized the transponder sitting near the window and stepped over to retrieve it when he accidentally stepped on a squeaking toy.

***

Justin roused and looked sleepy-eyed at the two strange men in his room. They looked just like the man in his sandbox that day. Two more Russians!

One of the strange men spoke a funny language. "Esdrast, mitsa moya pezuma voya drast necoproyovet nisha nasha druga." Justin rubbed at his eyes. "Huh?"

The strange man spoke again. "Hello, we mean you no harm. We are looking for our friend."

83

Wide-awake, and a little scared, he didn't know whether to cry out for his parents or answer. He saw the other Russian holding his treasure. "Your friend is with the army guys. What are you doing with my dinosaur egg?"

The first man smiled and kneeled down to bring himself level with Justin. "Where did you get this thing?"

"In...in the forest."

"Well, young one, we better go look for our friend with the army guys. But, tell you what, how about I take your egg and fix it so you get a real dinosaur. Would you like that?"

"Boy...would I ever!"

"Then until next time, child, may the heavens destine you." Immediately, the two slipped back out the window.

As soon as they were gone, Justin leaped from his bed and ran downstairs. "Mom! Dad! You won't believe it! I'm going to get a baby dinosaur!"

CHAPTER 13

It was late, and Wayne was still up, reviewing reports. Leaning back, he stretched and rubbed his eyes. God, what he wouldn't do for a good stiff drink. Lately, his tasks included reviewing all UFO reports and determining if any appeared valid, based upon his knowledge of the Traanusians. The job seemed pointless, as there were hundreds of them from everywhere around the globe. When the reports arrived, it took him only a moment to conclude they were false. What took up the hours was detailing the reasons he used to make those decisions.

Maybe there was still somebody up in the commissary that he could get a drink from. Closing up his office, he headed across the yard to the commissary. He glanced up. It was a full moon tonight, a good night for werewolves and vampires. Wayne chuckled at the thought that leapt into his head. If only the world knew about these Traanusians. Those Hammer films would be mere child play than what panic would erupt throughout the country from news of aliens on Earth. Wayne was just a child when Orson Welles pulled that prank on the radio. Maybe he should give Orson a call, invite him over for a drink, and show him the real thing.

Enough silly musings, the bar was calling. Wayne hurried, when out of the corner of his eye he detected movement. He stopped in the middle of the yard and turned to focus on whatever he spied, but could see no one. "Is there someone there?"

Nothing. Not a sound. He took a few more steps in the general direction of the movement. "Hello? Anybody?" It was dead quiet except for a few crickets chirping in the night. He smiled to himself. Now he was being paranoid. Thinking about werewolves and vampires, then seeing shadows in the night. He needed that drink more than he originally thought.

The major returned to his path to the commissary, but just before he entered the crickets stopped chirping. He paused for only a moment then entered the building in front of him. As chance would have it, there were two soldiers, neglecting their duty, sitting there, drinking coffee. The quartermaster was at the back of the room, doing some cleaning. Seeing the major, the two soldiers snapped to attention, spilling coffee everywhere in the process. Wayne would have to worry about their breach of conduct later.

"Stand up, get ready, and pull your weapons, safeties off." When they indicated their readiness, Wayne nodded. "All right then, follow me, I suspect we have intruders."

Wayne turned to the quartermaster. "Ring up security, get every man already awake, armed and down here ASAP."

The three exited out the back door of the commissary and circled around the building, trying as best they could to be out of sight. Rather than reenter the courtyard, Wayne led the men in a circumventive route. As they progressed along, one of the men broke silence to whisper to the major, "What are we looking for, sir?"

"I don't know. All I know is that there is somebody out here. I could tell, the crickets stopped."

The man behind him hesitated in his pursuit. "Crickets, sir?"

"Yes, Private, crickets. When anyone nears one, it stops chirping until it senses that danger has passed. You need a better understanding of your duties and how to perform them when on watch, soldier. Remind me to put the two of you on report after this is all over, will you?"

The trio made their way around the commissary. Nothing. Wayne stopped and listened carefully. The crickets chirped away. Whoever disturbed them before was now gone. Crouched, the three raced across the open lane until they reached the side of the next building. One of the men bumped into the other. "Shit! Sorry, I can't see a thing out here."

Wayne shushed them and pointed. "Quiet! Listen… I think I hear some noise coming from that direction."

"Lead the way, Major, I'll stay tight."

After they reached the next building, Wayne peeked around the corner. The building housing the Traanusians stood across the next lane. Out front, the night guard lay sprawled on the ground, an alien standing over him with a weapon trained, and Kraanox and the other Braannoo were emerging from the structure with five others.

Wayne signaled for the men to split up and provide him cover. Walking slowly, holstering his pistol, he came out from behind his cover, and in broken Braannoo, ordered the aliens to surrender.

The Braannoo closest to him hoisted his weapon to shoot, but a yell from Commander Kraanox stopped him.

Kraanox separated himself from the group to step toward Wayne. "Major Bucknell, we will not shoot. I have requested that Captain Vreedoo…" He pointed to the Traanusian on his left. "…and these countrymen of mine not harm any humans, and they have so far grudgingly agreed. But if you shoot, they will return fire, and standing here in the middle, I do not like my chances of survival."

Wayne scanned the group in front of him. By now his two men were in position that should a fire fight break out, they would have a crossfire advantage. "I can't let you go, Kraanox. You know that."

Captain Vreedoo stepped forward and spoke into Kraanox's ear. He nodded his understanding, then focused again on Wayne. "Major, I have enjoyed your company. You have always treated me and mine with respect, but I wish to go home, and my government has sent this rescue team to extract me, nothing more. The ship is here. and we will depart immediately."

Wayne took one step forward, pulled his weapon and aimed it directly at Kraanox. "I cannot let you leave. If you try, I will shoot. It appears that what we have here is a Mexican standoff."

Above him, the stars disappeared, and he heard a whooshing noise. The alien ship arrived directly overhead. Kraanox stepped away from Wayne and engaged in a quick heated discussion with Captain Vreedoo then faced him once more.

"I propose a compromise then, Major. I will stay, but you will allow my crewman to leave. His health continues to deteriorate, and I think that he will not survive much longer. Back on Traanu, they can treat him better, and perhaps he will recover there. Otherwise, we start shooting and see what happens. You must decide quickly, Major, or they will fire regardless."

Wayne heard the noise of approaching troops on the run, and the Braannoo began to raise their weapons in readiness. From above, what looked like a lift appeared to be lowering to the ground. A million possibilities ran through his mind in an instant, but at the end of it all, he nodded his compliance and stepped back one pace.

Kraanox faced his counterpart, engaged in one more heated debate, then finally turned and walked over to stand beside Wayne.

***

Captain Vreedoo was furious, Kraanox knew. He gave a quick command and the remaining Braannoo scurried onto the platform. "I will leave a transmitter beacon in space in case you change your mind." The six Traanusians were hoisted up and into the ship in a matter of seconds. And just in time, as a contingent of men, some half-dressed, emerged from around the corner, armed and ready.

Kraanox hung his head. So close, and yet so far. All around him, the humans buzzed as they discussed the departing alien ship. The major shouted orders, but Kraanox did not care to listen. His decision was made. He would remain a prisoner. His people took immense pride in honoring their word, and he was not going to break that tradition.

He submitted to having his ankles shackled once more. Looking down at the chains so recently discarded, despair overwhelmed him for a moment. Kraanox stared into space, watching the ship leave. He always felt in control of himself when others were with him, looking for his command.

He never felt more helpless, or alone.

CHAPTER 14

The singing, though largely off-key, was loud and accompanied by many cheers.

"The Motherland hears, the Motherland knows
Where her son flies in the sky."

He felt a familiar hand clasp down on his shoulder. "Isn't it wonderful, Vladimir? We have beaten the Americans into space. Even now, our great comrade, Yuri Gagarin, circles the globe looking down on all of us. This is a joyous occasion."

Vladimir pried himself free. Leonid's penchant for bear hugs made giving some personal distance a priority. "Yes, Leonid, a great day. I believe I have some vodka in my desk. What say we go and open the bottle?"

Leonid scowled. "Vladimir, you should not be drinking here at the Komitet Gosudarstvennoy Bezopasnosti. If word got back to the Politicheskoye Buro, we would all be in trouble."

Vladimir chuckled. "If drinking vodka is not allowed on a day like today, then when is it? Besides, I bet right now at the Politicheskoye Buro they aren't wasting time with vodka. They are drinking champagne!"

"Ah, I suppose you're right. Let's go to your office and do it privately, though. No sense in sharing with this rabble." Leonid waved at the other KBG workers still reveling over the space flight of the Vostok 1.

Vladimir circled in behind his desk, while Leonid closed the door and sat down in one of the leather Bergère chairs. "Now, Vladimir, where is that bottle?"

Pulling open the bottom drawer, Vladimir retrieved the bottle and two shot glasses. "See, Leonid, still unopened. What better occasion than this one?"

"Ah! Shustov Vodka! How much are we paying you, Vladimir?" Eh?"

Vladimir poured the shots and held his glass aloft to Leonid. "Nostrovia!"

"Nostrovia!"

Downing the liquor in one gulp, Leonid pounded his glass down onto the black walnut desk. "While you are pouring another, turn on the radio so we can hear more of what's happening with the space flight."

Vladimir handed Leonid the bottle and turned to the radio behind his desk. The commentator was replaying Gagarin's statement before liftoff.

"Dear friends, known and unknown to me, my dear compatriots and all people of the world! Within minutes from now, a mighty Soviet rocket will boost my ship into the vastness of outer space. What I want to tell you is this. My whole life is now before me as a single breathtaking moment. I feel I can muster up my strength for successfully carrying out what is expected of me."

Leonid finished his second shot. "Not so vast."

Vladimir looked from the radio to Leonid. "How so not so? Space is infinite. Right now, Yuri is all alone out there in the cosmos, looking for God."

"There is no God, and when I tell you this, believe me, Yuri is not alone."

Vladimir regained control of the bottle and began to pour a third drink. "What are you telling me, Leonid? Is there something going on that the KGB is unaware of? Is the Politburo withholding secrets? I know that overseas reports go to you directly. Have the Americans beat us to space? What is it?"

Leonid grabbed his vodka and held it to look through it in the light. "What I tell you, Vladimir, is not to leave this office."

Vladimir nodded vigorously. "Go on."

Leonid drained his glass once more. "Out there, there are aliens, from outer space. We know this for a fact, because the Americans have captured one of their ships. It crashed almost four years ago. Our radar picked it up back then, and we have since corroborated the details. The Politburo is deeply concerned over this. Should Americans gain alien technology, it might give them an advantage over us. Something that cannot be tolerated."

Vladimir sat back in his chair, dumbfounded. "Why have I not been informed?"

"Plain and simple, Vladimir. The news would be devastating. It would demoralize the entire Soviet Union. Our leaders have decided to keep this quiet and learn what we can through our agents."

"Khrushchev is weak. We should be attacking the Americans before it is too late."

"Patience, Vladimir, patience. In capturing these aliens, it is suspected the Americans have made an enemy of them. Even now, we hear persistent rumors that foul play is involved in the failed Mercury missions. It is said the ships' onboard systems are being compromised by transmissions from space. If true, then it would seem prudent to let the Americans alone deal with this problem, while we continue to advance our own program. Look at today's shining success. Yuri has already circled the globe for over an hour. What have the Americans achieved so far? Ten minutes? Bah! I, for one, believe our Soviet system is far superior."

Vladimir poured the fourth round. "What do you want me to do?"

Leonid smiled and hoisted the glass. "I need more eyes and ears overseas. How many agents do you have ready for infiltration, and what about others already there but not activated? Hmm? It is time to use those assets. Let the Americans assume the risks, while we benefit from all they learn."

Leonid stood up, drained his glass and smacked his lips. "Ah! Well, Vladimir, I must go. I look forward to your reports. When Yuri lands safely, it is important that I be there. Dosvidanya."

"Dosvidanya, Leonid."

The door to Vladimir's office closed, and he sat down once more, feeling somewhat befuddled. Aliens! From where? Reaching for the bottle, Vladimir decided to make the fifth a double.

CHAPTER 15

Television time! The dinner dishes done, Justin pelted into the living room, only to discover his father still watching television. "Uh, Dad? Isn't the news over?"

His father looked up from his wingback chair. "Sit down, Justin. The president is about to come on. Even though he's a Democrat, I think you should watch."

"Aw, Dad!"

"Don't 'aw, Dad' me now. Sit down. Maybe you'll learn something. Better than those stupid cartoons and that Mickey Mouse Club you're always watching."

Justin slumped to the floor next to his father. As he played with the carpet threads, he could hear the man on the television talking about how the president was at Rice Stadium today, addressing college graduates. "I'm not even in high school yet. This is going to be boring."

"You will sit there and listen."

Justin knew he might have crossed the line when his dad gave him a dark stare.

Finally, the man on the television quit talking and the screen showed this fellow walking up to a whole bunch of microphones. "Is that the president?"

His father threw his arms up in the air. "Is that the president? Honestly, Justin, what are they teaching you in school nowadays! Yes, that's the president."

"Sorry, I just thought that the president was some old guy with no hair."

"That was Dwight D. Eisenhower. He was the president before this one, and a good one I might add, being a Republican and all."

"Then how come you kept calling him an idiot?"

Justin's dad fumed for moment and then waved his hand. "Never mind. Just watch the TV."

Justin looked back at the screen. The applause appeared to be dying down. Maybe it was time for the president to talk.

At first, he was talking about a lot of history stuff. Really boring. Justin hoped he wouldn't talk too much longer. But when he spoke about exploring space, Justin's interest perked up. Maybe this wasn't going to be as bad as he thought.

"...We choose to go to the moon. We choose to go to the moon in this decade and do the other things, not because they are easy, but because they are hard, because that goal will serve to organize and measure the best of our energies and skills, because that challenge is one that we are willing to accept, one we are unwilling to postpone, and one which we intend to win, and the others, too..."

Justin was intrigued. "Gee, Dad, wouldn't it be great to go to the moon?"

"Justin, be quiet and listen. He's talking about beating those commies into space. We have to make sure we get there first."

"...And finally, the space effort itself, while still in its infancy, has already created a great number of new companies and tens of thousands of new jobs...the National Aeronautics and Space Administration expects to double the number of scientists and engineers in this area, to increase its outlays for salaries and expenses to sixty million dollar a year, to invest some two hundred million dollars in plant and laboratory facilities, and to direct or contract for new space efforts over one billion dollars from this center in this city..."

"Wow, going to space sure costs a lot of money!"

His father stamped his foot. "Shhh!"

"...Well, space is there, and we're going to climb it, and the moon and the planets are there, and new hopes for knowledge and peace are there. And, therefore, as we set sail, we ask God's blessing on the most hazardous and dangerous and greatest adventure on which man has ever embarked. Thank you."

His father harrumphed, then turned to face Justin. "Son, you don't want to be an astronaut. Go into space in one of those tin cans? No, son, the future is for the man who designs those spaceships. An astronaut, if he survives, will do what after it's over? A few speeches? Whereas the scientist... his skills will be in demand until the day he dies."

"Still, I think it would be really neat to be an astronaut."

His father patted him on the head and rose from his chair. "Now, I think you have some homework to do? You aren't going to become a world-class scientist sitting on the floor, watching television."

Justin rose wearily. "Yes, Dad." He made his way to the dining room table to work on his studies.

After some time, his mother passed by while Justin sat moping at the table, pushing a pencil lazily across some paper, doodling spaceships. "What's the matter, Justin?"

"Nothing."

Sitting down next to him, she rubbed his back. "Yes, there is, Justin. Now tell me."

"Dad won't let me be an astronaut! He wants me to be a...a scientist!"

His mother reached down and turned Justin's chair so that he faced her directly. "Justin, you are only twelve years old. You have plenty of time to decide whether you want to be an astronaut or a scientist. But let me ask you a simple question. Can a scientist be an astronaut or vice versa?"

"I…I guess so."

"Then your problem is solved. Work hard and you can be both."

His face lit up as his mother's simple solution sank in. He jumped up from his chair and gave her a big hug. "Thanks, Mom."

She gave him a squeeze and stood up. "Now the problem is solved. I'll let you get back to your homework."

Justin returned to his chair and got hard to work on the math questions before him. He'd always liked arithmetic, and the answers came readily now that he had an incentive.

Scientist and astronaut, what a great idea.

CHAPTER 16

"Captain, we are arriving."

"Bring the planet up on my screen."

Captain Pruutoc looked once again at the planet the natives called Earth. When he returned home and related the tale of how he destroyed the Braannoo ship, the Muurgu leaders expressed pleasure at the news. When he informed them of what could be gained from a return mission, those same men all but salivated at the prospect of nuclear weapons.

Then, when the war against Braannoo suffered a setback, the urgency to accomplish the task of retrieving this highly fissionable mineral gave the necessary momentum to bring Pruutoc once more so many light years from home.

The planet loomed on his screen. Blue, just like the blue of Traanu. Analysis of the atmosphere showed a very close proximity to the atmosphere of Traanu. Yes, this world could very well be their next conquest.

"Give me a tactical of the surface."

The image was superimposed with the outlines of hundreds of countries. From strictly a land mass viewpoint, it showed clearly which country dominated the sphere.

The ensign at tactical swiveled in his chair to face him. "Sir, I am identifying a number of satellites surrounding the planet. If you give me a few moments, I will be able to display them on your screen."

"Do you know whether these satellites are military or not?"

"No, sir, though based on mass, they all seem very small. More than likely they're communications."

Pruutoc waited until the screen lit with dozens of small lights indicating the satellites. This new development caught him by surprise. How quickly were these Earthlings advancing technologically?

"Captain, all the satellites are in a low orbit, barely above the atmosphere."

Pruutoc weighed his options. "Pulling into a close orbit would make searching for uranium signatures easier, but increase the risk of being spotted. No, it seems the better plan is to enter a high orbit until the uranium is located, then strike swiftly. Ensign, set us into a high geodetic orbit above this country."

Pruutoc marked his indication on his screen.

"Yes, Captain." The ensign moved the Emperor into the region of space just above the Soviet Union.

***

Vladimir sat in the back seat as his driver careened through the streets of Moscow. He picked up the file beside him one more time. There could be no doubt about it. The Soviet radar scanned the entire border in self-defense. Vladimir tried to verify his report with the military with no results. When questioned as to why he required the information, he evaded answering. It was not for anyone else to know how the KGB spied on her own people.

The small, spy satellite piggybacked into space with a weather satellite. Using radar, it tracked American satellites as they passed overhead. But when signal pings bounced down to the KGB radar station showed an object of such massive size, there could only be one possibility.

Pulling up in front of the Politicheskoye Buro, Vladimir jumped out and raced straight to Leonid's office. "Leonid, I need to speak with you."

"Come in, Vladimir, you look upset. What can I do for you?"

Vladimir dropped the report in front of Leonid. "There can be no doubt, the pings verify it. It's outside of the range of the military search pattern, but we picked it up."

Leonid chuckled. "So, your little spy in the sky has got you a bigger fish than you can swallow."

"This is no time to laugh! There is an alien spaceship directly over our heads!"

Leonid leaned back. "Sit down Vladimir. We will figure this out. In the meantime, your nervousness is bothering me."

Vladimir plopped into a chair. "I never thought there would be the day I would need to keep secrets from the Komitet Gosudarstvennoy Bezopasnosti, especially when I am in charge!"

"This ship is staying directly over us? Not moving?"

"Over Dzhezkazgan, to be exact. It's just…sitting there."

Leonid slapped his desk top. "I have the answer! General Bolkov is a friend of mine. They are conducting a high-altitude nuclear test tomorrow. With the Cuban missile crisis currently commanding complete attention of everyone, a little saber rattling is necessary. Give me the location. I will relay those coordinates to Bolkov. He will fire the weapon there. Poof! No more aliens."

"Will it work?"

"We can only hope so, comrade, only hope."

***

Pruutoc reviewed the possible Russian sites to retrieve either the refined metals or an actual weapon. All were military installations with troops and anti-aircraft equipment stationed nearby. He doubted whether the weaponry would have any real effect on the Emperor, but the necessary time to load the uranium would leave them open to attack. Another question lay before him, whether to go after the lightly guarded unrefined ore or gamble and go straight for the finished product, a nuclear weapon!

"Captain! A missile just launched from the site directly below us. I believe it is headed right for us!"

Pruutoc rushed to the console to examine the data. By the heavens, they were under attack. "Quickly, target the missile and begin evasive maneuvers!"

As he belted himself into his station, he turned first to his helmsman. "Move the ship laterally to evade the rocket."

Swiveling in his chair he pointed at his weapons officer. "Target that missile and fire!"

Beams of energy fired and lanced across the sky in an attempt to hit the oncoming missile. He watched as the missile neared until finally, his gunner managed to detonate it with a direct hit. Only then did Captain Pruutoc get a true sense of the devastating nature of the weapon. The sky filled with such brightness, that both sets of his eyelids instinctively closed for a moment. Initially, he was rocked by a thermal wave that scorched the exterior of the ship. The intense winds that followed buffeted them crazily.

But he became most frightened when the entire ship system shut down and the interior went dark. "What happened?"

His first officer hit the emergency lights. "It must be some kind of electromagnetic pulse.

"Engage backup systems now!"

The free fall lasted only until the backups kicked on and re-established the ship's propulsion system. The details on his console showed the Emperor fell all the way into the lower atmosphere of the planet.

Pruutoc sat back. This was a weapon the Muurgu Empire must have! Pulling up the site map, Pruutoc gave flight instructions to his navigator. "Battle stations everyone. I aim to capture at least one of those weapons for the glory of the empire."

The Muurgu ship sped down to the base that dared to fire on them and laid waste to the facility. The Kraganda power plant and the entire surrounding neighborhood exploded into flames as the Emperor's laser canons dealt their decisive blow.

After they left Earth's atmosphere, the first of his crew to fall at his station was the navigator. Pruutoc knew better than to make the same mistake twice. Only when he was satisfied all resistance was crushed, did he send in the retrieval team.

Mission accomplished. He gave orders to return to Traanu. They only managed to attain one warhead, but a hasty retreat was necessary. Tactical enemy aircraft were converging quickly.

His ship withstood the thermal and wind waves from the nuclear blast. They recovered from the electromagnetic pulse. Pruutoc was horrified to learn from the ship's medic, deadly nuclear radiation penetrated every inch of the hull. The silicate shielding was useless against this invader. Every Muurgu on board received a mega dose of radiation. Despite achieving their mission to attain the nuclear material, Captain Pruutoc was unsure as to whether he would even make it home.

CHAPTER 17

Steven Smeeton drove his car to the base. Too long a time had passed since his last stint here, that, and a couple of rankings. Reduced to a captain, he did not relish the role reversal he now faced with Major Bucknell becoming his superior officer.

The trial was a farce from the beginning. Brigadier General Francis Johnson relied on his cronies to staff the tribunal. The general's lawyers were able to persuade the court that the Geneva Convention did not apply, as these were aliens, not humans, and non-signatories to the convention. After six months of testimonies, and military political wrangling, the general was released without charge. He withdrew into early retirement, with full honors.

After that, Steven's life became hellish. New charges were brought against him for misuse of his authority and countermanding a superior officer's orders. With the general retired and the charges against him dismissed, Colonel Smeeton stood little chance of coming out ahead. In the end, his role in the military was significantly reduced, his goals and aspirations destroyed. All he had left was his honor.

His previous knowledge of the Traanusians was what allowed him to return to his post as head of security. There were those that wanted to punish him even further, but the demand for secrecy outweighed personal vendettas. He was now parked in front of the base, waiting for admittance.

The guard on duty seemed to be stalling. He'd called in Captain Smeeton's transfer orders some time ago and stood waiting in his booth rather than opening. Steven was just about to get out when he saw Major Bucknell jogging to the gate.

Wayne appeared glad to see him. More than likely, he would not have heard anything since the incident and was now bursting to know what happened. Funny, during his previous assignment at the base, Wayne and he clashed.

Wayne came up to his open window. "Sorry you were held up, Steven. When I heard you were being assigned here again, I gave instructions to the guards to delay things until I could greet you personally."

Steven felt perplexed. His memories of dealings with Major Bucknell were not fond ones. The major climbed in the passenger seat and they proceeded into the base, Major Bucknell chatting all the way as if they were old buddies. As he looked around, he noticed several new buildings. What was previously a fairly empty yard was now a good-sized facility. Security appeared tighter as well, with additional fences and guard towers that gave the place a fortress like atmosphere.

Wayne directed him to his new quarters and then walked him over to the mess for a drink. Walking in, he was surprised to find Kraanox standing at the bar. Wayne gave him a wink. "We give him a little more freedom now around the base. He likes brandy. Care for one?"

Kraanox approached him, hand outstretched. "It is nice to see you again, Colonel Smeeton."

Hesitant at first, Steven took the hand. "It's captain now, Kraanox, but thank you for remembering." Kraanox smiled. Some time had passed since he last saw the Traanusian, but the familiarity popped back quickly. Shaking his hand, watching him smile and laugh with the others, it was almost as if he was one of the men, not an alien from a distant world. He was even wearing fatigues. Steven guessed that his original suit of clothing could only last so long, and they needed to dress him in something, but military garb? "So how are things here? I've been briefed about the rescue incident, and your decision to remain."

Kraanox froze for a moment. Letting go of the captain's hand, he sighed deeply and appeared to gather himself. "I miss my home, my friends, and my family. I have been here a number of your years now, and though not the same, I have been afforded a new home, new friends, and new family."

Steven spent the rest of the afternoon at the bar with Major Bucknell, partaking of perhaps a bit more than he should. He was briefed about his duties by Wayne, then spent the rest of the time meeting the men as they passed through the commissary. A number of faces were familiar, but there were just as many new to him.

Steven listened as Wayne summed up all the research since his departure.

"The scientific studies have almost ground to a halt. Little has truly been learned from the remnants of the ship. The maneuvering rockets are no more complex than expected, the propulsion fuel for them similar to what we now use at NASA. The main interstellar drive is still a mystery as it was pretty well destroyed by the Muurgu attack and the crash on Earth. The shielding is a silicate composite, inferior to the strength of steel, though offers great promise in shielding against heat and electrical charges. The staff, with input from Kraanox, seems to spend more time dealing with mundane issues such as household goods, things that Kraanox *can* explain."

Wayne paused to take a sip of his drink, and then waved his hand around. "The base is now more of a clearinghouse for alien reports and phenomena. We beefed up security with an in-house radar station and more, to prevent a repeat of the rescue attempt."

"Plain and simple, without the onboard computers, nothing works. All that remains of them are shards of glass crystals, and, as of yet, we haven't been able to extract anything from them."

The three men sat quietly for a while, enjoying their drinks. Somewhere, a bell tolled six o'clock. Wayne asked the bartender to turn on the news.

The lead story featured President Kennedy making an announcement regarding the signing of the Limited Nuclear Test Ban Treaty.

"...In these years, the United States and the Soviet Union have frequently communicated suspicion and warnings to each other, but very rarely hope. Our representatives have met at the summit and at the brink; they have met in Washington and in Moscow; in Geneva and at the United Nations. But too often these meetings have produced only darkness, discord, or disillusion.

Yesterday a shaft of light cut into the darkness. Negotiations were concluded in Moscow on a treaty to ban all nuclear tests in the atmosphere, in outer space, and under water. For the first time, an agreement has been reached on bringing the forces of nuclear destruction under international control-a goal first sought in 1946 when Bernard Baruch presented a comprehensive control plan to the United Nations...."

Wayne looked over at Steven as the press coverage of the President went on. "I wonder what made the Russians give in on this. The United States has been trying to get this treaty done for a long, long time.

On the television, President Kennedy continued speaking.

. We have a great obligation, ...to use whatever time remains to prevent the spread of nuclear weapons, ..."

Steven turned to stare directly at Kraanox. "*They did.*"

A silence fell over the room as all stopped to follow his gaze.

Kraanox lifted his glass toward him. "You're welcome."

The president was still talking, and everyone's attention returned to the speech, without the response Kraanox required.

"...But now, for the first time in many years, the path of peace may be open. No one can be certain what the future will bring... According to the ancient Chinese proverb, "A journey of a thousand miles must begin with a single step."

The press coverage ended, and Kraanox turned once more to face Steven and Major Bucknell. "A man of such wisdom would serve as a great ambassador to the people of Traanu. It is moments such as this that make me appreciate the greater qualities that exist in mankind. A single step is all that is needed to begin a journey that is not only for my people a thousand miles but a hundred trillion more." Kraanox exaggerated a single step to stand before Steven and take him into a hug. Before the situation could become awkward, Kraanox released him, spun and hugged the nearest man, and then proceeding quickly, he embraced every man in the room, saving Major Bucknell for last.

Wayne, for a moment, played hard to get. "I'm a married man!" This immediately broke the room into a round of laughter. Kraanox completed the last hug, and Wayne turned to everyone in the room. "All right men, I need your silence on this one, so the next round is on me!"

Steven was momentarily surprised. When did the major get married? He figured Bucknell for a career man like himself. There never seemed to be time for a wife. He felt even further behind hearing of Wayne's matrimony.

Another burst of laughter, and once the drinks were poured the room settled down into quiet conversations once again. Steven sought out Kraanox one more time. "My apologies, Kraanox. Just like all humans, I would assume not all Traanusians are the same."

Kraanox nodded, and the two finished their drinks then drifted off into different groups to chat the rest of the night away. At the end of the evening, when Captain Steven Smeeton retired to his quarters, he finally came to terms with the turmoil within him. Taking orders from a man who served previously as his junior officer and one who never suffered the consequences of the trial with General Johnson should have proved a hard pill to swallow. The arrival of the aliens challenged his beliefs and put him in the crossfire with General Johnson.

But his reception seemed warm and genuine. It may have been tough to take orders, and difficult to face the Traanusian, but it felt good to be wanted again.

As a career soldier, to be wanted in a military role was all he truly needed.

Like Kraanox, he found a new home.

CHAPTER 18

It felt good to walk in the gardens—the flowers, the trees, the glistening pools all around. Jaaxxoo, King of Braannoo, walked here to relieve the pressures that weighed upon his mind. His wife by his side, the two strolled along, taking in the sights and smells. Flowers and birds abounded in a dazzling array of colors and scents that tantalized his senses.

"So, are you mad at Captain Vreedoo for failing to bring home Kraanox?"

The king stopped to lift up the chin of Floovaa, his queen. "No, my love, not angry. Proud, that our nephew should uphold our long tradition of honor and decide to remain, allowing his brethren to return unheeded, shows the true royal blood that flows through his veins."

Floovaa took Jaaxxoo's hand from her chin and held it as they continued to walk. "Still, Kraanox is popular with the people, and with the loss of his older sibling, he is the only son left to your brother."

"Yes, my brother still mourns for the loss of his oldest, a death most tragic. But he is not alone. Many are the extended members of my family lost, not in space, but through war."

The two walked silently for a time, the gardens of the castle being most extensive enough to allow them to meander through without having to retrace their way. Each step brought new delights and smells.

They reached an open glade with a large pond fed by a small waterfall. Jaaxxoo waved to the servants following them, who set about quickly setting up a small table and two chairs that the king and queen might grab a bite to eat on the lawn.

"The truth is, this on again, off again war with the Muurgu is a strain on the people, not just through the loss of sons, daughters, husbands, wives or any other extended family members. But the financial drain on our economy gnaws away at the minds of those who survive. Many, I hear, suffer with empty larders and threadbare garments."

The queen frowned. "Then perhaps we should be thankful that we have survived. Are not things turning our way lately? Have we not claimed a number of major victories recently? Are not the Muurgu also engaged on another front with the Bruutaan's? Perhaps the people need only a respite to refresh them. Rid their minds of their troubles. Maybe you should call a holiday. Open the royal coffers and provide a feast for all. Give them hope that we near the end of the tunnel, and daylight is just ahead."

Jaaxxoo stooped to kiss Floovaa once, quickly. "That is why, my love, I take these walks with you and not my advisors, for such delightful insights that do not involve a battle plan."

The table set, the king and queen sat to enjoy a light meal. Floovaa glanced over at the nearby waterfall. "And this is why I accompany you on these walks. There is still the romantic in you. I recall the midnight trysts we enjoyed at this very pond prior to our wedding. If our parents knew then, they would have been mortified. Your father would probably have exiled me from the country!"

Jaaxxoo chuckled. "And your father would have those brothers of yours beat me until I was a pulp! My one weakness in my code of honor is you."

"Then perhaps a dip in the pool for old times' sake?"

"This old body? In that pool once more? You must be planning my execution after all those years."

As they laughed together, a page came rushing forward to drop on one knee in front of him. "Your Majesty, we must get you to the shelters immediately. A suicide mission of the Muurgu has broken through our defenses and appears headed toward the palace. They sacrificed a large portion of their fleet to get this group in. We suspect that you are the target."

Jaaxxoo scanned the skies as if he might see these intruders. "How many got through, and do we have flyers on intercept?"

"Six or seven, my lord, and we have twenty of our own bearing down on them as we speak, but I fear the Muurgu may reach the castle before ours arrive."

Jaaxxoo turned his gaze toward the castle. Its armaments were vast and well shielded. "Then we shall wait in the cover of these trees and watch our forces route the enemy."

It was only a few moments before the siren sounded and the enemy flyers came into view. In the distance, the royal fleet could be seen fast approaching as well. The time differential was only a matter of seconds. The king relaxed. His armies should make short work of the incursive force.

He watched as the Muurgu fighters, still appearing out of range, unleash their payload towards the castle. He knew the defensive armaments would pick up the missile and tracked it to shoot down. Once in range, the laser cannons would fire to destroy the weapon as it neared.

For a brief second, Jaaxxoo and Floovaa huddled together, watching as laser cannon fire streamed out of the castle. What could such a suicide mission hope to achieve? Even now, it appeared the invaders were running away after falling short of the target.

As he expected, the laser cannons found their mark in the oncoming missile. The enormity of the explosion and the blinding bright white light accompanying it staggered the king. In the brief instant following, he realized with horror the impending devastation of the ensuing blast. The castle would all be but demolished, and most of the flyers hurled to the ground. His mind quickly turned to his loyal subjects. How many would die from such a monstrous blast?

As the blast wave hit, his last thought was to protect his wife by holding her tight to him. In the end, it mattered little.

CHAPTER 19

Justin was beyond excitement as he watched the countryside roll by the train window. Just like in the song from school, he watched as the spacious skies and amber waves of grain filled his vista.

The conductor approached, coming down the aisle. "Tickets! Have your tickets ready. Tickets!"

Fumbling through his carryon, he found his ticket just as the man arrived at his seat.

"Tickets!"

He handed his over. "Here you go."

The man punched a couple of holes in the stub and glanced at it before returning it to him. "Washington, D.C., huh. Going up to meet the president?"

"Actually, I am."

The conductor, chuckling, stopped, and looked down at him. "You are? I'm just fooling with you, son, no sense in lying to me."

"But I'm not! I really am going to see the President." Justin fumbled once more into his bag and produced the letter of invitation and handed it over.

Scratching the side of his head as he read, he finished and handed the document back to Justin. "My apologies, young sir. Teach me to open my mouth before I think."

He turned and faced the rest of the people in the car. "Ladies and gentlemen, we are honored to have a special guest on board today. Mr. Justin Spencer, on his way to meet with the President of the United States of America, Mr. Lyndon B. Johnson himself. Mr. Spencer is going to receive an award from the president." He turned to face Justin once more. "I'm sorry, son, what was the name of that award?"

"The Presidential Scholars Award."

Turning once again to the crowd, he continued. "The Presidential Scholar's Award, for academic excellence!"

A round of applause and a few cheers reverberated through the train car. Justin half rose, gave a tentative wave to everyone, and then sat back down.

The conductor leaned back over Justin. "Anything I can get you, young sir? Something to eat, drink? No charge today, it's on the house."

"Uh, well, thank you. I suppose. Do you think it would be okay if I have a *Coke*?"

The man laughed. "Young sir, you are a modest one, that you are. One *Coca-Cola* coming up!"

A chicken salad sandwich, two *Hershey* bars, and three *Cokes* later, Justin thought of home.

His mother wanted to come. But she needed to stay behind. His father wasn't well and felt that Justin could manage on his own anyway. He said it was time for him to take charge of his life. "Go on. Go alone, you're a man now. Have some fun. It's about time you start taking care of yourself. Say hi to the president for me."

His mother cried and gushed a lot. Her little boy was no longer so little. In truth, Justin was now a foot taller than his mom. But no matter how big he got, he still felt like a small boy in her presence.

So they bought him a ticket and made his hotel reservations. His father did his best to give a firm handshake. His mother hugged him hard and took a long time to let him go.

For Justin, it was a difficult moment. He knew both his parents loved him, but in different ways. He grabbed his suitcase and climbed aboard the train. The ride seemed long and quiet, and gave him much time to think.

He pondered the numerous ways his life would now go; which school would he go to. Whichever one he picked it would be out of town. This trip would be the first of many days to come where he would not come home every night to Mom's cooking and Dad's lectures.

***

The White House. It was simply exhilarating that he was in the building. Along with about a hundred and twenty other scholarship recipients, he waited in the east room. Looking around, he could see the other faces full of awe. He wondered if his own looked like theirs.

The chatter hushed as President Johnson entered. Every eye was glued to him. He was introduced and began his address to the scholars. Justin listened intently, but at the same time his gaze was scanning the room and the other people in it.

"I hope that you feel as special about this award and this event--at least as special--as we feel about those who have been selected for this great honor.

Certainly, we all recognize that we are living in a time which requires a great deal from all of us. ...this time in America has required us to endure events which seem unbelievable--and almost, at times, unbearable-tragedies of violence and unreason..."

Justin craned his neck, and from the corner of his eye noticed someone standing at the back of the room, leaning against the wall.

"...Every time for our country has been a difficult time. But every time has also been a time of hope, too..."

Justin turned in his seat to get a better look and the students beside him sneered at his inattentiveness.

"Ask yourself not what you can say or do that will create doubt or will plant fear, but ask yourself what you can do that will heal, build, and be constructive...."

He returned his gaze to President Johnson, but inside his mind a new agenda waited for the speech to end.

I have not the slightest doubt about the future as long as a country can develop young men and women with faith like you, with hope like you, with the leadership that I hope you will give all of us. Thank you very much."

When the speech was over, every other person in that room lined up to shake the president's hand. But Justin recognized the man in the corner and strode back toward him.

The man leaning against the wall straightened up when he saw Justin approaching. "You're going the wrong way, son. The line's over there."

Justin glanced over his shoulder at his fellow honorees. Turning back, he offered his hand to shake. "Mr. Shepard, could I have a moment of your time?"

Alan B. Shepard, Jr. smiled at him and accepted the proffered handshake. "How can I help you, son?"

Justin swallowed hard. "Since I was a kid, I have wanted only one thing in life. How do I become an astronaut? I want to go into space like you."

His visit with America's first astronaut felt like a dream come true. Though they only had spoken briefly, Mr. Shepherd paid attention to him and even hinted at advising NASA to keep an eye on Justin.

Justin felt spent as he changed to his pajamas in his hotel room. The continuous excitement of the day and the long train ride sapped all his strength. Before climbing into bed, he turned on the television. Although tired, he decided

116

to stay up to watch his favorite show, and it was just about to start.

"Space, the final frontier. These are the voyages of the starship Enterprise...."

CHAPTER 20

After the devastating attack on the Braannoo capital and the obliteration of the royal castle, the people of Braannoo went into a frenzy. When Vreedoo gave his report, the weapon was most likely obtained from the Earthlings, the military commanders agreed they should do what they can to prevent such a recurrence. Admiral Druugaan ordered a full scale counter attack with the sole purpose of destroying Muurgu space capability.

Vreedoo served in the air force and joined in on the attack against the Muurgu bases. He recalled how many of his fellow pilots were shot down by the Muurgu defenses.

Vreedoo thanked the heavens the Muurgu were preoccupied, with their skirmishes with the Bruutaan's. Otherwise, they would have swept into Braannoo with ease in those fateful days after the counter attack. Too many of their military's forces were depleted.

Though the loss of life and equipment was monumental, the mission was deemed as success, Muurgu space fields were, for the time being anyway, out of commission.

After the battle, Admiral Druugaan summoned him. "Captain Vreedoo, things are a mess right now. The people are without a leader. I need you to return to the human planet once more and succor the release of Commander Kraanox at all costs. You know the reason why."

"Yes Admiral, after so many of the royal family were lost in the attack on the castle, Kraanox now stands as the legitimate heir to the throne."

"Exactly, and the people know this as well. They will not take kindly to us should we fail to make every effort to retrieve him."

"I sincerely doubt I will be able to forcibly retract him. The humans will be ready for us now."

Admiral Druugaan rose from his chair to come round his desk and place a hand on Vreedoo's shoulder. "Diplomacy, man, use it. Shookaal is trained in negotiation tactics, put him on the job. Just remember, bring Commander Kraanox home, we're counting on you."

***

The Dragonfly slowed as it neared the planet. Already, it had passed within the orbit of the single moon that encircled it. Captain Vreedoo wanted to approach with caution. "Scan the surrounding space to make sure there are no Muurgu ships in the vicinity."

As tactical began the scan, Vreedoo mulled over the unlikelihood anything would be found.

On his last voyage here, the argument with Kraanox frustrated him. Rather than shoot their way free, Kraanox elected to stay behind so there would be no loss of life on either side. He would be disappointed to find out the crewman he saved died the day of the nuclear attack, along with everyone else in the main hospital of the capital city. Vreedoo's promise of no further rescue attempts, proved to be, in hindsight, a terrible decision on his part. Now, he must plead with Kraanox to seek release from his vow.

"Captain, a ship, near us, but not of Muurgu design. I suspect it is from the planet below."

Vreedoo strode over to the console and brought up the image of the Earthling ship on his view screen. "These creatures are simply amazing. Look at that contraption. It is surprising that it can fly at all, let alone achieve space flight."

A crewman interrupted the captain. "Sir, I am picking up heat readings from inside that ship. I suspect that there are three life forms aboard. I suppose humans."

Vreedoo bent forward to get a closer look at the screen. "As I said, simply amazing. Helmsman, get us nearer that ship. I wish to get a closer look."

"Captain! We are intercepting transmissions from the human ship."

"Where's Shookaal. I want to understand what they're saying. Get him up here, now."

***

So far, so good. The liftoff at thirteen thirty-two on July sixteenth proved flawless. Each section of the Saturn rocket fired precisely and jettisoned accordingly. They were now in space for three days.

Mike looked out the window because something caught his eye. "What the hell is that?"

Neil stretched over to stare out where Mike was looking "What is it? What do you see?" Mike pointed out the ellipsoid shape in the distance. "Buzz, you better have a look at this."

Edwin Eugene 'Buzz' Aldrin, Jr. moved to stare out the same window as his two fellow astronauts, Neil Alden Armstrong and Michael Collins. "Well, what the hell is that?"

The three Apollo 11 astronauts were in a quandary. Should they radio Houston about what was outside their ship? The men considered possible reactions. Would NASA panic? Would they abort the mission? It was finally decided that they would send a cryptic message to Mission Control.

***

Since the last visit, Vreedoo's linguist Shookaal was now fluent in six human languages. As communications officer he was picking up messages from the earth ship. "I'll relay in Braannoo each message to your console."

"Make it so."

Captain Vreedoo sat and watched the screen as the human communiqué were interpreted.

"Do you have any idea where the S-IVB is with respect to us?"

"Captain, they are receiving communication from the planet as well."

"Standby."

"Let's watch and listen for a while, I would like to get a better understanding of these aliens before we proceed with our mission."

"Apollo 11, Houston. The S-IVB is about 6,000 nautical miles from you now, over."

Vreedoo straightened up to look for the man who detected the earth vessel in the first place. "Ensign, are you detecting any other vessels out there?"

"No, captain, nothing else of sufficient mass shows on my screen. There appear to be a number of satellites in orbit around the planet, but nothing in our vicinity."

"Hmm, I wonder if they have detected us. At this distance, it is unlikely they are detecting us with old-fashioned radar, but they may have seen us. Perhaps we've been spotted, let's move off a bit. I don't want our arrival to be anticipated. It's time to get down to the surface and retrieve Kraanox."

***

Kraanox sat in the mess hall with a large group that included Major Bucknell and Captain Smeeton. Everyone sat watching the broadcast of the Apollo Eleven mission. "In our history, we do not have such an early event as this one. Our planet has no moons. Hence, we did not begin space travel until we were further in our scientific

121

advancement than you. In my time here, I am becoming a good study of this planet. Unlike you, we have no moon, so no close proximity space travel, no tides, and no werewolves."

A small chuckle rippled from all those around who were listening.

"There is a close proximity in size, your planet being slightly larger. I suspect heavier, too. I find the gravity tires me, though over the years I have become accustomed. And our days are as yours, only slightly longer."

"There is only one other planet in our system. A gas giant twice the size of your Jupiter. Our scientists surmise that this monster has absorbed all other planetoids in our system and has its eye on us as well. Much further out from our sun, it is on a slow eventual spiral inward. But it is no immediate threat. At its current rate it will take another three billion years before it reaches us."

"So, as a result, the nearest planet we could visit was in the next solar system. We achieved that goal when we finally developed interstellar space flight thirty years ago. Since that time, we have visited a dozen different systems and only yours showed life."

"So, as I sit here and watch these events unfold with your people, I am downhearted at the knowledge of what could have been. The people of our world should not be fighting; we should be united in reaching across the cosmos for new people such as you. Though reading of your two world wars, I guess that we aren't so dissimilar after all."

A soldier shouted, "Hey everyone, they've begun the lunar descent!"

***

Justin looked around with satisfaction. His chores done, he wanted to get in front of the television as quickly as possible to watch the lunar landing. With the lawn done, it was time to put the mower away in the backyard shed. As Justin emerged from the shed, he was surprised to discover two strangers in the yard. The pair seemed odd, both wearing toques on their heads, and gloves on their hands, despite the hot weather. "Can I help you?"

One of the men took one small step forward. "Do not be alarmed. You may not remember me, but some eight years ago, our paths crossed. I am in need of a favor."

Justin pondered running into the house, but as he looked hard at the two men, recognition set in. But that was eight years ago when he was only ten. Despite the hats pulled down on their heads, Justin could see these were not two men, but the two strangers who entered into his bedroom so long ago. He found their pointed ears, very flat noses, bulbous eyes and almond complexions unsettling now, as then. He thought that night in the dark of his room they seemed different. Now, in full daylight, despite their attempts to cover themselves, their differences were obvious. And they spoke with a weird accent. His childhood remembrances of the supposed Russian in his backyard flooded back and his curiosity overcame his fear. "What do you want?"

The first man smiled. "I am sorry. I did not get your name the last time we met. My name is Shookaal. This is Captain Vreedoo."

He was momentarily stunned. "My name is Justin, Justin Spencer."

Shookaal reached in his pocket, pulled out a small packet and offered it to Justin. "I need a letter delivered to the military base down the road, and we cannot go there ourselves. Would you please deliver it?"

His excitement rose. He was still trying to figure out their nationality, though doubt began to creep in as to whether they were even of this world. "I...I suppose I could."

"And before you go, I made you a promise that night, and we always keep our word." Shookaal reached into a pack on his hip and produced a large, round object. "Your dinosaur."

Justin hesitated, his gaze darting back and forth between the two strangers. "This isn't a bomb, is it?" Looking at the packet, he could tell it was nothing more than paper folded up, but the egg, he wasn't so sure.

Shookaal stepped slowly forward and held both the egg and the letter in front of Justin's hands. "It will hatch in a week, so you will have time to have it inspected if you like. But the letter must be delivered now."

Justin decided he would take a chance and took the letter and the egg. "Hey! This thing tingles! You're sure it's not a bomb?"

"No, Justin, it's just its way of identifying you as its kin."

Holding both the letter and the egg, he dashed for the house. "Okay, I'm on my way." He went to lock the shed, and when he turned back around, the two aliens were already walking away toward the woods. He yelled at the retreating figures. "Hey, how do you know I'll do it?"

Shookaal turned and waved back. "I don't. I am hoping that your honor will make you do the right thing as well." He spun again and in moments, they were out of sight.

Justin stared for a moment longer. Shaking himself from his reverie, he raced into the house. "Mom, I need to run into town, okay if I take the car?"

His mother appeared from out of the kitchen. "Aren't you going to watch the Apollo 11 land?"

"I won't be long Mom. I'll be back in time."

"Okay, don't be late. Your dad will be home soon."

Justin decided his parents need not know the truth. Grabbing the car keys, he jumped into the family sedan and headed off toward the base. He found it hard to concentrate

124

and not speed, with his mind racing so fast. He glanced at the letter packet, but did not recognize the glyphs on the outside. It must be some alien language!

He pulled up to the base and was halted by a number of armed men in uniform. "What is your business here?"

Justin waved the packet out the window. "I was asked to deliver a letter here."

"Get out of the car, please."

Justin clambered out and was searched by the men. One of them called in his arrival. "Hello, Captain Smeeton? …Yes, sir, we have a young man at the front gate who says he was asked to deliver a letter here…Yes, sir, I have it.…No, sir, I do not know who it is for. It has strange writing on it. … Yes, sir, I will bring him in immediately."

The guard came out of the booth and waved to the other guards. "All right, the captain wishes to see him. Bring him in."

***

He sat in a room guarded by a sentry. Based on the salutes and the uniform, He figured the man walking in was a senior officer. "Now, Mr. Justin Spencer, is it? My name is Captain Steven Smeeton. Now Justin, how can I be of assistance?"

"Well, sir, I was mowing the grass in my back yard when these two strange men approached and asked that I deliver this letter to the base here. I guess that would mean you."

Captain Smeeton held out his hand for the letter. "Well then, I guess we best have a look at it."

Justin turned the letter over to the captain who seemed startled and gave Justin a quick, hard look before opening the letter. "Who did you say gave this letter to you?"

"Just like I told you, two strange men."

The captain stood up. "Justin, I need you to wait here for a moment. I'll be right back."

The captain stepped out of the room and Justin slumped back into his seat. "Jeez! I hope this won't take long. I'm going to miss the lunar landing!"

The captain returned and required Justin to go over the events a half a dozen times. After soldiers searched his car and returned with the dinosaur egg, he became adamant. "See! I told you I was telling the truth!"

The man turned over the egg to Captain Smeeton, who turned it a few times in his hands. "It tingles. Did it tingle for you, Private?"

"No, sir. I am wearing my gloves." The private flashed his hands. Captain Smeeton motioned for the sentry to leave. "All right, Justin, we believe you. We are going to have to keep this egg though, I hope you understand. Guards, take Mr. Spencer to our holding cell until I determine what to do."

Justin shrugged off the guard's hand from his upper arm. "But that's my egg, they gave it to me!"

At that moment the door opened and another officer walked in. "Steven, what's going on? They are about to step out. Are you coming to see?" He stopped to stroke his chin. "Do I know you, son?"

Justin recognized the major as the man who visited his classroom so many years ago. "Yes, sir, my name is Justin Spencer; you made me an honorary warrant officer, remember?"

Captain Smeeton waved in Justin's direction while addressing the major. "It seems that Justin here is being used as a courier for our…distant friends. They gave him this letter to deliver and also gave him this…egg."

Major Bucknell went to reach for the object. "An egg? What kind of egg?"

Captain Smeeton blocked the major from reaching it. "Hold on, Major. Something funny about this thing. It tingles when you touch it. So far, as I understand it, only the boy and I have actually handled the goddamned thing. You never know what the hell it could be, possibly some kind of biological weapon."

The major glanced at the letter then looked back at Justin. "Yes, Justin, I remember you now. Captain Smeeton, have your man release him. I think he is merely an innocent in all of this. Justin, walk with me, will you? We need to talk a little."

Wayne and Justin stepped out into the courtyard. "Justin, it was one thing when you were a seven-year-old boy, quite another when you stand before me as a young man. To make you believe then that what you saw was a man was appropriate. Trying to convince you today is not realistic. Obviously, you have been drawn into this situation once again. What I need from you is your solemn promise that you will speak of this to no one, not even your family. Is that understood?"

Justin nodded his head. "You have my word, Major, but what about the egg? They gave it to me."

"I think you understand that we need to check it out first. As Captain Smeeton said, it could be dangerous."

"Well, if it is an egg, can I have it back?"

Wayne chuckled and clapped him on the shoulder. "I am sorry, Justin, but I can't have an alien life form roaming the streets. Perhaps, someday, you can visit again, but not right now."

"I don't think that's fair. But anyway, I gotta' go. The Apollo 11 will be landing soon and I promised myself to see it happen. Bye."

"Good-bye Justin. Somehow, I suspect we will see each other again."

***

After Justin was gone, the major headed back to the mess hall where Kraanox was still seated, watching television. Wayne sank down into a chair. "We need to talk."

"Certainly, Major, but I wouldn't want you to miss this."

"Houston, Tranquility Base here. The Eagle has landed."
"Roger, Tranquility. We copy you on the ground. You got a bunch of guys about to turn blue. We're breathing again."

After some time, Steven entered as well, still cradling the egg under his arm, and placed it on the table before him.

Before Steven could react, Kraanox reached across and lifted the egg with delight. "A crotuu egg! Where did you get it?"

Wayne looked over at Steven. "Well, I think that can debunk your theory on it being dangerous...What is it, Kraanox?"

Kraanox hoisted the egg close to his ear. "And close to hatching, as well. Why, my good major, this is a crotuu egg. From this will hatch one of our most revered pets, much like your dog, though perhaps a bit bigger. In all actuality, it is a reptile. Though quite smart, unlike the ones I have read about here. And warm blooded. I would think your closest comparison would be, oh, a dinosaur."

"A dinosaur! Tell me, Kraanox, when you say, a bit bigger, just exactly how much bigger?"

"Hmm, Oh I would think five to six hundreds of your Earth pounds. He is a ferocious creature, all muscle. Four footed, each with sharp claws that could rip a man to shreds, and bone plating around the head and shoulders."

Steven looked aghast. "My god! Who in his goddamned right mind would want such a creature as a pet? It could eat you alive."

"Well, certainly not me, Captain, nor you. But it will be devotedly loyal to all who touch its shell. It thinks of you all as family now."

"So, the tingling I felt when I held it. What the hell was that?"

"That, Captain, is an enzyme that draws DNA from your skin for the egg to absorb. This DNA is registered inside the animal as kin. His sense of smell is so sensitive that it can detect the trace DNA elements that float off your body. So, it is good that you have touched it."

Kraanox looked to Wayne. "And you, Major, have you touched it as well?"

Wayne reached out to take the egg from Kraanox. "Not yet, but I suspect that I better do so, if what you are telling me is true."

Wayne was pleased to see Kraanox so happy. It bothered him now to make him sad. "The egg came with this." Wayne placed the letter in front of Kraanox.

***

Kraanox stared at the packet with his name scrawled in Braannoo across the top. He carefully opened it and scanned its contents. Once he finished, he handed the letter back to Major Bucknell and sat quietly staring into space. Wayne carefully folded it and returned it to his pocket. "What does it say?"

Kraanox came out of his reverie to face Major Bucknell. "Unfortunately, it appears that the Muurgu do not suffer the same limitations for honor as I do. My entire family has been killed. I am all that is left."

"My people wish to negotiate for my release and to launch formal relations with your government. It is their hope that you will release me and establish a friendly relationship with them. You must excuse me. I wish to retire to my room. There is much for me to think about, and there are many for me to mourn."

Kraanox got up and left the mess hall with his security team in tow. As he left, the television continued to play out the historical event.

"That's one small step for a man, one giant leap for mankind."

CHAPTER 21

"These are disappointing times, eh, Yuri?"

Yuri sat across from him, a copy of the report in his hands. "You know, Leonid, why I even bother to bring this report to you is beyond me. You always already know the contents."

Leonid chuckled. 'Yes, often times that is true, but what I don't have is your opinion."

"My opinion?"

"Yes, Yuri. Take, for example, the alien ship above the United States. It has been there for quite some time now. The Americans know that. You know that. I know that. The Americans probably know that you and I know that. And yet, still it stays there. No action has been taken by the Americans. And the aliens? Well, who knows what they are thinking, but there have been no raids on American installations like what happened at Kraganda."

"A sad day for the Soviet Union. My predecessor felt a certain amount of fault for what occurred."

"Bah! There was no fault. We fired a nuclear warhead at these space invaders. A nuclear warhead! And they survived! No one could have predicted that. So now they are over America. Do you think the Americans know of the failure at Kraganda? Is that why they refuse to act?"

Yuri thought for a moment about rumors that the Americans were in negotiations with the aliens. This was of great disturbance to those in the Komitet Gosudarstvennoy Bezopasnosti. The disaster that occurred at Kraganda was not to be repeated. "My opinion is of little consequence. My job is to provide the intelligence reports. It is up to you to make the decisions on what to do."

"Yes, and we will, but you must have some insight into all of this. What are your agents overseas telling you?"

"Rumor has it that the Americans are negotiating with these aliens for the surrender of the alien prisoner they hold."

"There you go, Yuri. That is the kind of insight I am looking for. You see? You too must play a part if we are to succeed. Now tell me, what are you doing to verify these rumors."

"We are trying our best to get an agent inside the base where the alien is held. It is our belief that negotiations are probably involving two teams. One based in Washington and the other at the base where they can get input from their captives."

"Good, Yuri, good. A good plan. It gives us options. It would be most unfortunate for us, should the Americans successfully negotiate some alien expertise that would give them a significant technological advantage over us. Though I doubt that it will happen."

Yuri was startled. "Why would you say that?"

Leonid tilted his head so that he looked out from under his bushy brows. "Because, Yuri, the Americans are always cautious. The prisoners they hold are their only trump card. If they surrender them up, then they believe the aliens won't honor the bargain and will be free to do whatever damage they can from space."

"That is a most intriguing theory. Yes, when you put it that way, it does sound like what the Americans will do."

"Yes, it does. But that does not mean we can rely on that happening. We must take extra steps to ensure that nothing else occurs."

"Yes Leonid, but I don't see how."

"The Americans may think we are the enemy. We may think the Americans are the enemy. We play our little game of this cold war without really fighting. But the truth is, these aliens are the enemy. Not just of the Americans and the Soviet Union, but of all mankind. We need to be united against this 'out of this world' threat."

"What do you propose?"

"Pack your bags, Yuri. We are going on a little trip."

"A little trip? Where to?"

Leonid rose to slam the bottom of his fist against a world map on his wall. "To Helsinki! The Americans are proposing talks, the Strategic Arms Limitation Treaty, and during these negotiations, the issue of the aliens must be broached."

Yuri got up and walked over to the map where Leonid stood. "And what am I to do at these talks?"

"You, Yuri, will be talking about the aliens, not me. You will meet with their CIA people and find out what's going on. Let them know we know in case they aren't already aware that we do. Meet with these people behind closed doors, unlike the talks which will be watched by everyone."

"So it is your intention that I go to the SALT talks, meet my counterpart in the Central Intelligence Agency and negotiate a treaty in regard to the aliens."

"Yes, Yuri, that is exactly what I expect you to do."

He was quite sure something could be negotiated. Something could always be worked out.

CHAPTER 22

Wayne headed down to Kraanox's quarters. When he arrived, he found only the room attendant there. "Where is he?"

"He's in the pool house, sir."

Wayne cursed silently. Sometimes he wondered whether Kraanox even wanted to go home. Life on the base was becoming a vacation for him. Sure, there was a detail of men wherever he went, but his freedoms were extensive. And he spent a large amount of time in the new pool house, built for his health. He would sometimes go underwater for fifteen to twenty minutes at a time, forcing Wayne to install underwater speakers to get his attention.

Bucknell entered the pool house and found Kraanox on the deck playing with his 'pet'. The thing was now grown quite considerably since it hatched, and was probably around a hundred pounds of muscle, leather, bone and teeth. The men gave it ample space and it seemed to have a nasty temperament with them. It only was friendly with Kraanox and those who were there that night to touch the egg. Fortunately, he made that list. "Hi, Rex! How's my boy!" Wayne crouched to pet the beast, which charged him and bowled him over in its enthusiasm to greet him.

Kraanox came over to pull the animal back and give Wayne a chance to regain his feet. "He certainly does like you, Major."

Wayne got up and dusted himself off. "I still find it amazing that he likes me, but none of the men here."

Kraanox smiled as he threw Rex a *Milk Bone*, which he chomped instantly into pieces and devoured. "It is as I told you, Major. While still an egg, you handled his shell bare handed. The shell absorbed your DNA and passed it on to its host during incubation. As a result, the animal believes you are one of its relatives. That's why he likes you so much. He will be friendly with anyone who handled his egg prior to hatching, though the order in which the shell is handled determines the priority in the animal's mind. We carefully give the egg to our offspring for them to handle first. That is why they make such great pets, and excellent guardians of our children."

Having composed himself once again, Wayne found a chair to sit in. "Just how quickly will Rex reach his maximum size?"

Kraanox seated himself in the next chair. "He should reach a size of about ten feet in length in about two of your Earth years."

Wayne's eyes went from looking at the animal to the guards standing some yards distant. "I suspect that he is already more than a match for any man. He certainly will be quite formidable, full grown."

Kraanox's gaze followed Wayne's line of vision, which made Kraanox chuckle. "I would say so. In the next year he will grow armor plating as well, making him very formidable indeed."

Rex followed Wayne and Kraanox's lead and looked over to the men, giving a low-throated growl that caused the soldiers to take a step back. This elicited a few laughs from the two of them, which seemed to make Rex happy and wag his tail.

Wayne swiveled in his chair to give Kraanox his full attention. "Listen. Things aren't going well with our negotiations with your people. Though I am not involved in the talks, I have been getting some reports, which have been very ambiguous. I finally called in a favor. I chased down Lieutenant General Kelsey McTague. You might remember him. He's still alive and enjoying his retirement. Well, I told him of the situation, he made some calls, and here's what he told me.

"Plain and simple, the government doesn't trust you or your people. The attack on our installation some years ago has left a very bad taste in their mouths. Now, before you go protesting that it was the Muurgu and not you, understand that my government does not view it that way. They lumped you in altogether. An alien is an alien, regardless of what country from your home world.

"Besides, there was an attack in the Soviet Union as well. I can't give you many details, as we only learned of this recently at the SALT talks in Helsinki. The Soviets are convinced that all of you are a direct threat to humanity as a whole. The general couldn't confirm it, but he has been made to believe that there is a secret treaty between my government and the government of the USSR not to engage in any dealings with people from your planet. His remarks to me were, "Why do you think those commie bastards were willing to sign the SALT Treaty in the first place? We needed to give them something; apparently that something was not to deal with you.""

"So what has been happening lately is my people have just been stringing your people along in the hope of getting something for nothing. As a result, we have been notified your ship will be returning home. I have received commands to increase the security around you and limit your movements on the base."

Kraanox sat quietly, apparently absorbing what Wayne told him. Rising to give Rex another treat, Kraanox motioned for Wayne to walk with him. "Grave is the day, Major Bucknell. I suspect then, that your superiors are expecting another rescue attempt. Understand this. As a member of the royal family, at no time can my orders be disobeyed, and we are a people deep in tradition. I have extreme doubts that Captain Vreedoo would disobey my command. I made a promise to you, which I must keep, and Vreedoo has made a promise to me, which he must keep. So you need not fear of another attempt to free me, nor an escape attempt on my part, but if I am to be confined again, then so be it."

Kraanox slapped his thigh. "Come, Rex, we must return to our quarters."

Wayne remained where he was and watched Kraanox go. It was moments like this that made him wonder if there was anyone in charge who truly knew what was going on.

CHAPTER 23

Dinner proved to be a very quiet affair. As always, Justin's mom made a tremendous meal. It was just that Justin's father was ill. He ate slowly, said nothing, and looked poorly. The usual banter between his parents was gone, along with his father's very active newspaper reading. Watching his father eat and look the way he did was hard on Justin. The change for him was traumatic, having been away to school. Unlike his mother, who was here every day and watched the slow, cruel hand of fate curling around his dad.

Justin was digging into his dessert when his mother broke the silence "So, Justin, any word yet from your job application?"

"Not yet, Mom, but I'm hoping to hear soon. They said they'd let me know in a couple of days."

"Well, hopefully not too soon. You've been away so much your father and I have hardly seen you at all these past few years."

"Yeah, I know, Mom. But school's over now, so maybe I'll be able to be here more."

His mom got up to clear away some dishes. "You know, Suzie stopped me on the street last week, wondering if you were home yet. I told her you'd call her when you got back."

Justin stopped to look up. "Aw, Mom, why'd you do that?"

"She's a nice girl, and I don't think it would hurt you so much to go out on a date. After all, she is the girl you took to your high school prom."

"Yeah, I know Mom, but that was four years ago! I'm sure she's seeing someone else by now."

"You never know, Justin, you never know. Anyway, unless you're going to help me with the dishes, you and your father can just get up and get out of my way."

His father retired to the living room to watch the evening news. It took him some effort to rise from his chair at the table, but when Justin offered an arm up, he feebly brushed him off. "I don't need any help!"

Justin followed and sat then watched the television with little interest. His focus was more intent on his father. He was feeling so helpless. The president would be addressing the nation tonight, and his dad wanted to watch. His mother moved about, cleaning up after dinner, but keeping an eye on both of them.

After a brief introduction, the president came on the screen. Justin was amazed that the president sounded and talked just like his father. The only difference is the president ran the country—his father, the family.

"Good evening.

This is the 37th time I have spoken to you from this office, where so many decisions have been made that shaped the history of this Nation. Each time I have done so to discuss with you some matter that I believe affected the national interest.

In all the decisions I have made in my public life, I have always tried to do what was best for the Nation. Throughout the long and difficult period of Watergate, I have felt it was my duty to persevere, to make every possible effort to complete the term of office to which you elected me…"

The doorbell rang and Justin jumped up. "I'll get it, Mom." He strode over to the front door.

When he opened it, there was a brown truck in the driveway and a delivery man on the porch. "Justin Spencer?"

"That's me."

"Delivery for you. Please sign here."

Justin quickly scrawled his name onto the form and returned to the living room.

"...Therefore, I shall resign the Presidency effective at noon tomorrow. Vice President Ford will be sworn in as President at that hour in this office..."

His mother peeked into the living room. "Who was at the door, dear?"

Justin was turning the package around in his hand, trying to ascertain where it came from. "A package for me, Mom."

"...In passing this office to the Vice President, I also do so with the profound sense of the weight of responsibility that will fall on his shoulders tomorrow and, therefore, of the understanding, the patience, the cooperation he will need from all Americans.

As he assumes that responsibility, he will deserve the help and the support of all of us. As we look to the future, the first essential is to begin healing the wounds of this Nation, to put the bitterness and divisions of the recent past behind us, and to rediscover those shared ideals that lie at the heart of our strength and unity as a great and as a free people.

By taking this action, I hope that I will have hastened the start of that process of healing which is so desperately needed in America..."

Justin sat down. "I wonder what's in here, what do you think, Dad ... Dad? Dad!"

His father lay limp in the big chair. Justin sprung up to give his father a shake.

"Mom, come quick, something's wrong with Dad!"

His mother raced into the room. "Quick, call the hospital!"

Justin dropped his package and raced for the telephone. "What's the number?"

"Try that new 911 number. It's supposed to connect to emergency services."

Justin fumbled with the receiver and dialed 911.

"...Here in America, we are fortunate that most of our people have not only the blessings of liberty but also the means to live full and good and, by the world's standards, even abundant lives. We must press on, however, toward a goal of not only more and better jobs but of full opportunity for every American and of what we are striving so hard right now to achieve, prosperity without inflation...."

"Hello, hello, my dad needs an ambulance...yeah, it's 1947 Main...that's right, the Spencer place. Please hurry."

"...I pledge to you tonight that as long as I have a breath of life in my body, I shall continue in that spirit. I shall continue to work for the great causes to which I have been dedicated throughout my years..."

"The ambulance will be here right away. How is he?"

His mother was crying. "He's not breathing!" She was pushing on his chest, trying to get him to breathe.

"...I have done my very best in all the days since to be true to that pledge. As a result of these efforts, I am confident that the world is a safer place today, not only for the people of America but for the people of all nations, and

141

that all of our children have a better chance than before of living in peace rather than dying in war.

This, more than anything, is what I hoped to achieve when I sought the Presidency. This, more than anything, is what I hope will be my legacy to you, to our country, as I leave the Presidency.

To have served in this office is to have felt a very personal sense of kinship with each and every American. In leaving it, I do so with this prayer: May God's grace be with you in all the days ahead."

The ambulance arrived and the attendants took over from his mom. After a while, they looked over at her and shook their heads. She broke down again and cried in Justin's arms as the men took his father out on the gurney.

Later that night, when his mother was finally asleep, Justin returned to the living room. His package still lay on the floor. He picked it up and gingerly opened it so as not to rip the packaging. He read the letter through and placed it down on the coffee table, then stared at his father's big, empty chair. "I didn't get a chance to tell you, Dad. NASA has offered me a job. I'm going to be a scientist, just like you wanted."

CHAPTER 24

The world was changing just a little too rapidly for Captain Steven Smeeton. Lately, he felt old. Truth was, almost all soldiers his age were already retired. Steven had no family, no one to go home to, and so no desire to retire.

But as he listened to all the new recruits talk, he could sense theirs weren't the values of his generation. And the scientific advances were amazing. The changes in computer technology among other things were astounding. NASA was launching a ship called Viking to Mars. Mars! Hell, it seemed like only yesterday that humans were barely able to land on the moon.

One thing for sure. When that Viking spaceship got to Mars, scientists would be able to confirm whether or not the aliens came from there. He'd never believed that twenty plus light year stuff. If he understood correctly, light traveled at some six hundred and seventy-one million miles an hour! When you think of twenty-four hours in a day and three hundred sixty-five days in a year, it all added up to a hell of a lot of miles!

There were a lot of new whiz kids running around the base. Many of the original scientists found themselves at a standstill and been transferred out. The new breed coming in showed a greater amount of zeal to solve the riddles of the wreckage and postulate new theories on what did what.

Tonight, Steven was taking Rex out for a walk. The tighter security didn't allow Kraanox out at night, and the only other soldiers who Rex liked were on leave. So it came down to this, pet watcher. How low could he go? He laughed at himself and the ridiculousness of his predicament. Rex looked up and smiled at him, wagging his tail when Steven laughed.

"How's our dinosaur today? One thing boy... I never get an argument from you. Not that I would ever want one, that's for sure." He looked at the leather strap in his hands. As if the leash did any good. Rex could probably snap the strap like a wet noodle. Either that or drag him halfway across the camp without breaking a sweat.

Rex nuzzled up and licked his hand. He figured it would take less than a single gulp to swallow him up to the elbow.

The men had agreed easily on a name. A number of suggestions were originally floated. Canine Rex, General Rex, Martian Rex, all with one common theme, Rex. And so it was agreed. It hadn't taken long either for Rex to recognize his name.

Steven remembered his own childhood pet dog, and without a doubt, this creature was smarter than any canine. "You know, Rex, sometimes when I talk to you, I think you understand everything I say. You just can't talk is all." Rex always appeared to pay attention when talked to. Yes, it wouldn't surprise him at all if he really did understand.

Looking down at the creature, it was hard not to be a little afraid of him, even though Rex was always good to him. Somehow, Steven couldn't find himself liking the beast. The animal continued to grow. He currently stood at just under four hundred pounds, and the top of his head, neck and shoulders were encased in hard bony ridges. His mouth was wide and full of sharp teeth, and the claws on his feet looked like the talons of eagles, only much larger. His body was made up of a mass of muscle and Steven saw the creature only once in a full attack mode, when a pigeon landed in his path. The speed with which Rex pounced seemed a flash, and in one gulp, the bird was gone.

It was too bad that Rex was the only one here. A breeding program would simply revolutionize the armed forces. Imagine every soldier with his own pet crotuu. On the battlefield, as a vanguard, they would blow through

144

entrenched enemy forces. Their speed, natural armor, and built-in weaponry would be impossible to counter. Steven could just imagine the look on the faces of enemy troops seeing a thousand, heck even a hundred of these animals racing up to their position. There'd be a number of soiled shorts, that's for sure.

There were requests from men on the base that the animal be destroyed, but Major Bucknell held firm, Kraanox was alone on this world, not denying him this 'pet' was the least that we could do to make his stay comfortable.

Deep down, he liked the fact the men were somewhat frightened of the animal. It helped to keep things in line around here. After all, security was still his primary job, and old or not, he was going to keep doing what he did best.

As Steven rounded a corner, his path brought him near the main offices. Glancing at the building, he stopped in his tracks. Was that just the faintest glint of light from the communication room? He stood stock still, and Rex, recognizing his posture, followed suit and angled himself in a defensive position in front of the captain, a low growl emanating from deep within.

"Shhh, Rex! Be quiet for a moment."

Rex glanced at Steven, then returned to his posture, but without the growl.

Steven waited, there it was again, a small light, very faint and only for a moment. Steven waited a few more seconds, then decided to investigate.

He looped the leash around a porch post. "You stay here, Rex. I'm going to go in and investigate what that light is."

Rex whimpered.

Steven knelt to bring his face near to Rex's. "Now be a good boy and stay. If I need your help, I'll call and you just come a running, okay?"

Rex responded by giving him a huge lick and then sat down.

Standing up, Steven produced his master keys, opened the door, walked into the building and hit all the light switches. Standing in the corner near another new contraption, the facsimile machine, was one of the new lab guys. "What the hell are you doing here this hour?"

At first the fellow appeared startled, but regained his composure quickly. "I'm sorry, sir, I was just doing some last-minute work, and I didn't want to bother anyone this late."

He knew that he'd grown older, but that didn't mean his faculties were gone. Older yes, but wiser too. "I think you better goddamned come with me, son. Let's go see the major, shall we?"

Steven lowered his hand to his sidearm, just to be cautious, and the man watched this carefully. All right, let me just pack up my stuff." Bending down, the man scooped up a large valise and shoved some papers inside.

He approached Steven with the valise held before him. Steven stepped aside so the man could pass and go out first. At the exact moment he passed, the fellow swung the satchel and caught Steven by surprise. Together, the two men went down in a heap. Steven tried to grab his revolver, but the fellow proved quicker and restrained his hand from reaching the gun. He struck Steven several times, opening a severe gash on his forehead. In a moment the young man took the gun and rose to point it at Steven. He pulled a switch blade out of his jacket. "They shouldn't let old fools like you have a weapon. Any last words before I put you out of your misery?"

Steven struggled to a sitting position and wiped a shaking hand across the blood smear on his forehead. Looking up at his potential executor, Steven smiled feebly. "Yeah, I only have one goddamned thing to say…Rex!"

The fellow swung to look at the door as a howl emanated from behind it. In the instant that Steven yelled, Rex snapped the post holding him and crashed through the front door and part of the wall of the office building. Horror filled the face of the man as he fired off two quick shots at the charging monster, all to no avail. The first shot went high and the second ricocheted off the bony plates. Rex's jaw snapped across the man's shoulder, tearing off his arm and crushing the entire area. One of Rex's claws arced across the fellow's abdomen and his innards spilled out on the floor. In one quick instant, the man was dead. Steven leaned back against a cabinet and closed his eyes. In the distance, voices could be heard as people were running to investigate the shots.

Steven sat still, and slowed his breathing in an effort to calm down. Maybe retirement wasn't such a bad idea after all. Right now, he was just happy to be alive. He would wait right here and try to compose himself until someone arrived. It was hard to do, though, with Rex licking his face.

CHAPTER 25

"Goodbye, Justin. I love you. Take care of yourself."

Justin hugged his mom before boarding the train. "Are you going to be okay? I mean, without Dad and all?"

"Oh, don't be silly, Justin. I've been taking care of that house for the past twenty-five years! Your father, God rest his soul, never lifted a finger once in all that time. With both of you men out of the house, I'll have so much free time I won't know what to do with myself. Maybe I'll get a job to pass the day."

Justin hugged his mother again. "Don't worry about money, Mom. I'll send some home as soon as I get my first paycheck."

"Never you mind that! I'll be just fine, thank you. Now you get on that train and go become successful."

"Okay, Mom, I'll see you for the holidays."

Justin turned to get on board when he heard his name again. "Justin! Wait!"

Turning, Justin saw Suzie Derkins coming along the train platform. "You weren't going to leave without saying goodbye, were you?"

He felt sheepish. At his mother's urging, he'd taken Suzie on a date a couple of nights ago, but knowing he was going away to work, he just didn't feel comfortable about it. "Hi, Suzie. I…uh…I guess not. It's just the excitement of going, I guess. You know, you get all wrapped up with it. Um…how did you know about me leaving this morning?"

Suzie glanced at his mom. "Your mother told me. I hope you don't mind me coming."

"Um…no, no, not at all." Justin put his bags back down and gave Suzie an awkward hug.

Suzie clasped her hands and hunched her shoulders. "Well, I guess, good luck with your job." She gave him a peck on the cheek.

"Uh…um, yeah, I guess…thanks."

He looked back and forth between Suzie and his mother. "Well, I guess I better get going. Thanks for coming to see me off, Mom. Thanks, Suzie."

Justin picked up his bags and started to climb onto the train. Behind him, he could hear a chorus of goodbyes. As he walked down the aisle, he bent to look out the windows and saw his mom and Suzie still there, watching. When they spotted him looking, they both waved. Justin waved back feebly. The two then turned and headed off the platform, and Justin noticed his mom put her arm around Suzie as they went.

Justin found a seat and flopped into it. It was going to be a long ride.

***

"Tickets! Have your tickets ready! Tickets!"

The conductor arrived at his seat, leaned over, and punched Justin's ticket. "Well, well, well. If it isn't Mr. Justin Spencer. Been a long time, young sir, but I still remember. So, where we off to today? Washington again?"

"No, sir, NASA. It's my first job."

The conductor scratched his head. "NASA, huh? Young sir, you never cease to amaze me. What are you going to be, an astronaut?"

"No, not an astronaut. I'll be working in research and development."

"Oh ho! A scientist, then. Well, congratulations, young sir. I'm quite sure your father is real proud of you."

Justin felt his eyes moisten. "I'm quite sure he is."

The man straightened and stared for a moment. "Well then, you just sit there and enjoy the ride. Once again, your money is no good here. It's a good thing you don't take the train too often. Otherwise, I'd lose my job. *Coca-Cola,* wasn't it?"

Justin rubbed at one eye with the knuckle on his right hand. "Yes, a *Coke.* Thank you."

***

During his weeks of orientation, he visited many of the NASA facilities. He was impressed by the grandeur of the buildings and the large number of people employed therein. Justin got the opportunity to be introduced to a number of astronauts and other high-ranking officials within the NASA organization. During this time, he completed examinations that were conducted by some of the leading scientists in the country. He never got any results, so verification was impossible, but Justin felt he did well in answering the myriad of questions and solving the problems put before him.

So only a certain amount of dejection crept through him as he looked at the squat, unadorned, smallish building at the edge of the grounds where he was to work.

Perhaps he hadn't done as well as he'd thought. His mind raced as he ran over all the tests, questions and problems in his mind. Where did he go wrong?

When he stepped into the building, the director greeted him and gave him a short tour. There were only a handful of people working there, and very little equipment. They ended up in the small cafeteria, with only a couple of vending machines for coffee and sandwiches. The director bought them each a cup of coffee and sat down. "Justin, you are probably wondering what it is that we do here. Before you say anything, let me fill you in."

"This facility is focused on new concepts for interstellar flight. So far, we've only physically been to the moon and landed a scientific vessel on Mars. And that one

150

took six months to get there! If we're to get anywhere further, we're going to have to get there faster than a two-hundred-year trip to the nearest star. We have some ideas, some theories only, so what we're looking for is young bucks like you with new ideas to figure it out. Take us to the next level. Make space flight more than just a large bomb blasting its way off this planet."

"So, let's begin. Allow me to introduce you to the other members of your team. I'm sure once you get to know them you will have much to talk about."

His coworkers included six men who varied in age from twenty-nine to fifty-eight years of age, making Justin the youngest member. They welcomed him warmly to the team.

The director excused himself and the seven men sat down to discuss their progress and how Justin would fit into the team.

He looked around at the men staring at him, waiting to see what he would say. "Well, hi, I guess. So…as the new guy, do I have to go through any kind of initiation? In college, boy, those first few days were rough! I hope you guys go easy on me."

The others laughed, and the oldest fellow got up and wrapped an arm around Justin's shoulders. "Don't worry. When it comes to pranks, you'll find that no one is sacred around here. For now, get comfortable, read up on what we've done so far. As a team, we tend to throw the odd thing on each other's desk looking for input. So don't be shocked when you find something on yours that wasn't there the night before."

"Okay, I'll take it a step at a time. When you guys are ready, I'll be ready."

"Fine…fine. Your desk is in that office over there." He pointed to a small room near the corner.

Justin walked over to his new office and looked in. On his desk, he found mountains of files piled, with all sorts of sticky notes all over them. Behind him he could hear laughter. Looking back, he couldn't help but grin. "Okay guys, funny, veerry funny!"

CHAPTER 26

Even from space, in his mind, he could smell it.

He yearned for the feel of Braannoo soil beneath his feet, for the splash of Traanusian water on the Braannoo shores, for the love and comfort of family and friends.

But that wasn't the smell pervading him. The smell was trouble.

Once landed, Captain Vreedoo reported to his superior commander. "Things have gone badly since you left, Captain," the commander said. "The Muurgu are becoming much more aggressive. Their battle against the Bruutaans is over for now, and they are concentrating their forces against us. Things are going badly." He motioned Vreedoo to sit.

"How so, sir? I recall our last assault before we left. Yes, our losses were high, but we gained the high ground, control of near Traanu outer space. With the exception of the Emperor, they retained no battle cruisers. Just space stations, which lack the mobility for attacking, and are only effective in a defensive posture."

"And that is absolutely correct, even to this day. But it is not the battle for outer space we fear, but the one on the ground. The last of our island fortresses fell scant months ago, and as a result the Muurgu have been able to establish a beachhead on Braannoo soil. Although out on the Zeenda peninsula, Braannoo soil nevertheless."

Vreedoo rose to look at a map outlining the situation. "This is bad news, indeed. And I am sorry to report that I have failed in my mission. The humans are impossible to deal with. Like the Muurgu, they have no honor."

"I've received the report already on your mission. This news will not sit well with the public, or for that matter, the prince. We are cursed that only a fool remains of the royal family. The generals are marching all over him. Kraanox would have provided much needed stability in the military hierarchy."

"Surely, there must be something we can do."

The commander slumped into his desk chair. "Go now to the prince. He is waiting for you. He hopes you will bring tidings of Commander Kraanox's imminent return to relieve him of the burden of ruling."

"Then I will go now. Kraanox is not coming. I will have to tell him that only the heavens can save him and Braannoo now."

He arrived at the new palace to meet with Prince Druummo. Built to stand where the old palace once did, the structure seemed more of a bomb shelter than a royal hall. Gone were the splendors of Braannoo artistry which adorned the old walls and filled its hallways. Now, in its place, were reinforced blast walls, with additional trusses and support beams crisscrossing everywhere.

An older cousin of Kraanox, but more distantly removed from King Jaaxxoo as his bloodline followed that of Queen Floovaa. He doubted that many in the public even recognized his right to rule. If not for the war with the Muurgu, such an appointment might have led to a revolt.

Ushered in, Vreedoo knelt. "My liege, I am here."

"What news of my cousin? Has he returned?"

After rising, Captain Vreedoo bowed once more before his monarch. "I am sorry, my liege, I have failed. My attempts to negotiate with the Earthlings have been fruitless. They bear much in common with the Muurgu, these humans, full of lies and deceit. I knew not what to do. I gave Kraanox my honor bound promise that I would not try a further rescue attempt. In the end, we could delay no longer. I gave the order to return, empty handed."

The prince strode across the room to stare out at the landscape. Captain Vreedoo straightened up and watched the prince for whatever was to come, but Prince Druummo stood motionless, staring out. After a few awkward moments he ventured an interruption. "Sire? Are we to do nothing?"

Prince Druummo turned at the waist to look back at Captain Vreedoo. He smiled slowly, then turned back to look out the window. "Look at it, Vreedoo, the countryside, the trees, the streams, the ponds. See in the distance the mountains, the clouds, and the sky. See moving about the people, the animals, and the wildlife. Around us are the houses, the bridges, and the town. All of this is what we are; we are Braannoo."

Druummo motioned for Vreedoo to join him. He stepped forward until he was beside the prince, who wrapped an arm around him. "A long time ago, we were like them, Vreedoo. A country full of strife, where the people stole from each other, lied to each other, and yes, even killed each other. It was only a miracle that we weren't eradicated then. That our people didn't become extinct as so many peoples of this world before us. It was in those dark days that our forebears stepped forward and took a stand. They, as a family, led the people from that dark time, to this one of enlightenment."

"So now, when I look out at the land, and I think of the Muurgu on our shores, my heart weeps. I think, we should kill them all, do whatever it takes, poison them, annihilate them, and assassinate them. We should do whatever we can do to win this war, no matter how evil. But then I think of what would happen, what we would become. We would become like them, Vreedoo, full of lies, deceit and hate. They would win then, Vreedoo, they would win. The country that lies outside this window would not be the country I know, the country that I love."

"So, we will leave Kraanox alone. We will honor his commitment, his obligation. And when we are all gone from this life, we will see each other once again in the great afterlife that is due all Braannoo that follow the faith."

155

Vreedoo bowed again. "Yes, my lord. I apologize if I have offended you. It is just that my heart weeps as well for those of my people who die every day in the battle against the Muurgu."

"And you shall have your chance to defend those of your home land. I am appointing you a commander in the space division. Many will protest this appointment, but I have my reasons. Though the mission failed, your honor held true. Find a way to use the higher skies to win this battle for us. Go now. Take a day or two to recover from your journey. Your new command will wait until then."

He headed for his home. He was thankful his family was in a small town of no military value. The serenity of his village gave him a peaceful feeling. Walking through the streets, seeing the people go about their business, you would never know that a war front raged not far from there. Entering his house, the stress of his career melted away as he was greeted by his family, his four children, his wife, and her parents who lived with them. Though simple in fare as there still was rationing going on with the war, the home cooked meal was most exquisite after many months in space.

Late in the evening, Captain Vreedoo relaxed in his home pool in his living room. The kids were gone to bed and his in-laws retired to their private quarters. The vid screen was on, but he wasn't really paying attention to it. Nestled in his arms was his wife of eighteen years. Just to hold her felt such a thing that the emotions stirred deeply in him and he wept. Snuggled against him, she did not notice the tears.

The difficulty of the tasks he faced weighed as a deep stress upon him. The war is going badly and he failed in his mission to return Commander Kraanox to Braannoo. As well, unlike his Muurgu counterpart, he failed to retrieve anything useful for the battle at home. It was tearing at him that his home and family were threatened.

His people were one of faith and looked to their royal family to lead them. Now, with the king gone, and so many of the royal family obliterated, it was easy to believe that the faith of his people was being tested.

In fact, his faith suffered as well. He could not sit idly by and watch his beloved Braannoo destroyed. Over a million people died the day of the nuclear attack, and almost another million ailed from radiation sickness. Many of those would not survive.

The war itself was also killing people by the thousands. Soldiers mostly, men and women who understood the risks of the job. But innocents were being killed as well, and the cities and countryside being ravaged.

The weight of it all settled in, and he went to sleep with a troubled mind. As a result, he suffered a restless sleep and woke early. He sat alone in his kitchen with a morning beverage when there was a knock at the door. It was still dark out, and Vreedoo approached his front door with some trepidation. Upon opening it, he found a young cadet standing at attention. "Captain Vreedoo, your attendance is required immediately, I am to drive you."

Vreedoo reached for his jacket near the door and fumbled putting it on. "What is it, soldier, what's the crisis?"

"It's the military council, sir. They are meeting immediately, during the night. Prince Druummo has died. A suicide."

He went cold. Finishing buttoning his jacket, he stopped to scrawl a note to his family. "All right, let's go."

As he got in the back seat of the car, his mind returned to that last conversation with the prince only yesterday. He wondered how much longer he would be able to keep his own faith.

CHAPTER 27

The intercom buzzed. "He's on his way in to see you."

Yuri pressed down to reply. "Who is?"

"Leonid."

Ushering his staff out of his office, Yuri quickly stacked away the open files on his desk. Just as he finished, Leonid barreled in through the door. "Yuri! What's this I hear?"

"What are you talking about?"

Leonid plopped into one of the wing-backed chairs. "Don't play games with me, Yuri. You know full well what I am talking about. Your man at the American military installation where the aliens are held has been compromised."

Yuri reached into his credenza and pulled out a bottle of vodka. He knew that a few drinks would calm Leonid down. "I am sorry to say, that what you have heard is true. We do not have the details, but he is dead, all the same."

"Did he learn anything before being killed? What information have you received? Have the Americans gained any technological secrets from the aliens?"

"Very little, I'm afraid, but not due to the failure of our man. It seems the Americans have learned very little as well."

Leonid stopped to drink his vodka. "Bah! What is this? Stolichnaya? Your predecessor kept a bottle of Shustov in his desk for my visits."

"My apologies, Leonid. I will make sure to have some next time."

"Humph! Well, anyway, what have you done about replacing this man?"

"Why…nothing! We have agreed to Razryadka after all."

Leonid slammed down his shot glass. "Nothing! American détente is something we agreed to for political purposes. We have not changed anything in our efforts. Even now our Kosmos spy program is recording American movements."

"The Zenit satellites we launch are limited at best. Taking photos for fifteen days then crashing back here for us to retrieve is nothing compared to the American Kennan satellites. Their KH-11s transmit the photos from space and stay in orbit. Détente is a good thing until we can catch up with them."

"That is happening as we speak. The Almaz program is now underway. Not only will we catch up, but we will surpass the Americans with it."

Yuri poured again. Whether or not Leonid complained about the vodka, it did not stop him from drinking it. "How do you figure this, Leonid?"

Leonid leaned back in his chair and smiled. "The Greeks conquered the world by using horses and creating an armored cavalry. The Romans conquered the world with the development of roads to allow their troops to move quickly when in need. Britain ruled by controlling the seas. Germany came close with its Blitzkrieg tactic through the development of their tanks. The Americans defeated the Germans by the next advancement in air warfare and controlled the skies. The evolution of warfare is consistent. From foot soldiers, to cavalry, to mass transit, then movement across the seas, until finally the air. It only makes sense that the next step is the control of space."

"Will we really be able to do that?"

"Yes, Yuri, we will. Our Diamond program, using Soyuz spacecraft, is setting military space stations into low Earth orbit. These Salyut Orbital Piloted Stations are equipped with aircraft cannons. Once we have enough of those in the sky, we will dominate our American competitors."

"And tell me, should the aliens come back again. Can these Salyut's defeat them? Or will the aliens simply blow them out of the sky?"

"That is your problem, Yuri, always finding the negative in things."

"Here at the KGB, it is best to be a pragmatist."

"And I am an optimist! It takes optimism to have vision, to see things as they could be, as they will be!"

During his outburst, Leonid stood up to wag a finger at Yuri, but then slumped back into his chair and placed a hand to his chest. "I don't feel so good."

Yuri pressed on the intercom. "Quick, get the nurse in here right away." He came around his desk to stand beside Leonid's chair. "She is on her way."

The nurse entered and checked Leonid over quickly. "What seems to be the problem?"

"I think he is having a seizure of some kind."

The nurse reached into a bag and pulled out some pills. "You just need to relax. Here, take two of these."

Leonid swallowed the pills. "What are they?"

"Nembutal. It will relax you, help you sleep."

After a while, Leonid seemed to relax. "I'm feeling much better now, thank you."

"It is my privilege to have helped."

"Then you will come and see me again to make sure I stay healthy."

Yuri bent to help Leonid stand. "I will make sure of it. Let's get you to your car so that you can go and get some rest."

Leonid stopped to place his hand under the nurse's chin. "Remember, come see me again."

Once Yuri felt satisfied that the man would be okay and the driver was taking Leonid home, he returned to his office. Military space stations. This revelation changed his perspective on how things were going.

Maybe the end of détente was a good thing.

CHAPTER 28

There proved to be no doubt of the outcome. Prince Druummo never communicated his decision to elevate Vreedoo's rank, and the remaining commanders showed tremendous disappointment in his failure to bring home Commander Kraanox.

Now, no guiding hand of a royal family member existed to countermand any orders. Once again, Vreedoo returned to Earth to reclaim the last member of the family, this time through any means possible.

"Let's take this slowly, everyone. I do not wish to alert the humans to our presence just yet. Establish a high orbit until we determine the situation."

He sat and waited for each department to report in.

"Communications, sir. The buoy we left is still functional and operating."

"Helm, sir. I have established a high geosynchronous orbit."

"Tactical, sir. It appears there are a large number of satellites now circling the planet. Most appear to be in a low orbit, none set out as far as we are."

Vreedoo looked at his own screen for the tactical report. "Are you able to determine the capabilities of these satellites?"

"It will take some time, but between myself and communications we should be able to verify if any have military capability or are simply communication satellites."

"All right, let's start with that. Before I proceed, I want to know what I'm up against."

Captain Vreedoo sat and mused. There would be no doubt that a close approach to the planet would be observed. It was amazing how fast the humans were developing their space technology.

162

The challenge before him involved gaining the release of Commander Kraanox without breaching his honor. So a direct assault on the military installation holding Kraanox could be ruled out. Negotiations last time proved fruitless, so it made no sense to try the diplomatic route again either. He needed a more indirect tack to achieve his mission.

"Are we able to determine which of these satellites have been launched by the country holding Commander Kraanox?"

The communication officer turned to face him. "I should be able to do that, sir. By monitoring the uplinks, I can verify which are in direct communication with the Americans."

"Perhaps then, our first tactic will involve this. Let me know once you have made a complete inventory of them."

"We'll get on it right away. There are a large number of satellites around the planet, all on different geocentric orbits, some are geosynchronous orbits that vary from polar to equatorial, others are geostationary orbits, and chasing down each and every one will be no small task."

***

The following day, Vreedoo pulled up his tactical of the planet below. Now charted in red was each and every single satellite attributable to the American humans. All others were in white. "Clearly, these Americans are the dominant country on this planet when it comes to space flight. Over two thirds of the satellites are theirs!"

"Yes, sir. I think you should examine this one in particular. It is significantly larger than all the others." The tactical officer, made the necessary adjustments to zoom in on one satellite in detail.

Vreedoo looked at the display. "Is it a space ship?"

"I think not, Captain. Although large enough, the arrays on it and the propulsion system seem incompatible with flight."

Vreedoo weighed his options. "Helm, bring us to this...thing that tactical has on display."

"Right away, sir, but it will take a little jiggling and some time to match the orbit."

In close proximity they were able to examine the craft in more detail. Its configuration definitely included a crew area, but a lack of heat signatures indicated it was unoccupied at the time. Their space bridge would not match the entry portal so Vreedoo made a decision to cross over externally.

Two technicians and Shookaal were to accompany him. He took his cue at this point and donned his own spacesuit. Stepping out of the airlock into space was always an awe-inspiring thing.

As he floated across the void of space toward the satellite, he could not help but look all about him, the sheer blackness of space with the stars shining all around, and the brightly illuminated orb below him, this planet they call Earth. Looking down, he could see the vast oceans, the mountains, the swirling clouds. Except for the difference in the land configuration, this could be Traanu. It was moments like this that always humbled him.

The moment passed quickly enough though as Vreedoo reached the open hatchway into the satellite. Once inside, he and another crewman were able to seal the hatch from inside and enter the main area inside the satellite. It took a few moments to equalize the pressure and restore an acceptable level of breathable air before he chanced taking off his helmet.

"This must be some kind of orbiting station. Perhaps it can be our bargaining chip with the humans to regain the Commander."

***

In the cafeteria of the Johnson Space Center, Bill sat down to try and enjoy his ham and cheese sandwich. He was only finishing his first bite when one of his technicians came up to him in a hurry. "Uh, Bill…"

He threw a hand up in exasperation. "Can you believe it?"

"Um…no…uh…believe what…I mean…Bill, I need to talk to you…"

"This ham and cheese sandwich. I mean, really, what does it take to make a decent ham and cheese sandwich? I mean, really…"

"Uh…Bill, this is important…"

"You know, it's really quite simple, it really is, it's just bread, ham, cheddar cheese and some mustard—now what can be so hard about that…"

"Bill…I have to talk to you."

"It's really quite amazing, we can put a man on the moon, but make a good ham and cheese sandwich? I mean, really!"

"Bill!"

Bill stopped gesticulating at the sandwich and looked up. "What is it? Can't you see I'm eating?

"Bill, there's somebody on Skylab!"

Bill lowered the sandwich. "What do you mean there's somebody on Skylab? Who the hell could be on Skylab? The Russians didn't launch recently, did they? Nobody told me there would be somebody going up there. It sure isn't any of our people, so who the hell is it?"

"I don't know, all I can tell you is that systems are being activated and environmental is running."

165

"That can't be possible. Take me to your station." Grabbing a last bite of his sandwich, and coffee in hand, Bill followed the tech into the mission control room. "Here, let me do it."

After a few moments of reading displays, he got out of the seat. "Stay here until I get back."

Since confirming what he heard to be true, he straightened up, strode into his office, composed himself, and then picked up the telephone to make a momentous telephone call. After a few intermediaries he got the connection he wanted. "Mr. Secretary? You won't believe this, but we have visitors on Skylab!"

***

"As near as I can figure, this is an orbiting space station of some kind."

The simple analysis of the technician matched what Captain Vreedoo already suspected. Once they reestablished adequate environmental levels, they scavenged through the ship to learn what they could. The technicians, with Shookaal's interpretations, shook their heads at the rudimentary levels of technology.

"It's amazing they can obtain orbit at all. The computer technology here is less than the smallest handheld device on our ship."

Vreedoo heard a beeping. "What is that noise?"

"It's coming from over here. We think it's a communication station."

"Shookaal, man that station, I wish to talk to the Earthlings."

Once the technician showed him how, Shookaal sat down and turned it on. A voice could be heard speaking what Shookaal described as English and translated as it came in.

"Calling Skylab, come in Skylab…"

Vreedoo stepped close. A face appeared on the screen. *"This is the secretary of state of the United States of America. Do any of you speak English?"*

Shookaal looked to Vreedoo for consent and received a nod, then focused on the screen. "I do."

"Well, that is most fortunate. I must inform you, that you are treading on sovereign property. I demand that you leave at once."

Shookaal translated for Captain Vreedoo, who spent a moment thinking of a response. "Tell them that they are in no position to give orders."

After Shookaal translated into English, the man on the screen continued. *"I am prepared to take whatever actions I deem necessary to remove you. Leave the station now."*

"Human, we have been more than patient with you. We tried to extricate our national without harm, which you resisted. We tried to negotiate his release in an honest and fair manner, which you failed to honor. I am left with little choice myself. I am sure that this station is an expensive venture for your people. Release Commander Kraanox to us immediately, and I will spare this outpost from harm."

"Now, you listen here, spaceman! The United States will never buckle to any threat. Do you understand me?"

"I will give you one day to capitulate to my single demand. After which time I will destroy this station and every other satellite you now have in orbit. Failing that, I will examine what ground based assets to target next."

"You will get our response well before then, I promise you."

The connection signed off and Vreedoo felt pleased. They were going to respond. "This is a good sign, Shookaal. We just might get Kraanox back after all."

Shookaal stroked his chin as if lost in thought. "I'm not sure, Captain. I heard the same words as you, but when you did not hear is the inflections attached to those words. I

167

am far from fully understanding their entire language. It is filled with commonalities and overlaps that make it a most confusing dialect. Many words have multiple meanings, and inflections can imply entirely different things from the original definition."

"What are you saying, Shookaal? That he is lying?"

"Not quite, Captain. Lying, no, but his intent I believe to be other than anticipated."

One of the technicians reached over to grab Vreedoo by the arm. "I'm sorry to interrupt, sir. It is important that you put your helmet back on. The humans have turned off the environmental by remote control."

"What?"

Before the technician could respond any further, the four Braannoo stumbled as they felt thrust shift them. "They're moving the station!"

Vreedoo's communicator buzzed from the Dragonfly. "Captain, the Earthling space station is moving away. Tactical reports that it is descending toward the atmosphere. Entry will most certainly cause it to break up. I suggest you depart immediately. Helm is maneuvering now to maintain proximity."

It took a few moments for the four of them to put their helmets and gloves back on. They depressurized the cabin and exited quickly into the black vastness of space.

The two technicians returned immediately to the ship. Captain Vreedoo, with Shookaal at his side, stayed in space to watch the Earth vessel. They floated there in silence. He watched and watched as the space station grew smaller and smaller. All the while his mind raced as to what he should do.

Once back inside the ship, Shookaal sat with him as they pulled off their suits. "So, what now, Captain?"

"Nothing."

"Nothing?"

Vreedoo stood up to look out a window at the planet below. "Yes, nothing. These Americans would rather destroy their own than be honorable. There is no amount of pressure that we can impose on such that would have any effect. We go home."

"Home? But what about Commander Kraanox?"

"May the heavens help him, for there is nothing we can do. At least, back on Traanu, we may yet help in the war effort. Containment of the Muurgu from returning here is still a priority. Unless they return here, I shall not."

CHAPTER 29

Justin faced Robert Grimmson, the project director. "So, Bob, what are you here to tell me? I'm fired?"

Robert shook his head and laughed. "Fired? Where did you ever get such a crazy notion?"

"Hmm, well, let me see. I have been on this project for a long time and with no results to show for it. Although the theories we are working on seem sound from both a physics and quantum mechanics viewpoint, we simply don't have the technology to test them." Justin studied Bob's face for signs to see if he was on the right track.

Robert nodded. "Yes, yes, go on."

"Well, now you're telling me that NASA budgets are cut back, making any further equipment development a virtual impossibility. So the only thing left for me to work with is a pencil and paper."

"Well, I wouldn't put it so dramatically."

"And now the department is to be downsized, and since I'm the low man on the totem pole, that means I get the axe."

"A reasonable deduction, Justin. One thing for sure, we didn't make a mistake in hiring you. But for once, your intuitive skills are incorrect."

"So, then what, Bob? You just asked me to clean out my desk."

"And that I did, Justin, that I did, not for termination, but for a transfer."

"A transfer? To where?"

"I'm not even sure where. All I can tell you is I was asked to make a recommendation of one bright mind and I chose you."

Justin felt sheepish. Talk about the wrong guess. "Okay, once I get my foot out of my mouth, I'll go pack. Thank you, Bob."

Robert got up and gave Justin a friendly slap across the back. "No problem, Justin, you made it an easy decision. They're sending a plane for you this afternoon."

***

The small plane idled on the runway. Justin climbed aboard and, much to his surprise, found out who waited on board for him. Army, no doubt, and though unsure, Justin thought the rank of his insignia indicated a Major. And his face appeared strangely familiar.

"Hello, Justin, so nice to see you again."

Justin's eyes went wide with final recognition. The graying hair on the man's temples made instant recognition impossible, but when the man greeted him, the memory of their last meeting flooded back. "Good day Major Bucknell, long time, no see."

The door to the plane closed and the pilot asked Wayne if it was all right to take off. Wayne consented and told Justin to make sure his seat belt was secure. In moments, the plane thundered down the runway and took off.

Once airborne, Justin stared out the windows at the landscape that dropped away below him. The fields planted with their various crops made a colorful patchwork on the land below. As the plane continued to rise, the land fell away, a blanket of clouds separated them from the ground, and Justin returned his focus to the major.

***

Wayne sat quietly watching his fellow passenger staring out at the world. He smiled as he watched Justin marveling at all he could see, the wide-eyed innocence that obviously made up a part of the character of this young man. Once he was confident of Justin's full attention, he

171

unclasped his hands folded under his chin and opened a small table that folded down from the wall. He opened two cans of cola and placed one on the table in front of Justin.

"So, Justin, you're probably trying to figure out what all this is about." He leaned back and took a sip of his own cola to allow a moment of silence to whet Justin's appetite for the answer.

Wayne smacked his lips. "Ah, nothing like a cold pop. It still reminds me of being a kid. Eh, Justin? Why, I remember when you were just a lad and I gave you a ranking in the army—Honorary Warrant Officer, if I recall correctly. You were as proud as a peacock that day."

Justin reached for the cold drink. "Yes, Major. I still have the badge you gave me."

"You know, Justin, I have a son now, about the same age as you were when that happened. Just like you, he's all wide-eyed about the world and everything in it." He leaned forward to place his can down into the little circle depression in the table that would hold it in place as the plane rolled slightly with the cross winds. "What I need to tell you now, Justin, is that there has been a slight change to your title. The word Honorary has been removed."

Justin blinked a few times. "Wait a second, are you saying that I've been drafted?"

As Wayne leaned back into his chair, he returned his hands to the folded position below his chin. "It's a little different than that, Justin. This isn't joining the military in the same sense. Consider it an appointment to continue your work, but in a military venue. The reports I've reviewed state you were at the top of the field in your department. Some of your research reports showed promise, your hypotheses verifiable. Needless to say, you come highly recommended."

Justin appeared rattled by the news, for when he put his can of pop down, he missed putting it into the circle depression and instead caught the edge, which caused his soda to tilt and slip from his hand. In a small shower of cola, both men shied from the table as Justin scrambled to catch the now rolling can, spewing pop as it went. Justin managed to nab the can just as it rolled off the edge, while Wayne, now standing, retrieved some towels to mop up the pop. Justin muttered his thanks and proceeded to wipe down the counter.

Just as Justin finished, Wayne dropped a tri-folded document in front of him. "Take a moment to read this."

Justin unfolded the papers and perched himself on the edge of his seat, elbows on knees, holding the papers in front of him. The document was very official looking, and there in bold script, was Justin's name and the title Warrant Officer just below that. Without really reading all the fine print, Justin's eyes were drawn to the bottom of the page. There, in a deep blue ink, was scrawled the signature that authorized the document. Justin's eyes grew wide and he looked up at Wayne. "The...the president?"

Wayne smiled and gave a polite nod.

Justin straightened up. "Of the United States?"

He couldn't help but chuckle. "The very one. I was serious Justin about this being an appointment. Now you have the right to refuse this selection. I can order the pilot to turn this plane around right now, and take you back to NASA. What's it going to be?"

Justin pivoted his head right and left, as if looking for cars at a busy intersection. Finally, his gaze returned to the major. "The president of the United States has appointed me?"

Wayne leaned over and placed a hand over top Justin's hand. "Yes, Justin, the president of the United States. He has great faith in you."

Justin collapsed back into his seat. "The President of the United States has appointed me. Me. This is an honor.

Wayne returned to a comfortable position in his own chair. "I take it that the answer is you'll take the job."

Justin blinked again and refocused on the major. "What...what? Oh, oh yes, I'll take the job...the president..."

Wayne reached down to grab a magazine to read. "All right then, I am glad of it, I thought you would take it. I will finish the briefing when we get to the base."

Justin's gaze returned to look back out the window. The cloud cover now behind them, a clear view of the countryside could be seen.

***

The ride to the base was quiet. Sitting in the back of the jeep, Justin watched the road go by and the scattered houses between the air base and the army compound. There was the old Jenkins house, with Mr. Jenkins still sitting on the porch in his rocker. It seemed to him like he'd been sitting there forever. And the Miller house, farther down the road, with its big apple tree in the front yard. As kids, he and his friends climbed that tree to steal the odd apple. More memories flooded back into him as they continued down the road.

The jeep came to an intersection and turned off the main road to head to the base. Here, things were changed. Instead of one checkpoint, there were now two. And the extra set of fences, complete with razor wire, gave the camp a more foreboding appearance.

Once they reached the main grounds, Justin noted the newly-constructed, corrugated steel buildings. They parked the jeep outside an office structure. Justin followed Wayne in and made himself comfortable in one of the easy chairs in front of the major's desk. Major Bucknell picked up the phone and gave instructions for some people to come to his office. After hanging up, instead of sitting down at his desk, Wayne parked himself on the corner. "Well, Justin, let's talk a bit about what's happening here. You worked at NASA in pioneering new propulsion systems for our endeavors into space. Unfortunately, budget restraints, and upper management commitment became sorely lacking. What is here is an opportunity for you to continue that work."

Just then the door opened and two men stepped in and greeted Major Bucknell. Both men were in the same field as Justin, and after a round of introductions Wayne got everyone seated and regained his perch on the desk corner. "Okay, continuing from where I left off. Justin, these are the men whose theories you have been passed while at NASA. It is my hope that the three of you together can sort through your individual limitations and arrive on a consensus of theory and put such theory into practice. All the necessary technicians are on hand to assist in building whatever you decide to build, and we can get going again on what has turned into a stalled venture."

After a few more pleasantries, the men excused themselves and Justin was taken to his new quarters to settle in. Major Bucknell invited him to meet later at the officer's mess. Justin stepped out into the early evening air to head over to the hall. A slight breeze picked up and it felt good to have the cool air rush over him instead of the heat of earlier in the day. As he crossed the compound, he was startled to hear some type of animal baying, but unlike any hound he knew, this one had a deep, throttling sound to it. It unnerved him as he stepped through the doors into the building.

Major Bucknell was already there, along with the two scientists he'd met earlier, and standing next to him was a bald fellow that he seemed to recognize. It was only when they were mere feet apart that his eyes grew wide with recognition.

Kraanox smiled and reached out to take his hand. "It is so very nice to see you again. Justin, it has been such a very long time. Tell me, does your mother still make that wonderful carrot cake? Now that you are back here, do you think you could get her to make me one? The food around here is atrocious!"

As his jaw dropped, Wayne burst into a hearty laugh. "Come on now, Kraanox, don't be so hard on our chef, he does his best. Let's sit down, shall we?"

As they worked themselves around the table, Justin banged against a couple chairs and nearly fell, unable to take his eyes off Kraanox. Kraanox reached out and grabbed Justin just before he fell over. "Now, Justin, it doesn't have to be a whole cake, just a nice slice or two would do."

Shakily, he managed to right himself into the chair nearest him. "Uh, shhh…shhh…sure."

Kraanox released his grip on Justin's arm. "The major felt it was important that you meet me as soon as possible."

Wayne leaned in and gained Justin's focus. "Sorry, Justin, I didn't mean to startle you. I just felt it was important that you understand what we are working with here. When you encountered Kraanox all those years ago in your backyard was the beginning of a new chapter in the history of mankind. Kraanox crash-landed in the woods near here, and your encounter with him proved to be the first one with an alien species. Kraanox has been our…guest since then, and with the remnants of his ship combined with what knowledge Kraanox has been able to impart to us, our scientists have been struggling ever since to understand the technology involved."

Kraanox spread his arms in a gesture of surrender. "I have been trying to tell the good major for many years now that I am but a simple soldier and not a scientist. How all these things work is just as vague to me as it is to him.

176

But alas, here I am, having to stomach one more meal from the hands of the men who call themselves quartermasters and are working diligently to poison me, having reduced me by a quarter already! Do you think we could get your mother to come here and cook?"

Justin turned to stare back at Kraanox in incredulity. "I'm sorry... what are you talking about?"

Kraanox clasped his hands together in a pleading posture. "Okay, I will settle for one slice, one slice only."

Major Bucknell burst out laughing. "Enough Kraanox, he's as befuddled as can be, as it is. I'll get you some carrot cake."

Before they could go any further, their conversation was interrupted by another of the strange howls that Justin heard before entering the officers' mess, only this time it was much closer. He twisted in his chair to look at the door. "What is that?"

As if in answer to his question, the door burst into a hundred pieces, and what appeared to be a small dinosaur charged into the room, headed straight for him. He raised his arms to shield himself as the animal bounded upon him and knocked him to the floor. The huge jaw, with its rows of jagged teeth, perched over his face, and for one moment, he feared for his life. What followed was even more surprising, as the creature began licking his cheeks. The animal totally filled his vision, but he could hear the bedlam that was going on in the room.

"What's going on here? How come Rex isn't confined to his pen?"

"I'm sorry, Major. He was all excited so I decided to take him for his usual walk. Once I undid his chain from the post, he bolted. I grabbed his leash and was doing my best just trying to hang onto him. I couldn't stop him. He's way too strong, and he charged all the way here, dragging me along like a rag doll."

A number of the men in the room began to yank hard at Rex's chain and pull him away from Justin. After the initial tug somewhat dislodged Rex, Justin scrambled out from under him to stand up. Rex looked back for a brief second at the men holding his chain then simply pulled them along as he returned to cozy up to Justin and nudge him affectionately.

Kraanox put a hand on Justin's shoulder to calm him and used his free hand to rub around the bone plates on Rex's head. "There, there now, Rex, it's okay. He isn't going anywhere. Be a good boy and sit down, will you?"

Rex looked up at Kraanox and whimpered. "Now Rex, be good, sit down!"

Major Bucknell came to stand behind Kraanox. "Sit down, Rex!"

Rex whimpered once more, but then hunkered down to the floor looking back and forth between Justin, Kraanox and the major. Justin took two steps sideways to place himself somewhat behind the other two men. "What is it?"

Kraanox, while still petting Rex, craned his head around to look him in the eyes. "To him, he's your son."

Justin looked wildly from Kraanox to Major Bucknell. "My son?"

Wayne reached out to pet Rex as well. "Kraanox, you told me that only those who touched his egg before birth were recognized as parents. You also told me he would reach a weight of four to five hundred pounds, whereas, he's probably closer to eight hundred now."

Kraanox straightened and turned to fully face them. "As to his weight, I can only assume that the iron rich food and slightly different gravity has led to Rex becoming the giant crotuu that he is. And obviously, Justin had contact with his egg, and before us, I might add. Watching Rex's reaction, I would suspect that Justin was, in fact, the first to handle the egg, which I seem to recall, was what Captain

Smeeton told us. In the mind of Rex, this makes him Rex's father. Only his mother would have a closer bond."

Justin hesitantly put his hand out to touch Rex who shuffled forward to make the touch happen quicker, and his hand recoiled for a moment from Rex's movement. Once the giant beast stopped, he tried again and followed the example of scratching around the bone plates as Kraanox did. Rex began to purr, although the rumble sounded much deeper than any cat. "He...he likes it!"

Major Bucknell straightened up, barked a few orders to get the men to clean up the mess, and then found his seat once again at their table. Kraanox joined him, and as Justin moved over to sit down, Rex shuffled along to stay within hand reach of Justin. Justin sat down and continued to pet Rex. Eventually dinner was served and Justin let go of Rex to attend to his dinner. Rex laid his massive head onto Justin's foot.

After the meal, the five men sat and chatted about the project and all its implications. Rex finally consented to being moved, and sat in the corner. It was time to turn on the television. The president planned an address to the nation, and everyone wanted to watch.

"Good evening. This is a special night for me. Exactly three years ago, on July 15, 1976, I accepted the nomination of my party to run for President of the United States. I promised you a president who is not isolated from the people, who feels your pain, and who shares your dreams and who draws his strength and his wisdom from you."

Kraanox interrupted. "This...democracy of yours, it really is quite an interesting concept. I believe the Bruutaan on Traanu practice something similar."

"...I invited to Camp David people from almost every segment of our society—business and labor, teachers

179

and preachers, Governors, mayors, and private citizens. And then I left Camp David to listen to other Americans, men and women like you. It has been an extraordinary 10 days, and I want to share with you what I've heard..."

Major Bucknell leaned into the group "I had the special honor of meeting with the president some days ago. He was most anxious that our work proceed, and that what sciences we discover can have domestic applications as well."

"...These 10 days confirmed my belief in the decency and the strength and the wisdom of the American people, but it also bore out some of my longstanding concerns about our Nation's underlying problems..."

Once again, Kraanox chirped in. "Yes, quite interesting, that the common man could so easily approach and influence your leaders."

"...I want to talk to you right now about a fundamental threat to American democracy. I do not mean our political and civil liberties. They will endure. And I do not refer to the outward strength of America, a nation that is at peace tonight everywhere in the world, with unmatched economic power and military might. The threat is nearly invisible in ordinary ways...."

Kraanox continued. "Of course, one of its weaknesses is the paralysis that occurs when consensus is absent."

Justin's mind drifted to his one trip to the White House, and how he failed to speak to the president then. He wondered, if given a second chance, whether he would have done anything differently.

"In closing, let me say this: I will do my best, but I will not do it alone. Let your voice be heard. Whenever you have a chance, say something good about our country. With God's help and for the sake of our Nation, it is time for us to join hands in America. Let us commit ourselves together to a rebirth of the American spirit. Working together with our common faith we cannot fail. Thank you and good night."

They all sat and discussed the president's message and more details on Major Bucknell's visit to Camp David. As the evening wound down, Kraanox returned to his quarters and the other men decided it was late enough and time to call it a night. After some whining, Wayne convinced Rex to go with him and return to his pen. Justin returned to the room assigned him and tucked himself in for the night. At the end of his amazing day, his confidence in the work he was doing felt restored and he fell into a deep, peaceful sleep.

CHAPTER 30

"Turn it off, Yuri. Turn it off."

Yuri reached and turned off the television. "You must admit Leonid, this new "old" man that the Americans have elected as their new President is someone who is a threat. Analysts in the Komitet Gosudarstvennoy Bezopasnosti have described him as a hawk of the most vicious kind."

"He is just another President. I have seen five others before him. This one is probably no different."

"How can you say that, Leonid? He is proposing a lot of hard-line talk."

"Yes; and what will it get him. Just more debt for his country to pay."

"True, but what will we do to match it? Already the country reels from financial pressures. Maintaining the large military forces in Afghanistan and around the world is draining us."

Leonid slammed the desk top with the flat of his hand. "Our economy is as strong as ever!'

Yuri sighed. Turning to his credenza, he produced a bottle of vodka and two glasses. "Leonid, you may be able to fool the rank and file with that speech, but we have been friends for a long time. You know that I know better."

Leonid reached for the drink. "Thank you. I grow tired sometimes, defending the government. You know my health isn't so good. I shouldn't even be having this."

"I know, Leonid, I know. But whatever happened to that speech you gave me about the evolution of warfare. Our tanks and armies are at levels never seen before, and yet they scrapped the Almaz program. And now this new president is talking about establishing a Star Wars program, complete with a militarized space station!"

Leonid chuckled. "Yuri, you have it all wrong. Yes, they want to build this so-called Star Wars station, but not for us, for them! You know who I mean."

Yuri straightened up in his chair. "You...you mean..."

"Yes, Yuri, the aliens. It was not mechanical failure that brought down Skylab to splatter all over the deserts of Australia. It was the aliens who did it."

"But I thought they haven't been seen for some time now."

"They haven't, at least not on Earth. And even so, the Skylab thing appears to be an isolated incident. No, the aliens may seem to be gone, at least for now, but forever is a very long time."

"Then we should also prepare against them. The Almaz program must be resurrected."

Leonid stood up. "Well, I must go. I leave you with these words. Leave it to the Americans, Yuri. Let them spend the money."

"But if we leave it to them, then they will control space."

"Then they will control nothing, Outer space is very big, and very empty. Now, I am just an old man, Yuri, too tired to think much more on these matters. I am going home. Tell the nurse to come see me."

Yuri walked Leonid to the door and watched as he was driven away.

Standing outside, he decided to stroll out into the streets. Sometimes the fresh air would help clear his head when he felt depressed. Two security agents joined him, and he set off in a brisk pace.

As he walked down the street, he headed into the market area. Rounding a corner, he noted a large line of people. His curiosity piqued, he approached a man standing near the end of the line. "What are you lining up for?"

"I don't know."

"What do you mean, you don't know?"

"That's just it, I don't know. But when you see a line, you know that you must get into it, or else you will not get anything at all."

"But what will you get?"

"When I get to the front of the line, I will find out."

This was incredible. He stepped away from the line and followed it as it snaked down the block to the local grocery.

When he stopped by the door to look inside, others in the line cursed at him. "Get to the end of the line!"

"I'm only trying to see what's going on."

One old woman eyed him and the two KBG agents who were walking a respectful distance behind. "It's your fault! People like you! You are starving us to death. Look at me. I am an old woman, and I have to stand in line five hours just to buy a loaf of bread! And by the time it is my turn, the price will have doubled again. You should be ashamed! When I was a young girl, before communism, we were a proud people. Now look at us, lining up for half a day just to buy a loaf of bread!"

The old woman returned to her place in line. The two agents behind him were stepping forward, probably to arrest the old woman for speaking against the government, but he stopped them. Looking at the woman, he saw in her his since departed mother—proud, defiant, and a part of mother Russia that no longer truly existed.

She continued watching him and the two men, and did her best to straighten her bent back. The pose said, let them arrest me, I don't care anymore. A tear trickled from her eyes. Dabbing at it with her kerchief, she turned so he wouldn't see.

It was enough for him. Barking orders at the agents, he ordered that the grocer be arrested for price gouging. The men dragged the grocer away on his knees, pleading for a second chance. He went inside and reached behind the counter to grab a loaf of bread. When he exited the store, he found the old lady in line. "Here, take your bread." The old woman walked up, spat on the ground, took the loaf of bread, and then slapped him in the face.

Rubbing his cheek, he headed back to his office. Once he returned, he summoned the staff doctor. When he came in, the doctor noted the red mark on the Yuri's face and went to look more closely. "Not that, you fool, sit down! I wish to discuss the medication you are currently supplying to Leonid's nurse."

The doctor gone, Yuri saw the bottle of vodka, still sitting out from earlier. Pouring a large drink, he toasted to the empty air. "I'm sorry, old friend. It is time for a change."

CHAPTER 31

"Happy birthday!"

Justin blew hard and managed to blow out all the candles in one breath.

"Make a wish!"

"Thanks, everyone. Let's have some cake!"

His mom produced a large knife and handed it to him. Cutting the first slice and placing it on a plate, he passed it round the table. Seated around to his left were his mother, Major Bucknell and his wife, two colleagues from his department, and to his immediate right, Suzie.

His mom held up a staying hand. "Don't make mine too big. Save some for that friend of yours at work who likes it so much. It's too bad he couldn't come today. Anyone who praises my baking that much is all right in my book. Major Bucknell, as I understand it, you're in charge. You should have made arrangements that he could be here today."

Wayne passed a piece of cake to his wife. "My apologies, Mrs. Spencer. I'm afraid he's somewhat tied up for now."

"Hmm, well I do declare that I find that disappointing. Work is an important thing. But after all, if you can't enjoy a few of the simpler pleasures in life, than what's the point of living?"

Mrs. Spencer got up from the table. "I forgot to put the coffee on."

After reading the birthday cards, Justin began to wonder what was taking his mom so long in the kitchen. Excusing himself from the table, he went in to check. "Hey, Mom, how's the coffee coming?"

His mother stood by the coffee pot as it perked away, obviously finished. She held a Kleenex to her eye. "I'll be in, in a minute."

"Hey, Mom, what's the matter?"

"I'm just worried about you, Justin. Life is passing you by. Perhaps you should consider moving out. Live a little. Don't waste your life here."

"Mom, who would take care of you?"

His mother balled the Kleenex into her fist. "What do you mean, who would take care of me? I've been taking care of me for a long time now, thank you very much."

Justin stuck his hands in his pockets and absently toed at the kitchen floor. They had argued this out before. With his dad gone, Justin felt it up to him to maintain the family home. At first his mother seemed to enjoy having him around the house, but as of late, she hinted more and more that he needed to move out and find a place on his own.

The fact she chose to make this argument again with company in the dining room put him in an awkward position.

"Not now, Mom, we have guests."

"Guests schmests! It's time, Justin. You're thirty-five. Do you think that poor Suzie out there is going to wait for you until I die? Well, I've got news for you. I intend to live a very long time!"

His mother, pot of coffee in hand, marched out into the dining room. "Tell me, Major, how old were you when you moved out of the house?"

Startled at the question, Wayne uncrossed his legs and sat straight. "Uh, well, Mrs. Spencer, I went to military school when I was young and signed up right after I graduated. The army has been home for me for a long time now."

"Exactly my point. I've been trying to get my boy here to go find a place, get out from under my skirts. Life is passing him by hanging around here."

Justin followed in. "Mom, please!"

His mother spun around and fired off the same question to the other guests. When she finished, she returned her gaze to Suzie. "And what about you, young lady? I haven't heard your opinion on the matter."

Before Suzie could answer, Justin interposed himself by taking the coffee pot from his mother's hand. "Okay, Mom, you made your point."

As the coffee was being poured, an uncomfortable silence fell over the table. Major Bucknell coughed and everyone looked to him. "You know, Justin, you could stay on the base. Just for a while until you can get settled somewhere."

Wayne's wife elbowed him in the ribs. "Shush! Leave the boy alone. After all, it is his birthday."

"What? I'm only trying to be helpful."

"With help like that, who needs it."

The conversation broke open with a few other suggestions making the rounds. Justin piped in. "Look, everybody, thanks, I'll look around. I have some ideas anyway. I just am not ready to discuss them tonight."

Wayne raised a glass. "To Justin Spencer. A long and happy life."

Justin waved his hand over the table in a downward motion. "Hold on, hold on. There's something I need to say first."

Everybody returned their glasses to the table and looked at Justin. He cleared his throat and took a deep breath. "First of all, I want to thank everybody for coming tonight. You give me an example of what I can expect in my old age."

A few guffaws from around the table caused him to pause. "Mom, thanks for the dinner. It was wonderful, as always. And everybody, thanks for the nice cards and gifts. I have been thinking that it is time to make a move, though not in the way discussed earlier."

Justin stood up, raising a couple of eyebrows. "The only thing missing tonight is the one last gift I am looking for."

He turned to his right and held out a hand to Suzie. She took a quick glance around the table and then took his hand to stand up with him. "The last gift I need is one simple word. Suzie, will you marry me?"

Suzie lifted a hand to her mouth in surprise, then threw her arms around him and hugged him tight for a second. When she pulled free, her eyes glistened with tears. "Yes."

The table erupted into a cacophony of cheers, whistles, and clapping. Justin smiled and gave her another big hug, followed by a long kiss.

His mom stood up, came over and gave Suzie a hug as well. "Welcome to the family." She then turned and gave Justin a hug. "I'm proud of you. All I have to say is, it's about doggone time!"

Everyone laughed. Wayne stood up and once again lifted his glass. "To Justin and Suzie Spencer. May you have a long and happy life together."

Everyone else stood as well. "To Justin and Suzie!"

Before people could drink, his mom interrupted. "And to grandkids!"

Once again, the laughs went around, and everyone drank to the toast.

Justin sat down. Suzie moved her chair to snuggle against him. It was his best birthday ever.

CHAPTER 32

The Emperor moved silently through the cosmos as it neared the planet.

Captain Pruutoc mused over the coming mission. Many years having passed since his last visit to Earth. The Braannoo kept them penned in with orbiting space stations. Their cursed ships, although smaller, proved a constant harassment on the Muurgu Empire. They maintained a superior edge on land, but control of the skies belonged to the enemy.

He hit a button on his console. "Have the good doctor report to me."

In a few moments, the ship's medical officer came onto the bridge. "Yes, Captain?"

"You are certain that this medication will halt the effects?"

"Absolutely. It will prevent your body from absorbing any significant amount of radiation."

"Well, I have some doubts. It took years for me to recover from the radiation sickness, and half of my crew died. Why is that so?"

"Understand, Captain, your bodies already were exposed and absorbed what they did. This treatment is a preventative, not a cure. Extracting the radiation poisoning from your system was a much more difficult process. We were fortunate to save those we did, including you."

Pruutoc leaned forward into the doctor's face. "All I can tell you, doctor, is I better not get sick this time. Because if I do, I promise that you'll go before I do."

"Take the medication as prescribed in the moments prior to your encounter with the materials, and your systems will remain immune for half a day. Likewise, make sure the men are wearing the new, protective clothing we designed for this mission. You follow these steps, and everything will be fine."

"Thank you, doctor. Go make sure you are ready to administer the doses. We will be entering the planet's orbit momentarily. I intend this to be a quick strike mission. My orders are to obtain the raw material this time. Apparently, our scientists back home have perfected the technology to create their own devices with a much higher expected yield on detonation."

They tried in vain to mine enough of the isotopes at home, but it was impossible to find sufficient quantity. No, better just to steal it. And Pruutoc knew just where to look, but this time, the plan was to avoid any military installations. He was not prepared for an armed confrontation as the new suits designed to ward off the deadly isotopes provided little defense against the weapons of the Earthlings.

"Helm, place us into a geocentric synchronous orbit above our target. We will wait until later to conduct our raid under the cover of darkness."

"Aye, Captain."

The tactical officer turned to face Captain Pruutoc. "Sir, there appear to be a much larger number of satellites now circling the planet since our last visit. Until communications can verify them, it is possible they may be able to track us."

"These are stupid Earthlings. How far can they have advanced in a few short years? Follow my orders."

***

Passing directly below the Emperor, in a near Earth orbit, the cosmonauts aboard the Mir Space Station were the first to detect the entry of the Muurgu ship into the area. It wasn't long before senior staff at the Russian Aviation and Space Agency Rosaviakosmos was alerted.

"Captain, it is now the middle of the night. Shall I proceed as planned?"

"Take us down. Assault team to the lift."

They lowered the lift, and eight Muurgu alit a short distance from the target facility. Sensors displayed live feedback to the Emperor so that Captain Pruutoc could follow their progress.

The premises were encircled with a chain link fence and guard posts at the entries. At the gates, it appeared a lot of humans were exiting, indicating a shift end. Pruutoc hoped that the level of on-duty staff at such an hour would be minimal, giving his team an advantage. The men made quick work of cutting through the fence and approaching the main building.

The team commander looked into the camera. "Everything so far, so good, Captain. Our approach has apparently been undetected. We're proceeding toward the back of the building now to what appear to be loading docks."

"Remember, Commander, the longer you remain undetected, the greater the amount of the refined material we should be able to obtain."

"Yes sir, proceeding now."

The team reached the docks and began to look for an entry point. The doors were locked, and it would take a moment to cut through.

Tactical interrupted. "Captain, I am tracking several human aircraft approaching at high speed!"

Pruutoc swiveled to look over. "What? ...How?"

On his station monitor, an alarm began to sound. The team commander was shouting at his men to hurry. "Captain, our position is compromised, awaiting instructions."

"Get your team out of there."

At that moment, the doors burst open and several armed Earthlings rushed out, yelling something at his troops. When the men continued to run for the cut in the fence, the humans opened fire.

The captain spun in his chair. "Helm! Close the gap. Rescue who we can."

The Emperor pulled into close proximity of the building, and the remaining Muurgu men were quickly climbing onto the lift when the human aircraft arrived. Tactical continued to advise.

"Enemy aircraft have locked onto us. They have fired two missiles!"

"Quickly, veer off, close the lift!"

The oblique angle presented to the missiles as the Emperor pulled away provided some protection. The same shielding that warded micrometeorites came into play, and the two missiles skipped off the Muurgu ship. The first slammed into the roof of the structure, the second, following only two seconds behind, veered directly into the main building.

As explosions rocked the facility below them, the Emperor began to climb quickly. The Earthling air ships continued to fire their projectile weaponry at them as they rose.

"They're dropping off pursuit."

"How many of the team did we retrieve?"

"Medical here. We only have three men alive on the lift; all others are down, including the team commander."

"How, by the heavens, did they react so quickly? Engineering...is the hull compromised?"

"No, sir, some minimal damage, but nothing that would threaten us immediately, but I wouldn't be looking to do an atmospheric re-entry at high speed. The friction would rip us apart. We're going to need to affect some repairs. As for space travel, without total hull integrity, the shielding system for micrometeorites would be flawed. We might as well travel through a shooting gallery. But we should be okay to obtain orbit."

Captain Pruutoc stewed. Plainly, their arrival had not gone unnoticed. The humans were prepared. He cursed himself for not having heeded the warning from tactical when they first arrived. This proved to be a setback, but not one they could overcome.

There was no choice but to retreat. He misjudged these humans badly. Returning to Traanu, empty-handed, would not sit well with his superiors.

The disappointment over the failure below still hung heavy over him. Down below, the Chernobyl Nuclear Plant burned through the night.

CHAPTER 33

Vladimir sat comfortably on the restaurant's veranda, enjoying the view of the Mediterranean Sea. "Pass me the binoculars, please. I would like to see if I can make out who's on deck."

William passed over the binoculars. "I don't think they're strong enough to do that, but give them a try."

Vladimir adjusted the focus as he examined the cruise ship anchored just outside the Grand Harbor of Malta. He could read the lettering plainly, the Maxim Gorkiy. Looking from the bow to the deck, there were people moving about, but he could not make out the faces. "Too bad. I was hoping to see if your president was on the deck. I have only seen pictures of him. It would be interesting to meet him in person."

"Yeah, I bet it would be. He had my job as director, you know, some years ago. The two of you would have more to talk about than you originally thought, I bet."

Vladimir turned to look further out at the sea. "Where is your vessel?"

William got up and crouched behind him so that when he pointed over Vladimir's shoulder, he gave a clear line of sight. "In about that direction. You won't see much at all from here."

Vladimir scanned around a bit, and then found his target. "Ah, I see it. I can only make out the profile. So that is what a guided missile cruiser looks like."

"Yep, that's the USS Belknap, loaded with Harpoon, Terrier and Phalanx missiles. She's one tough little tug."

"I seem to recall hearing that this ship was sunk, was it not?"

"No, not sunk, but it was banged up a bit in rough weather off the coast of Sicily. They refitted it. It actually, at one time, served as a flagship for the navy."

"Hmm, rough weather, like we are experiencing now. Too bad. Originally, we were to meet on board your vessel. But I suspect that the comforts on board the Gorkiy are probably more to everyone's tastes anyway."

"I've always wanted to try some of that Russian caviar. Is it really all that good?"

"The best in the world. But no matter, neither you nor I are going to try any today." Vladimir handed the glasses back to William. "It was better that we met this way. So many things have happened in the past few years. What with perestroika and glasnost in my country, our business, like your secret service, will no longer be all that secret."

William chuckled and poured himself another glass of wine. "Well, since that incident at Chernobyl, it's plainly obvious that we both have bigger fish to fry."

He calmly received the wine bottle from his American counterpart. "Yes, with the cold war ending, we both need to focus on, is what's out there." He pointed toward the sky.

The waiter came with their meals. "Enjoy."

William looked over. "I don't know how you can eat that."

He looked down at his plate. "This is Fenek, the Maltese national dish."

"It's a rabbit. It's hard to imagine eating such a soft and cuddly creature."

"Well, you know what they say, when in Rome…"

"I'll stick to my steak. Being born in St Louis, the American heartland, we like our beef."

Vladimir chuckled. "Then you should learn to read Maltese menus better. That is Laħam taż-żiemel, horse meat!"

William took a bite. "Tastes okay, guess it will have to do."

With the meal finished, William reached down to grab a dossier from his portfolio and opened it on the table. "Okay, comrade, down to a little business. We've got the Hubble telescope going up soon, and it should be useful in giving a closer look at any alien ships, if they enter our area. Avoiding using land-based telescopes will help us keep this stuff quiet. I assume that, like us, you intend to keep this issue under wraps. The public reaction to aliens would be catastrophic. I know that you have kept an eye as well, with what you've loaded onto Mir. I think, as does my government, that a more concerted effort is necessary if we are to collectively remove this threat. What we would like to propose is a few joint ventures."

The papers were spread out so he could look them over. He tapped with his fingers as he shuffled through the pages. "These are all well and fine, my capitalist friend, though I am concerned as to the financial strain that this will put on my government. What would really help would be the live capture of one or two of these invaders from space. We would like to understand the physiology of these people better. Examining the corpses we retrieved from Chernobyl is just not enough for us in dealing with these aliens. If you should capture one of these creatures, would you be kind enough to share such information freely? And if you should retrieve any alien technology, then an understanding of these things would help immensely in our joint struggle against these creatures."

The American started to pack up his papers. "Well, it's time for me to go. If we do capture any aliens and or alien technology, you'll be the first to know. In the meantime, I'll have my underlings follow up on these proposals with your people."

William said goodbye and left Vladimir alone at the table. Behind the restaurant bar, the television was broadcasting USSR Leader Mikhail Gorbachev addressing US President George Bush while standing together at the podium discussing the results of the Malta Summit.

"The world is leaving one epoch and entering another. We are at the beginning of a long road to a lasting, peaceful era. The threat of force, mistrust, psychological and ideological struggle should all be things of the past."

Thinking of the evasive response from his earlier table guest regarding the incarcerated alien in the United States, Vladimir smiled and thought, "Not so fast, comrade, not so fast."

CHAPTER 34

"Stay in formation! Attack action plan four-four! Stay tight! We'll only get one chance at this!"

"Confirm, attack action plan four-four, maintaining vector."

"Confirm."

"Confirm."

Captain Vreedoo and his four-jet squadron screeched across the landscape, barely yards from the surface. Muurgu troop movements advancing from their beachhead threatened to break through Braannoo lines. He knew his daring plan put him at risk from both enemy and friendly fire.

The Muurgu column would appear right over the next rise. His missile payload depleted, as well as that of his team, left them only their pulse lasers. Normally used in close dogfights, their limited range made them ineffective against ground troops from any significant distance.

As they neared the ridge, the transonic wave drag threatened to tear the jets apart.

"All right boys...just over this rise..."

He cleared the hilltop and found himself facing an enemy armored force of forty or fifty vehicles and the surrounding complement of ground troops. Practically flying between the vehicles at supersonic speeds, the miracle would be not to hit one.

"Let 'em rip!"

Scant yards from their targets, the pulse lasers from the four planes emitted a deadly stream, cutting a swath of destruction through the length of the column. Return fire beamed all around them, but the trajectories were all wrong as the Muurgu were anticipating fire from much higher targets.

In an instant, it was over, and Vreedoo maintained the same low course. "Break left on my mark...Mark!"

As one, the four jets executed the maneuver as enemy fire concentrated on their previous trajectory.

"Pedal down, boys. Let's get out of here before it heats up."

***

Setting down at the airbase, he taxied up to his hanger. "Reload me! We need to run another sweep!"

"Captain Vreedoo, please deplane, you are required inside."

"Deplane! What kind of crazy talk is that! We need to go back out now. Our troops need all the help they can get or we'll lose the whole sector!"

"Vreedoo! This is Admiral Duurgaan. Deplane now. I will meet you in the debriefing room."

Pounding his console, he killed the engines and climbed out of the cockpit.

As he strode into the debriefing room, he found Duurgaan waiting with another officer. "Begging your pardon, Admiral, why was I pulled out? My team is still functional."

"You're required immediately at the spaceport. I want the Dragonfly in the air within the hour. I have already ordered Space Station Magna, the only one fitted with interstellar drive, out of orbit. With your lighter mass, you should pass them in transit."

"I apologize, sir, but the battle is here! Retrieval of Commander Kraanox is not possible. You need every available pilot right now."

The Admiral looked to the man standing with him. "Lieutenant, brief the captain."

"Yes, sir." The lieutenant produced a holo-player from under his arm. Turning it on, he motioned for

Vreedoo to stand close. The image showed Traanu from space and a large quantity of colored lights circled in various orbits. Many of the lights held stationary positions right above their respective countries. These were battles stations, positioned in a defensive mode.

"This image was recorded several days ago. You note right here…" The lieutenant singled out an orange light. "…a Muurgu battle station leaving orbit. At first, we thought it was only looking to establish a new, higher orbit, but it kept moving until it left Traanu space."

Vreedoo tapped the light and it expanded the image to where the general configuration could be made out. "That's a battleship class. I thought that the Muurgu didn't have any stations capable of interstellar flight?"

"So did we. Obviously, this one has been refitted. Fortunately, the Magna is designed and should overtake them, we hope, in time." The lieutenant changed the image. "This is from last night. Note the trajectory of this new light as it leaves the planet surface."

He watched as it set out on the same course as the battle station. Touching it once again, the image expanded. There could be no mistaking this one. "The Emperor."

"Correct, Captain, the Emperor. We have correlated the trajectories, and they match exactly. We need to ensure the Dragonfly and the Magna can intercept these Muurgu ships."

Vreedoo shook his head. "I don't know. The Dragonfly is no match for the Emperor, and the Magna no challenge to that Muurgu battleship."

The admiral placed a hand on the lieutenant's chest, causing him to nod and step back. "Captain Vreedoo. I do not give this order lightly. At this moment, I have only one other ship available for interstellar flight, and I'm not prepared to put all of them at risk at once. Obviously, the Muurgu space program has recovered. I am trusting in you to do your best for Braannoo. Your intimate knowledge of the Dragonfly and its capabilities makes you the only choice."

"Yes Admiral, I will report right away. What is the trajectory of the Muurgu ships? Where are they going?"

"Back to that planet, that one they call Earth."

CHAPTER 35

Rex nuzzled against Justin again, and he stopped to put his hands on his hips and stared down at the living dinosaur. "Rex, you have to let me be! I am trying to work here. You are lucky to even be in the same building with me. I have half a mind to have you put in your kennel permanently."

Rex shrunk down as much as his monstrous frame of muscle and bone would allow. "That's a good boy. You certainly know what I mean when I talk about the kennel."

For the past several months, they granted Rex the run of Justin's work area. He stopped and thought about the animal once more. Just how intelligent was Rex? He was sure that Rex understood just about anything said to him. Some tried to say they were conditioned responses to certain words, but he did not believe that. Just the way he seemed to listen gave the appearance of intelligence.

"Good morning, Justin."

He spun to see Major Bucknell and Kraanox entering. "Good morning, Major... Kraanox."

Wayne carried a bag from which he retrieved a child's plaything. It was one of those toys where you put the round pegs and square pegs in the proper holes. "I thought I'd give Rex a little test this morning. See how smart he really is." He placed the main board down and dropped the pieces about. "Now, Rex, I want you to pick up the pieces and put them in the board."

They watched as Rex tried to move the little colors squares and tubes of wood with his claws. Not designed for grasping. Rex gave up and picked one up with his teeth. Dropping the square piece onto the board, Rex tapped at it until it fell into a hole. Justin watched with excitement. He got one in! Rex next got another square and dropped it on the board as well. It landed above a round hole and Rex tapped at it without success. Rex then slammed down on it hard and the board shattered, pieces flying everywhere.

The look on Rex's face showed complete disappointment at the results. The three of them broke up with laughter. Wayne went and gave Rex a good scratch on the head. "Well, one out of two isn't too bad. That was a good try, Rex."

Wayne stood up and folded his hands behind his back. "There's no doubt that the food here agrees with him. I thought you told me, Kraanox, that these animals only reach around five hundred pounds or so, Rex must be nine hundred if he's an ounce."

Kraanox took up the task of scratching where Wayne left off. "Obviously, your Earth environment is a factor. As I said before, maybe it is the heavier oxygen content or the slightly higher gravity or the iron rich food. Either that or your chef is feeding him better than he feeds me."

Justin dodged over to the table and produced a big cardboard box. "That reminds me, Kraanox, my mother has sent over another carrot cake for you. She thinks she's feeding the whole base. I don't have the heart to tell her that an alien eats it all!"

Kraanox, in the process of taking the package from him, looked indignant. "I don't eat it all Justin, Major Bucknell eats some too!"

Wayne broke out laughing. "If I'm lucky enough to get a piece! You hoard that stuff as if it were gold. I knew something was up when you asked to come with me to visit Justin."

Kraanox offered Major Bucknell a slice, which Wayne politely waved off. "How are things coming, Justin? I understand you've made some recent progress."

"Oh, nothing really. We've only managed to complete some physics equations."

"Nothing! The way I hear it is you've solved the necessary quantum mechanics to back up the theory. And the boys want more than anything for you to get all the credit. They say you are the one who solved it."

Justin offered Wayne a seat and clambered over another, sitting backward so that his arms rested on the back of the chair. "Yes, Major, it's taken a long time, but we think we understand how the Braannoo ship operated. Now that we comprehend the process, it's only a matter of replicating it."

Kraanox sat down, joining them, piece of cake in hand. "Just make sure that you are absolutely positive you have everything worked out. I wouldn't want anything to go wrong."

Justin looked over. "Why, Kraanox? Did something go wrong with you?"

Kraanox wiped carrot cake crumbs from his mouth. He sighed heavily. "It was a momentous occasion for us, interstellar space travel, to visit other planets, no longer bound by the limits of our own system."

"We thought that we had everything figured out. The maiden voyage was watched by everyone. Millions of people cheered as the crew of that ship lifted off and began their voyage into history. As they sped away, we all waited patiently for their much-anticipated return. What would they find? Would they encounter intelligent life? Or life at all? The questions that burned through the minds of everyone were soon to be answered."

"Finally, the time for their return came upon us. But they didn't come home. Days passed. The scientists were under fire. What went wrong? Months passed and still no sign. Everyone feared the worst."

"News then came from the scientific quarter. They'd identified the wrong magnetic signature. What they thought to be the signature of the nearest star proved to be incorrect. Our scientists assumed that the strongest signature would come from our closest neighbor. What they locked onto instead was the signature of a black hole in the same direction, though a little closer. The ship, before slowing enough to adjust course, must have crossed the event horizon. They were drawn into that swirling vortex of no return."

Justin popped his head upward. "That's horrible!"

"If you get the signature wrong, the heavens take you. My oldest brother served as the commander of that first mission. He would have been king. His loss will be forever mourned by my people."

Kraanox hung his head and returned to eating the carrot cake. A heavy silence hung in the room.

Wayne looked back and forth between Justin and Kraanox, slapped his knees, and stood up. "Well, the situation is changing as we speak. Whether we want to or not, we find ourselves being driven into interstellar space. How long until we can actually build a ship?"

Justin scratched his head and rose from his chair as well. "That's the fun part. By the time we develop and test the propulsion system, figure out the magnetic signatures of where we want to go, and then actually build the ship, it will be a very, very long time. I wouldn't be surprised if it didn't take at least twenty or thirty years."

Wayne slumped back into his seat. "Twenty or thirty years?"

"At least."

From the far side of the room, noise could be heard. Rex found the unattended box of carrot cake. Kraanox, raced over to pull the box away from the creature. Too late. Kraanox shook the empty box. "Better have your mom send more cake."

CHAPTER 36

The planet appeared on the helmsman's console. It looked lifeless, with a dusty, red appearance. No oceans, a barely perceptible atmosphere filled with dust clouds, desolate and forlorn.

"Captain Pruutoc, we've cleared the last planet before the target."

"Good. Helm, slow to one one-hundredth speed. I wish to enter the planet's outer range at my leisure. I'm not going to let them know of our presence until our escort arrives."

Pruutoc swung around in his chair. "Tactical, any sign?"

"None yet, sir, as expected, we passed them on the way due to the mass differential."

"Then we'll just have to sit and wait out here. Helm, set us in an orbit behind their moon. We should be unobserved there."

"Aye, Captain."

"Communications, start a repeating signal to the Hammer. When it enters the solar system, I want it to know we are already here. Once it achieves orbit, we can begin our mission."

"Yes, sir."

"When the Hammer gets here, we will teach these Earthlings a thing or two."

***

Captain Vreedoo paced the bridge. "Helm, do not brake to anything less than a quarter light. I'm not going to get caught by the Muurgu slowing to orbit speed. We'll blow through the area and return after a swing around their star."

"Aye, Captain."

"Tactical, I need a complete sweep of the planet's area. We need to verify whether the Muurgu have beaten us here before we enter orbit."

"At that speed, sir, I'll never have a chance to single out a Muurgu ship from all the satellites around this planet."

"Concentrate on mass. Only look for something equal to the size of a battleship station. If there is anything that size, it will most probably be the Muurgu."

The Dragonfly sped through the system and raced past the planet, using the gravitational signature of the system's star to fly past. "Anything tactical?"

"Sorry, sir, I just couldn't get any kind of a reading at this speed. My sensors indicated nothing, but I only can give any assurances over a very small fraction of space."

The communications officer interrupted. "Captain, the beacon on our space buoy is still operating. I believe I can set it to identify the Muurgu battle station. We can use the signal from the buoy to tell us its location without nearing the planet."

"What about the Emperor? Will it be able to identify the Emperor as well?"

"I'm not sure. The battle station will be emitting a homing beacon for any Muurgu ships to locate them. Only if the Emperor signals the station in such a path that the beacon can pick it up, then it is unlikely."

"Nevertheless, good job. Set the buoy to notify us as soon as the battleship approaches. We'll continue the wide sweep in an effort to spot the Emperor."

"Helm, swing around that star and do it again. Use the signature of that gas giant of theirs to compensate, and cut speed to one fifth. We're going to do this until I'm sure of the situation."

***

The Hammer slowed as it neared the planet. Unlike the Emperor, the station showed none of the sleek lines necessary for atmospheric flight. More of a bulky ball with numerous protrusions that housed the pulse cannons or docking ports, its dark mass equaled almost ten times that of the Emperor.

"We're receiving telemetry from the Emperor now, sir."

Captain Droostaad sipped his drink before responding. His chair sat on a catwalk in the middle of the bridge room. All of the stations below him were on the main floor. The wall before him featured no windows, but a concave screen with a multitude of different insets showing him the visual, tactical, and statistical reports. To his right, the three-dimensional image of the ship and its positioning in the system displayed the planet and its satellite, as well as the location of Pruutoc's ship.

"Helm, bring us into orbit as per the recommendations from the Emperor. Tactical, give me a complete analysis of the orbital defenses of this planet."

"Yes, sir, beginning my sweep now. Initial readings show a heavy concentration of orbiting satellites. It will take some time."

"Communications, get Captain Pruutoc on my console. I want to hear it from him one more time how these barbarians made him run with his tail between his legs on his last visit."

***

Vreedoo examined the report. Communications informed him the buoy still operated, and they used it to spot the Muurgu battleship as it entered orbit. He felt a moment of despair as it was identified as the Hammer, the class of the Muurgu fleet.

Still operating from a large distance, it seemed unlikely that the Hammer would spot him. When the Emperor appeared from the far side of the planet's moon, his decision not to enter orbit now seemed all the wiser.

"Communications, the Magna should be arriving shortly. Feed out the telemetry and the details on the Hammer, so that Captain Hraakoo knows what's waiting for him."

***

Captain Hraakoo of the Magna sat at his console, examining what specifics were believed to be available on the armament of the Hammer. His weapons officer at his side debated tactics against the battleship class Muurgu station. "There's no doubt about it, Captain. In a straight fight, we don't stand a chance. They outgun us. And they more than likely have a better range with their pulse cannons."

"Yes, I'm afraid you're right. Even with the Dragonfly assisting, we might be outmatched. Our only chance lies in tactics, speed, and perhaps a little luck."

"Helm, how long until we reach the Earth system?"

"Not much longer, sir."

"All right, I'm not looking to get in a confrontation with them. Once we get logistics from the Dragonfly, we will set up in orbit directly opposite the planet from the Hammer. Hopefully, they'll never catch us, and should the Hammer make a move toward the surface, they will need to enter the planet's upper atmosphere, slowing them considerably. That would open them up to our attack. Even then, it will be touch and go with their superior firepower. We'll keep them pinned in orbit for as long as it takes."

CHAPTER 37

Kraanox sat with Major Bucknell in the commissary, eating dinner and watching television. The CNN commentator engaged in a lively debate about the war in Kosovo and the use of the "G" word, genocide.

"This is one of the big differences between Traanu cultures and Earth ones."

"What is, Kraanox?"

"Genocide. A comparative word does not even exist in my language. In the history of my world, this has occurred many times before."

"Genocide? You mean that whole peoples have been wiped out?"

"Unfortunately, yes. Today, there are essentially only nine different races remaining, and each has its own country. The last one obliterated was the Jaaqqaa. When that small nation was overrun, my uncle gave refuge to the royal family, a decision not popular with the people of Braannoo."

"Did they manage to integrate into your society?"

"No. And now they would be gone. The refuge they were given was on the grounds of the royal palace. When my uncle, the king, died that day, the Jaaqqaa were no more."

Wayne pushed his plate away. "Now I've lost my appetite."

He looked over the major carefully. "I fail to understand. Is this not the way of nature that the strong should survive?"

"That may be the way for dumb animals. Not for an intelligent species."

"And yet, as I learn more and more of your history, this practice of genocide has been tried time and again. I wonder why you resist it. The struggle seems constant."

"It is because there are always evil people in the world who ignore their humanity in their quest for power."

"Humanity. I have been here a long time now, Major. Only recently have I begun to understand this concept. It is filled with incongruences as people try to equate perceptions against reality. Though I suspect you believe, at the heart of it, is an altruistic purpose."

The major turned in his chair and appeared ready to argue the issue when a private appeared at the table with an envelope in his hand. "Sorry for the interruption, sir. This just arrived for you. It's marked urgent."

"Thank you, Private, you're dismissed."

Kraanox watched as Wayne opened the envelope and read its contents, leafing through a number of pages and finally banging the package down on the table.

"Grave is the day, Kraanox."

"I have not heard that expression from you in some time, Major. This must be something very serious."

"I just received a report from Washington, and apparently we have a few new visitors out there."

"Visitors, Major? Are you talking about my people or the Muurgu?"

"The Muurgu. But unlike the previous visits where they were in solo space ships, this time they brought friends, big ones." Wayne dropped a satellite image in front of him, showing the outline of a massive structure in space and a second ship nearby. "Our Russian friends tell us that the ship with it is the same one they've encountered in the past, meaning the Muurgu."

Kraanox picked up the picture. "Hmm, it appears to be a space station, my guess is battleship class, though it has been a lot of years."

"Washington needs to know the capabilities of this station. I am to get what details I can from you to help us prepare to deal with this threat."

He tucked his chin into the webbing of his fingers in thought. "Grave is the day indeed, Major. Unlike that second ship, this station could wreak great havoc on this planet. Its pulse cannons could devastate your cities from a great height. And the weapons constantly recharge, so they can fire endlessly."

"How high?"

"As I understand your distances is somewhere in the range of twenty to thirty miles. In outer space, the ranges are far, far greater, since there is no atmosphere to interfere with it, perhaps four to five hundred miles."

"At such a height, we should be able to return fire with missiles and shoot them down."

"They would intercept your missiles long before they neared them."

Kraanox came to a sudden realization, and a cold feeling overcame him.

"If the Muurgu are bringing those here, that is not good news at all. It may mean that the war back home is over and the Muurgu have defeated my homeland."

Wayne handed Kraanox a second photo. "Well, I wouldn't jump to that conclusion just yet, a second one settled into an opposite orbit, and we think the ship docked to it is one of yours."

He looked closely at the picture. "Yes, I believe that to be Captain Vreedoo's ship, and a destroyer class station. All is not yet lost. Though they are significantly outgunned against the ship you showed me earlier."

"The question is, are they working against each other, or together?"

"Major, if there is one thing I am sure of, it is that the Braannoo and the Muurgu would never cooperate. I told you earlier of the plight of the Jaaqqaa, and you should know that it was the Muurgu who wiped them from the face of the planet. Just as they would do to the Braannoo, should they win the war at home. And just as they would do to mankind, should they come here in force. Genocide is not a crime on Traanu, it is victory."

CHAPTER 38

The Komityet Gosudarstvennoy Bezopasnosty existed no more. Now, the Federal Security Service of the Russian Federation took charge of the same duties the KGB held back in the cold war days.

Nikolai leaned back in his chair, put his feet up on his desk and lit a Cuban. The jumbo, *Montecristo Double Corona,* in his hand was a small token of satisfaction. He liked a large cigar but these double coronas were huge and often wasted. Nevertheless, he couldn't downgrade one size as it just didn't sit right with him to be smoking one named Churchill.

An aide entered to tell him it was time. He grudgingly put out his smoke and headed down the hall. Another fine one wasted. No matter. There was business to attend to.

The room hummed like a beehive. Small, compact, but full of a huge amount of activity. A long time went into the planning and preparation of this mission. The numerous stages of getting the necessary equipment and supplies ready, and in place, alone took many months.

Nikolai glanced over the tactical display on the main screen. "Are they still being tracked?"

"Yes, sir. We have a constant data feed from observatories around the world who are following their movements. There has been no change in their orbits for many days now. They appear to be in some kind of détente, neither prepared to make the first move."

"Obviously, the intelligence reports we received from our American friends are correct. They are indeed combatants. As a result, our actions are being ignored as they focus on each other."

"Yes, sir, all is proceeding as planned."

"What is the status of the American satellites?"

"We have them charted on the screen—the blue lights. They are masked as Global Positioning Satellites. What are a few more, when the Americans have launched so many."

He chuckled. "Only the Americans would use a military payload to hide a military payload. But it seems to me they are not on the same orbit level as the aliens."

"No, sir, that would have been too obvious, I suppose. They are about five thousand miles below them, in a low Earth orbit. Their positioning thrusters are armed and ready."

"Good, and where are we on here?"

"The red dots, sir. This one is the Mir station, and as of today's liftoff from Kazahkstan, we now have two Soyuz ships in space, one docked with the ISS."

"Where are the Americans?"

"The space shuttle will be rendezvousing shortly. A full payload of liquid hydrogen is ready to be transferred."

"All right, I'm going to wait until all vessels dock with Mir, then it will be time to call our friends in Washington."

He went over to sit by the telephone. This was a call that would make history. Whether it would be remembered as a glorious moment or a tragedy was still to be determined.

***

General Beauregard surveyed his crew in the war room. He needed to trust these people due to the uniqueness of the situation. Examining the instrumentation, he almost felt at a loss.

"Lieutenant, brief me on the status here."

"Yes, sir, General. We are currently using both a number of on-Earth telescope systems, and our GPS satellites to track everything in orbit. In deference to our

Russian friends, they are indicated in the red lights, here, here and here. They are of course, the two Soyuz and the International Space Station."

"I see they are all together with a blue light, what is that?"

"That, sir, is the Columbia, our space shuttle, linking up to receive refueling from the Soyuz."

"Damned inconvenient, if you ask me. We should have just sent up our craft with extra fuel. The enemy is going to wonder about our ships meeting like this."

"Then we would have needed to sacrifice the space in our cargo hold."

Yes, Lieutenant, I know. The logistics were all explained to me a long time ago. I just hate to rely on those Russians for anything."

"Remember, General, the six Novator KS-172 AAM-L missiles they gave us as well. The Russians specifically designed them as outer space interceptors."

"Yeah, it's a crying shame we need to use their weaponry. Ya'd think we'd developed something of our own."

"Don't forget, sir, the Extravehicular Mobility Units we provided their crew. I think it's a bit of an even trade, wouldn't you say?"

"I suppose your right. Well, Lieutenant, until I get the call, I'm going to make myself comfortable. Keep me informed."

"Yes, sir."

He made his way over to a station set aside for him. Sitting down, he noticed there wasn't an ashtray. Patting at the package of cigarettes in his pocket, he mused about the good old days when it was okay to smoke indoors.

He leaned back to look at the big screen in the center of the room. The display showed a tactical positioning of the alien ships in a bright yellow, in contrast to the red and blue of the Russian and American vessels.

The secondary screens showed actual live footage of the two alien battle stations. Fore and aft cameras on both the Soyuz and space shuttle made up the balance of the viewers.

"Lieutenant, are our friends in Russia getting all of these feeds?"

"Yes, sir, in fact some of the feeds are from them."

A man approached and handed him a headset. "General, the White House."

Placing the headset on, he listened to his superiors at Strategic Command. "Yes, sir…we're ready…yes, sir."

When the line disconnected, he looked about the room. "All right, everyone, Operation NIMBY is a go. Let's get this show started."

Enough was enough for him. He reached into his pocket and pulled out the cigarettes. He didn't care anymore about the no smoking rules. "Lieutenant, have someone get me an ashtray!"

Lucky Strikes. He hoped they would be.

CHAPTER 39

Captain Pruutoc grew tired of the game. "Tactical, where are the Braannoo vessels now?"

"The Magna still orbits on the opposite side of the planet from the Hammer. The Dragonfly is still circling, further out, at high speed."

"How, by the heavens, do we get them to engage? I cannot enter the atmosphere without threat from above. And yet each time I try and catch them, they elude me. I cannot attack the Magna, as they would blow me apart, and the Hammer is unable to catch them as well. This stalemate must end. I am open to suggestions."

"Captain, I know the armament of the Hammer. After studying the Magna, I feel confident that it is no match for the Hammer, even with the assistance of their frigate."

"That may be true, but should the Hammer look to enter the atmosphere, it will have to slow and its range of fire will be severely curtailed. The Braannoo station would destroy it from space."

"I am not suggesting it enter the atmosphere, merely remain here in orbit until we get back."

"Back from where?"

"From Traanu, sir, with Muurgu reinforcements."

Pruutoc sat down to think on it. Returning empty handed for a second time and asking for reinforcements might be a greater risk to his career than the potential benefit of succeeding. He would have to gamble. "As plausible as that suggestion is, I cannot follow it. No, I think it's time to chance it. Let me know the instant the Dragonfly completes its next flyby. Then order the Hammer to proceed toward the planet. We'll take our chances on timing."

***

"Captain, the Hammer is moving toward the surface."

Hraakoo smiled. "It looks like our ploy has paid off. We out-waited them. Move to a position above them, but make sure they've entered the atmosphere before you do."

He looked at his display. Yes, there could be no doubt as to the Hammer adjusting its orbit. The Emperor showed itself nearby. "Get Vreedoo to come in. I'll need him to engage the Emperor while I attack the Hammer."

"Aye, sir."

"Battle stations everyone. Pulse cannons to full charge. Everyone in battle suits. I'm going to chance surviving their initial assault to get off a closer one of my own. Let's hope their gunners don't aim too well."

Captain Hraakoo belted himself into his seat. He was scared, but exhilarated. Entering a fight against a bigger, tougher opponent would make any Braannoo nervous, but it is moments like this from which glory comes.

***

"And so it begins. Helm, bring us about. We need to engage the Emperor before they enter the atmosphere. At this speed, we'd tear apart."

"Aye, Captain. I have the positioning from tactical now, plotting trajectory, it's going to be close."

Vreedoo pulled on his space suit, but left the helmet off, propped next to his console. "Everyone get ready, my intention is to draw the Emperor away, but it doesn't mean we won't get singed."

All about him, the crew of the Dragonfly donned their outfits. He feared for all of them. The Dragonfly was no match for the Emperor, and everyone aboard knew it, but they all went about preparing all the same. His heart swelled with pride at the display of Braannoo courage.

"Laapitoo dooraad aallissuu!"

A cheer went up from everyone. "Laapitoo dooraad aallissuu!"

He gritted his teeth and gripped his chair. He knew they were in for one wild ride.

***

Captain Droostaad felt confident. *It's about time. How Muurgu command gave Captain Pruutoc lead authority on this mission is beyond me. When this is over and we return to Traanu victorious, I intend to submit a full report as to the man's cowardice.*

"Weapons, when we get within range, target the military installations to completely disable their defenses so the Emperor can quickly extract what we came for. I don't want to be down in the atmosphere for too long."

"We'll need to provide air cover for them as well, sir. The Earthlings have a great many fighter jets to intercept the Emperor."

"Once we start picking them off from above, they'll retreat quickly enough. I doubt their commander is prepared to sacrifice a huge portion of his forces just to defend one facility."

The helm interrupted. "Entering low Earth orbit now, synchronizing our orbit to remain positional over target."

The tactical officer offered his contribution. "Sir, there are a large number of small satellites in the vicinity, I am sending logistics to the gunners now, in case any approach too close."

"Don't the reports state that they are non-military? No, stand off on that order. I want the phase cannons to remain fully charged until needed."

"Aye, sir."

"Onward, for the glory of the Muurgu Empire!"

***

As he pulled on his seventh cigarette, the images on the big screen changed. "Lieutenant, what's going on? I need a report now!"

"General, sir, it appears the enemy craft are nearing the planet."

"Quickly then, son, send commands to the rogues to intercept, arm the warheads on board. Notify the Russians of what we're doing. The Soyuz headed for that ship will need to adjust. How long until detonation?"

"Calculating now, sir, instead of the original eleven minutes, I'm now estimating four minutes until they blow. But that's strictly a guess on my part. As the rogue satellites move out and the enemy space stations move in, they are closing the gap in a hurry."

"What about the second station?"

"It's moving as well. We'll need to act quickly, General, or they will move out of range. The change in their orbit is playing havoc with our scheduling. The shuttle is going to be awful close when detonation occurs."

"Then quickly, son, quickly, order the Columbia to shut down all systems in three minutes, we can't have them caught in the electromagnetic pulse."

"We're on it."

***

Nikolai looked over the schematics of the adaptations to the supply attachment of the Soyuz one more time. Originally designed to bring extra materials to the Mir space station, its current refitting included six Novator KS-172 AAM-L missiles, just like the American shuttle. They should reach their targets in less than twenty seconds from firing. The big question was whether they would get there. All the missiles now featured specialized shielding. Scientists believed the adaptation would provide the best defense against the weapons of these aliens. He thought it seemed funny they didn't use it in their own shielding. American intelligence figured that, plain and simple, the aliens didn't have access to silver.

"Sir, the Americans have moved the countdown forward to less than four minutes!"

"Four minutes! Notify the Soyuz to prepare for the blast."

"Already communicated. Actual countdown now down to three minutes…mark!"

He saw the countdown posted on the screen in front of him. With less than three minutes to go, he felt a sudden urge to get up and pace. It took all of his willpower to stay seated and watch the countdown. Two minutes and counting. It felt as if time was slowing down, and he wondered if it would ever reach zero.

CHAPTER 40

The images of the two alien battle stations disappeared from the screen in a blinding flash of white light. General Beauregard shielded his eyes with his right hand, and lit the cigarette tightly held between his index and middle fingers. The screens next filled with a wash of gray static. "What's happening? Did we destroy them?"

A few more moments passed. The pictures cleared, and the images of both stations re-appeared. Detonations of the eight rogues ranged from seventy-nine to three hundred and fifty-two miles from the targets.

"Initial reports show the Braannoo space station floating freely. They're powerless, the pulse worked. Not so though with the Muurgu. They appear to be up and running."

"I thought the electromagnetic pulse from these explosions would have knocked out their power."

"That was the plan, General. I can only surmise that the Muurgu have learned to shield themselves somehow from the effects of the blast."

"When will the Columbia intercept with the Braannoo station?"

"We're still calculating that. The battle station starting moving before the pulse and its momentum is carrying it toward the other one."

He took another drag on his cigarette. "How long until intercept by the Soyuz?"

"Tough to help you there as well, sir, the Muurgu battle station is now moving toward the Braannoo one.

"Are you telling me that they are all moving together?"

"It appears to be that way, sir."

"God help us all."

Captain Hraakoo sat calmly amid the ensuing panic. The ship, only moments ago in total darkness, slowly came back to life, station by station. He listened as his officers reported in.

"Lighting restored…environmental is back up…engine systems check out, we're doing a startup cycle of the interstellar drive…positional thrusters operational…helm operational, but without the interstellar drive, operating on thrusters only…tactical display waiting for external sensors to complete their readings…laser pulse cannons operational, beginning recharge of cannons now…"

He opened a com link to his engineering section. "Engineering, what just happened?"

"Engineering here. As near as I can guess, we got hit with multiple waves of electromagnetic pulses that totally shorted out our systems. Our backups couldn't handle the overload. The ensuing shock waves bounced us around a bit, but no real damage to the ship."

"Tactical, I'm sitting blind here. How long until you're up and running?"

"Not long now, sir, switching to visual until I get full telemetry."

The blackness of space filled the screen. In one corner, the planet below showed its two faces, half in daylight, the other in night, the twinkling of the lit cities matching the myriad of stars filling the black sky.

"Have you found the Hammer yet? Did she enter the atmosphere?"

"Not yet, sir, I searched using the last projected trajectory, but it isn't there. Maybe the blasts knocked it out of the sky."

Hraakoo looked closely at the screen before him. One of the stars appeared to be quickly growing larger.

"Never mind tactical, I think I've found it. Sound the alarm, battle stations everyone. Cannons, be ready to give me whatever you have. Helm, prepare to fire thrusters on their first volley."

He stood and watched the screen, the Hammer now clearly visible, then spoke in a whisper audible to no one but himself. "The heavens take us all."

***

"Recharge the cannons. Fire again!"

"Should we not try and board her, sir?"

"No, I want that thing destroyed. Our victory will be complete only after we attack the planet and Pruutoc can finish his mission. I want to return to Traanu in all good haste. Towing that scrap heap out of here would double our journey home."

"Cannons recharged, firing again."

The battle proved to be an easy victory for the Hammer and Captain Droostaad. Pruutoc's report of the electromagnetic pulse from the discharge of one of the Earth weapons proved vital in this conflict. Despite the number of blast waves that hit them, the fail safes in the ship's system protected the ship from the complete blackout the Magna suffered. Once his ship returned to being fully operational, tactical informed him of the drifting of the Magna and its lack of an energy signature. He knew instantly what occurred and ordered his helm to intercept the Magna before she could recover.

Surprisingly, the Magna put up a little fight, even managed to hit the Hammer with a full volley, and he lost two laser pulse cannons in that assault. With two others still operational, his ship still served as a deadly force and that was exactly how he intended to apply it.

"Captain, two vessels are approaching our location."

"What? I thought only the Dragonfly remained, what is the other?"

"Actually, sir, neither is the Dragonfly. They appear to be two different Earth vessels of different design."

Droostaad quickly brought the tactical display up on his screen. He could not help but laugh. There were indeed two ships approaching, and from different vectors. But they showed to be no threat. There appeared to be no gun mounts. He suspected they could only intend to fire projectile weapons, which his gunners would pick off long before they reached his ship. "Weapons! Rotate the cannons to greet these silly Earthlings."

"Targets acquired. Waiting for targets to be within range."

He produced a drink pouch and paused to imbibe. "Once in maximum range, shoot them down. We have no time to waste on these fools."

***

Nikolai watch with amazement at the obliteration of the Braannoo space station. The energy weapons of the Muurgu were truly devastating. What remained of the station looked to be no more than a smoldering mass of junk. He doubted whether anyone could have survived in there.

"Get me the Americans. We need them to alter their target to match ours."

"One moment…General Beauregard is now online."

"General, the Braannoo station is no longer a threat. Have the Columbia alter target to match."

"Way ahead of you, Nicky! You should be seeing our new telemetry by now."

Nikolai looked up at the main screen and the new vectoring of the Columbia did indeed show a course correction toward the Muurgu battle station. "We have it. I show thirty-nine seconds to launch perimeter for the Soyuz. The Columbia now at seventy-five."

Once more he watched the countdown, this time to missile launch. American intelligence reported the battle station weapons ranged up to five hundred miles in space. To minimize the risk of the missiles being shot down, launch was planned at five hundred and fifty. Forward momentum would carry the two ships within range of the Muurgu guns scant moments after launch. Everything rode on the shielding protecting them until impact.

"Wait until we reach the perimeter. That way we can launch simultaneously, hopefully more than their defenses can handle."

"As you Americans say, let's give them hell!"

"Hoorah, Nicky boy, hoorah."

CHAPTER 41

When he received notification that the Hammer intended to attack the drifting Magna, he ordered the helm to vector out quickly and plot to intercept the outlying Dragonfly. Tactical reported the Dragonfly now coming toward them. If he could eliminate the Dragonfly, and the Hammer defeat the Magna, then victory over the humans would be assured and with it the ultimate victory over the Braannoo, back home.

When he neared the Dragonfly, it changed course to elude him. "Helm, match their new trajectory. We might actually have a chance at nabbing them this time."

The communications officer interrupted them. "Captain, you should look at this, I am receiving a live feed from the Hammer. Enemy vessels have launched an attack on them."

"What enemy ships? I thought the Hammer destroyed the Magna."

"Human, sir. They have fired what appear to be twelve missiles."

"The Hammer will simply shoot those down and then destroy their ships."

"That's just it, sir. The missiles are surviving the laser cannon pulses."

Pruutoc switch his console to the tactical feed from the Hammer. "That can't be, the fire power of those cannons should obliterate a human missile on contact."

He watched as the missiles approached rapidly. Finally, two winked out, indicating their destruction. That still left ten on an intercept with scant moments before contact. One more winked out, then the remaining nine merged with the tactical display of the Hammer. *How could this be happening? They must be direct hits!* Then the display itself winked out.

"Captain, we have lost contact with the Hammer."

He stood frozen, looking at the blank screen for just a moment. "Quickly, helm, take us to the Hammer. If we lose the station, the mission is lost. Make haste."

"But what about the Dragonfly, it's already on my scope."

"Forget the Dragonfly for now. We must save the Hammer!"

***

Vreedoo checked his tactical display once more. The Emperor was definitely veering off. His miscalculation in trying to enter orbit almost led to a direct confrontation with the Emperor. "Communications, any sound at all out of the Magna?"

"Nothing, Captain. I'm afraid the Magna is lost."

"Use the beacon. Get me a fresh telemetry on the Hammer."

"Yes, sir, it will take the beacon a few moments."

"Helm, move us closer to the planet. I want to be able to enter orbit if the need arises."

"Aye, Captain."

Vreedoo sat at his captain's station, waiting for the telemetry on the Hammer. *What would draw off the Emperor at such a critical moment?* He hoped he would have his answer shortly.

"The telemetry is in from the space buoy. Tactical now up, sir."

The display showed the Hammer with two small ships in close proximity. In fact, one appeared to be docked with the Hammer. "What's going on here? I need eyes on this. What are they, Earth ships?"

"Nothing else makes sense, Captain. We detected no other vessels from Traanu entering the system, Muurgu or Braannoo."

"Helm, plot a course in. If the humans are attacking the Hammer, it may be an opportunity for us."

As the Dragonfly started in toward the planet, he watched the tactical of the two human ships and the Hammer. The docked one appeared to be moving off, along with the other. There was no doubt the Hammer was drifting. The Hammer broke into a number of smaller parts. The humans must have planted an explosive inside.

That left only the Dragonfly and the Emperor.

***

Gone. It was inconceivable that the humans could destroy Muurgu's finest battleship. Yet there it was. The floating mass of space debris that once comprised the Hammer.

His assault team commander appeared on his console. "Captain, I am preparing an away team now to search for survivors. Please advise me if communications receive any helmet chatter while we're out there."

Captain Pruutoc continued to stare at the wreckage.

"Captain?"

He shook his head and turned his attention to the commander. "Negative on that foray. Prepare your men for combat. We're going after the humans who did this."

"Yes, sir."

"Tactical, where are the human ships?"

"They've moved in two different directions, Captain. I suspect they're both looking to drop into the atmosphere. I also suspect one is from the Americans and the other from the Russians."

"Helm, take us to the closest ship as fast as you can. I wish to catch them before they enter the atmosphere. I will make them pay for this insult to the Muurgu Empire."

"Yes, Captain, the nearest is the American ship—trajectory plotted and engaged. We'll be on them in an instant."

"Captain, they're entering the upper atmosphere now."

"I see. Commander, are you ready to fire?"

"Target acquired. We're in range. Give the word."

Pruutoc took one deep breath. "Fire."

The laser pulse flashed across the intervening gap. The ship, already encased in re-entry flame, exploded the instant the beam made contact. The remaining pieces flared brightly as they combusted in the planet's upper atmosphere. Pruutoc allowed a small grim smile to cross his face. "That's one down. Where's the other?"

"Still in orbit, Captain. Plotting trajectory now."

***

"One of the Earth ships has been destroyed, Captain."

"Where is the other?"

"We're receiving our own telemetry, instead of relying on the space buoy. On screen now, sir."

Captain Vreedoo examined the screen on his console. The second Earth vessel was nearly a third of the way around the planet from where the Emperor destroyed the first one. "Are they de-orbiting as well?"

"No, sir, it appears they've pulled out of their descent path. They must recognize the rate the Emperor is gaining on them. I suspect they're planning on making a stand."

"The heavens take them! Making a stand! With what?"

"It appears, Captain, they are exiting the vehicle, and I count four humans now floating in space next to their ship."

Captain Vreedoo stood up and looked about him. His crew all turned and appeared to be watching and waiting for his decision. "Such bravery deserves our support. Helm, set a course to intercept the Emperor. For Braannoo!"

A cheer sounded on the bridge. Though further away, because of their superior speed, the Dragonfly would arrive at almost the same time as the Emperor.

The tactical display showed the gaps closing quickly. What tactic were the humans using? Handheld weapons? At the speeds all three ships were now traveling the pass would seem practically instantaneous. Only computer programed laser weapons firing at the speed of light could stand a chance of a direct hit. Even then, it would be possible to miss. What chance would ordinary men, floating in the cold dark of space, have with simple, handheld weapons?

His head bobbed back in understanding. The gap between all three ships was now frighteningly close, visual contact would be momentary. "Helm! Adjust to pass over the Emperor, roll the Dragonfly that we might be able to fire, don't expose our underside, and, keep the Emperor between us and the humans. Force them to pass closer to the Earth ship."

Captain Vreedoo changed from tactical to visual on his console for the last, brief moments before engagement. No doubt the captain of the Emperor would be targeting the Dragonfly, instead of the humans, saving his pulse charge at maximum for a fatal strike rather than taking all the shots necessary at multiple targets. Now, if all things went as he planned, the Emperor should pass over the humans in the precise moment before engaging his ship.

"Gunner…ready…fire!"

Captain Vreedoo felt as if time froze as he watched both his ship and the Emperor fire simultaneously upon one another, both hoping their beams cut through the other.

The solid beam flashed before Vreedoo's eyes, immediately replaced by a different burst and then gone.

"Helm, hard about. I don't want to get caught from behind."

He felt no tremor. "Engineering, were we hit?"

"No, Captain, they missed us. I don't know how, but they did. Oddly, we were struck by a couple of micrometeorites at the exact moment, but they only pierced the hold. No one got hurt. No real damage."

"Tactical, where's the Emperor? It's not on my screen."

"I...I...it's gone, Captain... it must have exploded!"

The crew cheered, and Vreedoo smiled. "Gunner! Fine job! Remind me to promote you."

"Thank you, sir, but I don't think I did it."

His tactical officer looked over. "What happened, Captain?"

Vreedoo chuckled, and then was overwhelmed by laughter. Once he gained some measure of control, he looked about at the crew. "The humans did it, and quite ingeniously too. Knowing they stood no chance against the laser pulse weapon of the Muurgu ship, and their vessel was probably doomed, they entered space in just their suits and waited for the arrival of the enemy. While they waited, they used their projectile weapons, not to shoot at the Emperor, but to fill the intervening space with...I believe they call them...bullets. They created a micro-meteor storm of kind never seen before—all solid steel. The Emperor passed through it and was punctured so many times, in such an instant that it blew up. By keeping the Emperor between us and the Earth ship, we avoided the most of this storm to live another day."

"So now what, Captain?"

So now we go over to the remains of the Magna and see if chance has favored a survivor or two, then we go home. Our job here is done."

***

Nikolai got up from his seat. It was a tragic thing, the loss of the American space shuttle, the Columbia. After giving General Beauregard his condolences, he realized how he needed to get up and leave. All in all, the mission proved successful, encasing the missiles in mirrors succeeded in their surviving the laser weapons. It was a long walk back to his office where the rest of his cigar waited.

CHAPTER 42

Major Wayne Bucknell finished reading the reports. He rubbed the back of his neck, tense from both the length of the task and the new path in front of him. It was late morning, and he placed both hands firmly on his desk to rise. It was time.

He walked across the courtyard to where Justin Spencer was working. Sure enough, Kraanox was there, along with Rex. "Come on, Kraanox. We need to get Rex back to his kennel."

Justin looked at Wayne. "What's up?"

Wayne stopped in his tracks to look back. "You come too, Justin. You need to get out of the office now and then." Once they were in the yard, he figured, what the hell, and commandeered a Humvee. He opened the back hatch and ordered Rex to climb in. Although it was designed to hold heavy loads, when Rex clambered aboard, the vehicle sank substantially. "Jeez, Rex! You put on more weight?"

He climbed into the driver's seat. Justin took shotgun as Kraanox sat in the back. "Here, put these on, will you?" He handed Kraanox a large toque, sunglasses, and a pair of gloves.

Kraanox accepted the items without comment. Justin appeared bewildered, but likewise said nothing. Wayne put the vehicle into drive and headed for the gate. They were waved through quickly, none of the gate patrol questioning where he was headed or even glancing at his passengers.

The Humvee headed down the road until it reached the cemetery. Pulling in, they found the company chaplain waiting next to an open grave. Moments later, a military procession arrived and carried a coffin to the site. Wayne got out and joined in the proceedings, Justin with him, but he ordered Kraanox and Rex to remain in the vehicle.

After a short, military funeral, the pastor and the others left the field, leaving Wayne and Justin standing alone next to the still un-lowered coffin. He got Kraanox and Rex out of the Humvee and brought them over to the grave. Kraanox looked at the marker. Rex, sniffing, recognized something and whimpered.

Justin looked up from the coffin. "How old was he?"

Wayne placed a hand on Justin's shoulder. "Captain Steven Smeeton was eighty-six, a long, healthy life."

Kraanox reached down, took a flower from the bouquet left by the military and placed it on the coffin lid. "You humans die so young. I calculate that, in your years, I am about one hundred and ten years old, and I am in the prime of my life. I suspect that, if my health holds up, I should live to approximately two hundred and fifty of your years. A long time to spend in captivity."

Wayne stepped forward and hit the lever that lowered the casket into the ground. Rex let loose a howl that could probably be heard for miles. He took that as a cue to load up and leave. The three men and Rex climbed into the Humvee and headed away.

Wayne took them into town to find a local pub. On the way, they stopped at a butcher shop and bought a rear quarter of beef. Throwing it in the back for Rex, he wasn't worried about any mess, Rex would eat everything, including the bones, and lick the place clean.

In the pub, he found a corner booth and ordered lunch. He wanted Kraanox to be as comfortable as possible, and while this unique treat of taking him from the grounds was no doubt a serious violation of his duties, it was one he felt was warranted.

After lunch, Wayne ordered drinks for the three of them—the best brandy this lowly establishment could serve. It wasn't anything fine, but better than standard fare. "Kraanox, I have some news for you. Yesterday, my country, the United States, and Russia launched an attack on two space stations and their accompanying ships, one Muurgu, one Braannoo."

He waited for Kraanox to absorb what he was telling him. Kraanox sipped his brandy and then placed his hands on the table. "Go on."

Wayne reshuffled in his seat. "The mission was a success. Both stations were destroyed, and the Muurgu support ship as well. The remaining Braannoo ship seems to be at the remains of its battle station, performing some type of either rescue or salvation mission. Obviously, a lot of your countrymen were killed yesterday. I felt you should know."

Kraanox picked up his drink and sipped once more. Instead of looking at the major, Kraanox studied the glass in his hand. "As I said to you at the graveyard, I have a lot of years left in your custody. I will get over it."

The three men spent the rest of the afternoon drinking. At one point, a local drunk came in to have a drink at the bar and appeared to be staring at the three of them, most notably, at Kraanox. Finally, his curiosity got the better of him, and he wandered over to the table, his eyes never off Kraanox. "Hello, Major."

Wayne looked up. "Hello, Bobby. Gentlemen, meet Bobby Vance. Bobby, meet Justin Spencer and Kraanox."

Bobby all but ignored the offered handshake from Justin and kept his focus on the Traanusian. "Kraanox? That's an odd name. You foreign?"

Kraanox smiled and offered his hand to shake. "You might say that, though where I come from, it's a popular name. I was named after my great grandfather."

Bobby accepted the handshake, and Wayne tried his best to hide his smile and not snicker. Bobby pulled away quickly. "Well, a pleasure to meet ya. Guess I'll let you gentlemen alone now." Rubbing his hand, he retreated to the bar with one last long look backward.

When Bobby was gone, Wayne burst out laughing. He knew exactly how strong Kraanox's handshake was. The three men resumed drinking, but the talk turned significantly lighter.

Justin spilled a drink. "Oops! Sorry about that, Major. Guess maybe I've had one too many."

"Well, maybe it's time we got going anyway. Come on, I'll give you a lift home."

Once they got back into the Humvee, Rex let them know that he was unhappy at having been left alone so long, and he really needed to go to the bathroom.

Justin waved to the left. "Stop at my mom's. I'll take Rex out back to the field and give him a chance to do his thing."

They got to the house and pulled the truck into the backyard. Rex was quick to get out and make use of the open area behind the fence to relieve himself. Kraanox looked around the backyard and reminisced about his first and second trips to this location. "Tell me, Justin, did you ever get your pails back?"

"What's going on out here?"

The three men turned to face Justin's mother. "Justin Spencer! Why don't you invite your friends in for some coffee?"

Wayne bowed politely. "Thank you, Mrs. Spencer. I suspect we could all use some."

Kraanox went up and took her hand in both of his. "Ah, the infamous Mrs. Spencer. I am an ardent fan of yours."

Justin's mother glanced over at her son. "I take it this is the one you told me about, the fellow who eats all the carrot cake?"

Justin, hands in pockets, nodded. "The same."

Mrs. Spencer placed her glasses on her nose to peer at Kraanox. "You look a bit different. You aren't from

239

around here, are you? Kraanox, that's an odd name. Are you from out of the country?"

"You might say that. I have definitely come from very far away."

At that moment, Rex bounded back into the yard. "Oh my, a monster!"

Justin grabbed hold of Rex to guide him to the truck. "It's... it's a ..."

"It's a clone, Mrs. Spencer, a dinosaur clone. Amazing what science can do these days. Obviously, no one knows about this yet. But we wanted him to get a little fresh air. In discussing where to do it privately, Justin suggested here." Kraanox interjected smoothly.

Rex hopped over to stand next to Mrs. Spencer and give her a lick across the face. "Well, he's certainly not the monster he looks to be, is he?"

Mrs. Spencer led the three men into the house and seated them at the dinner table. In short order, she produced a steaming pot of coffee. Wayne accepted a cup, and Justin appeared to be glad for the stuff after all the alcohol. But Kraanox sniffed at the coffee and politely declined a cup. "I'm sorry, Mrs. Spencer. Coffee is not to my taste. Do you perchance have any brandy?"

Justin slapped his hand to face, and Wayne simply chuckled. Mrs. Spencer picked up the coffee cup and saucer and gave him a bit of a sideways look over her spectacles. "Sorry, no brandy. Perhaps something else might do. Justin, go look through the liquor cabinet. Your father put a bottle of bourbon in there."

Justin got up to rummage through her liquor cabinet and produced an unopened bottle of 12-year-old *Wild Turkey*. He handed his mother the bottle, which she wiped clean and held out in front of her. "I think it's about time to open this. Your father bought this as a gift for you for when you got your first job. Of course, with his death and everything, I completely forgot about it. So much was happening. I know he would be proud of you."

Justin took the bottle reverently from his mother's hand. She produced four glasses and Justin, after some hesitation, opened the bottle and poured. "You too, Mom?"

Mrs. Spencer sat down between Kraanox and Wayne. "Just one, I think, in memory."

Wayne gave his bourbon a little swirl and looked around the table "To Mr. Spencer, then."

Kraanox chimed in. "To Mr. Spencer."

Justin's eyes moistened. He rubbed them with the back of his hand, and then added, "To Dad."

They all drank and then Kraanox reached over, grabbed the bottle and poured another round which Mrs. Spencer declined

. "Wonderful taste this stuff, Major, I think you'll need to commission some of this for the days ahead."

Mrs. Spencer got up to put her glass in the sink. "How long will you be visiting, Mr. Kraanox?"

Kraanox waved his hand in dismissal. "It's just Kraanox, I will be the major's guest for quite some time to come."

Mrs. Spencer bustled about seeing who needed more coffee, of which Justin took full advantage of. "Visiting distant places is nice, but I find it's always nicer when you get back home to your family."

The three men exchanged glances. As the evening wore on, Mrs. Spencer made sandwiches and the bottle of Wild Turkey was soon half-empty.

It was getting late, and Wayne decided it was time to get back to the base. Throughout the day, he maintained contact via his cell, but sooner or later, he needed to show up. "I want to thank you for your hospitality, Mrs. Spencer, but I need to get these boys home."

Back in the Humvee, Wayne felt bothered by Mrs. Spencer's remarks. As they rolled down the road, he suddenly turned down a narrow lane.

Justin looked around. "Where're we going, Major?"

"Just somewhere to sit for a bit and get a little fresh air."

Wayne pulled up to a small, squat building with a sign out front that read: Communications Tower Station #4. The tower loomed behind, with its night lights blinking in the evening sky.

Wayne went over and tried the door, but found it locked. After a few half-hearted attempts to force it with his shoulder, he went around the back of the truck to get Rex out. "Come on, boy, I need you to do something for me."

He led him to the door, and imitated his previous attempt at knocking it down. The door and frame were steel, set in a concrete block building. Nevertheless, once Rex put his mind to it, he ripped the entire door apart and pulled the frame right out of the wall. "Good boy!"

After petting Rex, he turned to Justin. "Okay you're the brains of this outfit. Contact the Braannoo still in space."

The equipment necessary to send a signal was all there, but Justin appeared stymied. "I don't know how to reach them. I need their frequency. It would take too long to broadcast on all frequencies.

Wayne smiled and pulled the alien closer. "Don't worry, Justin. He has what you need, don't you, Kraanox?"

Kraanox blinked a few times. "Well, yes, I do, though I am at a loss to understand how you know."

Major Bucknell found a chair and sat down. "Seriously, Kraanox, you don't think we haven't tracked the beacon satellite your people left years ago. "Now, here is what you're going to say…"

***

In his space suit, Captain Vreedoo worked side by side with his crew in an attempt to breach the exterior of the remnants of the Magna. They managed to speak to two surviving crewmen through their helmet communicators. Just as they completed making an opening for the two trapped Braannoo to escape, his own communicator came to life. "Captain, you need to report in immediately. We are receiving a message from the space buoy."

***

The three men pulled the chairs from inside the communications building out into the yard. Mrs. Spencer insisted they take the bottle of Wild Turkey with them, and Wayne pulled it from the truck and unstopped the bottle. Taking a hard swig, he passed it to Kraanox, who did the same, then passed it to Justin.

In a short while, Wayne's cell began ringing. He picked it up and listened for a moment. "Stand down soldier. I am aware of the situation. Do not, I repeat, do not mobilize forces. Hold the base, no one in or out until I arrive."

It wasn't long until the dark hull of the Braannoo frigate appeared, hovering overhead. A lift lowered and Captain Vreedoo, along with an armed security team, stepped out onto the long grass to confront the trio. Kraanox rose, and turning, gave Wayne a hug. "I am unable to express myself any other way. May the heavens protect you."

Wayne freed himself from Kraanox's grasp. "Hurry up now. Get going. It will be only a few minutes before the F-18's show up, and you'll have to fight your way out. As I said, I release you from your bond. Now, take Rex with you and go!"

243

Kraanox shook Justin's hand, then headed for the lift. "Come, Rex!"

Rex followed halfway, but then stopped and looked back with a whine when Justin did not follow. Justin stepped forward, crouched down and rubbed Rex between the plates on his head. "It's okay, Rex. You go with Kraanox. Go on, be good." Rex shuffled onto the lift, and the others were forced to crush aside to make room for him. Captain Vreedoo placed his hand on Kraanox's forearm, as if to reassure himself that he finally had him. He then put a hand on Rex. "By the heavens, he's huge! He must be the biggest crotuu ever!"

Kraanox reached down to pet Rex. "I'm sure he'll be a hit with all the lady crotuus back home."

The lift went up and the ship floated away at an accelerated pace. As if on cue, two F-18's screamed overhead in pursuit, but it seemed unlikely that they would catch the ever faster moving Traanusian ship.

Major Wayne Bucknell and Chief Scientist Justin Spencer climbed into the Humvee and headed back to the base. They would have to answer a lot of questions.

CHAPTER 43

The Dragonfly entered Traanu space. Kraanox looked through the viewer at his home planet, something he last saw over half his lifetime ago. "Home, I almost can't believe it. It's been so long. I was afraid I wouldn't even recognize it anymore."

Vreedoo leaned over his shoulder. "Even in the comparatively short time I have been gone, I've missed it as well. It will feel good to get my feet back on firm land."

"Excuse me, Captain. Admiral Duurgaan wishes to speak with you."

Vreedoo moved over to his own console. "Captain Vreedoo here."

"Captain, you return home alone, where is the Magna?"

"Destroyed by the Muurgu."

"That is grave news indeed, and the mission, is all lost?"

"Not...exactly, Admiral. I suggest you prepare a meeting of the military council, we will be landing shortly, and I prefer to do my debriefing before all of them."

"As you wish, Captain, though I must confess, it might also denigrate into a prosecution."

"I accept that risk, Admiral. Vreedoo out."

Kraanox rose away from the viewing window. "You didn't tell him I'm aboard, or that the mission a success."

"I am afraid the Muurgu might be intercepting my transmission. After all these years, I'd hate to be shot down when I am so close to returning you home."

***

The shuttle from the spaceport to the military headquarters sped along almost deserted roads. Kraanox looked out and could sense the despair of his people. Houses were unkempt, and many of them appeared empty. Those he did see outside gave long sad stares as they drove by. "Where is everybody?"

The driver looked over his shoulder. "Muurgu bombing runs have managed to penetrate this far inland. Everyone generally stays indoors nowadays."

"This is a sad state of affairs. Why haven't we found a way to repel them?"

The driver took a harder look at Kraanox. "Do I know you? You look familiar. What's the matter with you anyway, you hiding under a rock lately?"

"Something like that."

***

Kraanox and Captain Vreedoo stepped into the council room together. With only a quick glance up from his console, Admiral Duurgaan began the meeting. "Well, Captain, we're all ears. Let's hear your report, though I must admit I am somewhat disappointed to see you here."

Kraanox stepped in front of Vreedoo. "Admiral, it's good to see that you're just as affable as ever."

The admiral looked up again. "My...my liege, is it really you?"

"Commander Kraanox reporting, sir."

"Report...reporting! Never mind that! It's good to see you, my lord." Duurgaan rose from his seat and bowed toward Kraanox, followed by all present.

"Sit down everyone, please. We have urgent business to attend to. First, I need affirmation as to my right of ascension to the throne. Are there to be any challengers?"

"The throne has remained empty since the death of Prince Druummo. The military council has been filling the seat by proxies. It was felt, until the crisis with the Muurgu settled, it would be unwise to begin a search for a new royal. There will be none who stand in your way."

"Then, before I begin, I ask for your oaths of fealty."

Duurgaan looked about. A few murmurs went about the table. After what seemed too long a pause, Duurgaan stood again and crossed his wrists, palms out. "You are my lord and king, and I swear my fealty."

Slowly, all the others around the table rose and swore their oath. Only then did Kraanox feel satisfied to proceed. "Now, the first order of business is to offer our supplication to all other countries of Traanu. All, that is, except for the Muurgu's."

"What do you hope to achieve, Sire?"

"I intend to gain their assistance in defeating the Muurgu Empire."

"But surely, what reason would they have in helping us. They are just as much our enemy as the Muurgu."

"We will share the technology of interstellar flight."

A number of shouts of indignation arose and made Kraanox frown. He slammed his hands down onto the table. "Silence! Do you wish to go the way of the Jaaqqaa?"

The murmurs died away. When he felt that he once again controlled the attention of those in the room, he began anew. "While in captivity on planet Earth, I learned many things about their cultures. They call the eradication of another country genocide, and they have formed a central body to help them in the struggle to enforce coexistence between its various peoples. They call this body the United Nations. Think of how many different peoples of our world are now gone. We have dwindled down to only eight. On Earth, they all still exist by the hundreds!"

Straightening again, he walked around the group. "We will willingly give our knowledge and aid to these other countries. We will form a military alliance in mutual defense. We will create a United Nations of our own to ensure the greater good for all. We will subjugate ourselves to the others to show we hold no delusions of loftiness or superiority. And when they all agree, we will offer membership at the last to the Muurgu, that they too, do not go the way of the Jaaqqaa."

"But my lord, this is madness! We will give all away and end up with nothing. I cannot believe it will work."

"It is for exactly that reason that I cannot entrust the negotiations to any other than myself and Captain Vreedoo here, who has witnessed firsthand the strength of their unity."

Captain Vreedoo stepped forward. "Gentlemen, what our king says is true. I witnessed two nations, once at war with each other, neither with the technology of laser cannons or interstellar space flight, join together to destroy the flagship of the Muurgu space force, the Hammer."

Gasps were followed by silence. Finally, Admiral Duurgaan looked up at Kraanox. "What, Sire, would you have us do?"

Kraanox smiled. "Well good sirs, we shall start with my visitation to the Bruutaan…"

CHAPTER 44

A few totally unproductive months passed. Justin found himself floundering, without direction. He missed the Major, Kraanox and Rex. Staring at his meal while sitting in the commissary, he found himself simply pushing the food around his plate as he did as a kid.

As he sat there, to his surprise, Wayne walked in. "Major! Are you back? I'm glad to see you. How have you been?"

Wayne motioned for Justin to remain seated and found an empty chair to plop himself into. "No Justin, I'm not back. I'm just here to collect my things. The army has decided to drop the charges and let me retire with honor."

Several people stopped by to wish the major all the best, as the two men shared short histories of their lives over the past months. Justin was waiting for television coverage of the Conference on Future Security In Space. The US ambassador to the conference started to give his opening address.

"The United States continues to recognize the common interest of all countries in the exploration and use of outer space for peaceful purposes, as declared in the 1967 Outer Space Treaty. When our astronauts walked on the moon for the first time, they left the message that they "came in peace for all mankind." The United States and other nations have sent unmanned probes to explore outer space and the celestial bodies, to explore the surfaces and atmospheres of the other planets in our solar system in order to understand the environment beyond our world..."

Justin gave Major Bucknell a sideways glance. "Do you think he made it home okay?"

"...The commitment of the United States to the exploration and use of outer space by all nations, for peaceful purposes and for the benefit of humanity, is clear. But the peaceful exploration and use of space obviously does not rule out activities in pursuit of national security goals..."

Wayne looked up to listen for a moment. "Yes, I think he made it home okay."

"...Free access to space and the use of space by space-faring nations are central to the preservation of peace and the protection of civil, commercial and security interests. The United States sees no justification for limitations on the right of sovereign nations to acquire all forms of information from space..."

Justin turned in his seat so that he could more squarely face Major Bucknell, while still keeping an eye on the screen. "Do you think they will come back someday? Either the Braannoo or the Muurgu? Will the Earth be under attack once again? Or will they come in peace?"

"...Most important, however, is the Outer Space Treaty, to which the United States remains firmly committed. ..."

Wayne folded his hands under his chin. "Something tells me we have seen the last of them for quite some time. The joint effort of the United States and Russia in eliminating the previous threat will make them think twice about whether it's worth the trouble."

"...The United States is committed, through its national space policy, to ensuring that exploration and use

of outer space remain open to all nations for peaceful purposes and for the benefit of all humanity ..."

Justin returned to his previous position, facing the screen and speaking sideways to the Major. "I hope you're right. I am going to miss them, though, both Kraanox and Rex. Perhaps someday I'll see them again. I am glad we beat them though. Can you imagine what would have happened if we lost?"

Major Bucknell unfolded his hands to reach across and clasp Justin's shoulder. "The thing to remember is that we did win. And we won because, whether American or Russian, we shared a commonality that united us. We are human. Born and bred on the planet Earth, and prepared to defend it."

".... The reality is that US-Russian relations are broad and strong enough to weather this sort of disagreement. As the Moscow Summit showed, it is a new and better day..."

Wayne rose from his chair and nodded from Justin to the television. "Just as he says, the cold war and the space race are over. Now the time has come for the next step together. Something like what you are trying to achieve. All in all, I am leaving things in good hands. I wish you well." Wayne shook his hand and headed out the door. Justin had risen to shake Wayne's hand, and still stood as he turned back to the television one more time.

"...The United States continues to recognize the common interest of all mankind in the furtherance of the exploration and use of outer space for peaceful purposes, as declared in the 1967 Outer Space Treaty. We see no need for further outer space treaties. We should move on to

other themes that address immediate and serious threats to mankind."

The crowd in the commissary was mostly oblivious to what just aired. Justin slowly scanned the entire room and finished at the television again, as the US Ambassador received his standing ovation. Justin smiled to himself, and thought, how right you are!

CHAPTER 45

A lot of years, a long struggle, but finally Justin would know the answer. He sat in the tower looking out at the open field. About five hundred yards away, the prototype rested on the grass. "Power up."

His staff were all about watching their monitors, making sure their data telemetry feed remained constant. Out on the field, there was no sound to indicate anything operating. The prototype remained dormant. He'd pulled a lot of strings for the young captain seated in the prototype to be the first to attempt piloting it.

"Power's on, Dad. Everything seems a-okay."

"That's Dr. Spencer to you. Don't forget it. I thought your mother taught you better manners."

A sharp elbow in the ribs reminded him his wife sat by his side. "As if you had nothing to do with it."

He turned to her. "Now, Suzie, this is a big day for me. Just because I want you here to share it, doesn't mean you get to be in charge."

"You tell him, Mom!"

"Now that's enough, let's have a little decorum here."

"Sorry, Da...Dr. Spencer. I'm ready to go through my checklist, now."

Together, along with everyone else who worked on the project, they went through the checklist, item by item. When all indicators showed green, the senior technician gave Justin the thumbs up. "Okay then, Captain, just as we rehearsed, lock on to the gravitational waves. Let's try first things first, getting it airborne."

"Locking on now. Everything is a go. Give the word."

"All right, let's start simply. Five feet up, no more."

"Five feet up, trajectory set, initiating now!"

The prototype jumped up the five feet and stayed there, hovering silently over the lawn. A chorus of cheers filled the room--the test a success. "Congratulations, Captain. You're the first man to pilot an interstellar drive system."

Suzie leaned in. "Way to go, Son!"

"Thanks Mom, uh, I mean, Mrs. Spencer."

Justin turned and received a big hug and kiss from his wife. "You did it, honey."

The applause in the room continued, and Justin rose to acknowledge the accolade. It would be only a matter of time now, until they could build their first interstellar space ship.

"Captain Spencer to control. Request permission to take her for a spin."

"Easy as it goes, Captain."

"Easy as it goes, yes, sir."

The prototype shot upward and cruised around the practice field with ease. Justin watched out the window for a few maneuvers. "How does the control of the craft feel?"

"Just two words to describe it, sir. Yee Haw!"

CHAPTER 46

In the many years since his return, a lot of changes altered the political landscape of the planet.

The first negotiations proved to be the toughest, but in the end, the Bruutaan came to terms with him and the Braannoo. When word reached the other lands, they lined up quickly to join the new consortium of aligned nations. None of them wanted to miss out on receiving the interstellar technology.

When all the other countries aligned under the new United Nations of Traanu, the Muurgu Empire resisted joining. Privately, the other nations were all pleased, as the Muurgu were the friend to none. The empire's quest of world domination came to an abrupt end when the combined armies of the alliance soundly defeated them in the field of battle. It took all of his negotiating skills to stop these nations from proceeding onto Muurgu soil in an attempt to wipe them out.

In the following years, internal discontent in the Muurgu Empire led to embitterment and finally revolt. Their economy collapsed, and its people were near starvation. The first to lend aid were the Braannoo, much to the surprise of the others. A new government formed in Muurgu, set to a format provided by Kraanox—a democracy.

The world of Traanu was, for the first time in a long time, at peace.

***

Kraanox often found enjoyment when visiting the restored gardens and pools of the rebuilt palace. A page notified him of a request for an audience. Rather than return to his seat of authority, he invited the guests to visit him where he was. This was the pool his uncle most favored, and the memory still strong in his mind.

Vreedoo, now his personal advisor, approached with the delegation behind him. "Your majesty, the visitors from Earth."

He rose from where he was lounging and used the English language he learned long ago. "Gentlemen! I am pleased to welcome you to Braannoo."

A tall, handsome, young human stepped forward. "Greetings from Earth, your Majesty, I have a number of issues to discuss with you. But first, please allow me to honor our visit with a few tokens of goodwill. My mission leader has sent you these gifts."

The fellow handed over a package and two boxes. With the package was a letter Kraanox opened first.

Dear Kraanox,

I hope you enjoy the gifts. The package contains all the necessary seeds for you to one day have the ingredients you need to make your own. I have enclosed my mother's secret recipe. Hoping all is well. Justin

PS: I have sent you one last one. I made it myself. Enjoy.

Kraanox bent to the first box and opened it to discover a fresh carrot cake. "It's still fresh! And cold!"

The young human clasped his hands behind his back. "Grave is the day I let that spoil on the trip. We ordered a refrigeration unit specially built for that thing."

He looked up quickly to stare at the young Earthling. "What did you say your name was?"

Bending to open the second box, the young man held it up for Kraanox to see. "My name is Captain Steven Bucknell, your Majesty. I smuggled this gift on board myself. My grandfather said you'd like it."

Inside were twelve bottles of *Wild Turkey*!

OTHER NOVELS by MICHAEL DRAKICH

THE BROTHERHOOD OF PIAXIA

Years have passed since the overthrow of the monarchy by the Brotherhood of Warlocks and they rule Piaxia in peaceful accord. But now forces are at work to disrupt this rule from outside the Brotherhood as well as within! In the border town of Rok, a young warlock acolyte, Tarlok and his older brother, Savan, captain of the guard, become embroiled in the machinations of dominance. While in the capital city, Tessia, the daughter of Piaxia's most influential merchant, begins a journey of survival. Follow the three as their paths intertwine, with members of the Brotherhood in pursuit and the powerful merchant's guild manipulating the populace for their own ends.

Great, well-rounded characters? Magic running rampant? A lost princess? Yes, this book has it all. – tHe crooked WorD

If you love fantasy that mixes magic, lost royalty, sacrifices, heroes, and strong characters, I would suggest The Brotherhood of Piaxia. – Captivated Reading

The Brotherhood of Piaxia is what it wants to be - a real entertaining fantasy story. It comes along with more characters than you normally get but a lot less then you meet in a famous series you can watch at HBO. It has definitely more magic than a famous fantasy trilogy you could see in cinemas. There is less blood and gore than in a book with a title how to serve a drink. It is also a book which does not drown in romance. For me is a book which you like to read when you want to have a well dosed mix of well-known books. Or in simple words The Brotherhood of Piaxia is like the espresso you enjoy after a good meal. – Edi's Book Lighthouse

LEST THE DEW RUST THEM

Terrorism in America has a new game…decapitations!

Homeland Security Director Robert Grimmson faces the task of catching five men in New York City. They call themselves the Sword Masters with a single-minded plan of terror through decapitations.

Barely has the task begun when a new arrival at JFK is a man importing thousands of swords! Alexander Suten-Mdjai is a trainer in the deadly art of swordsmanship and Robert cannot help but believe there is a connection between him and the Sword Masters.

As he goes about the task, each step in his search is made more difficult through the interference of politicians, the media and his own government.

Robert's examination constantly draws him back to Alexander who regales him with a tale of swordsmanship from his lineage featuring events of mankind's bloody past and often oddly having a connection to the case before him.

With the clock ticking as New York collapses into a deep panic, he must catch the Sword Masters before it is too late!

This is one of the best suspense thrillers I have read in a long time. – Voracious Reader

This book was really, really good. It was action packed from beginning to end. I could hardly wait to finish and see what would happen. – The Book Worm

This entire book was nothing but entertaining. I have never read a crime-type book that I liked and this book was so good that it's going on my favorite's shelf. – Angels In The Underworld

THE INFINITE WITHIN

Going into outer space calls to Astronaut Brooke Jones like the sirens of old, and when the chance to be part of the first manned mission to Mars arises, she is ecstatic. But little does she know the fate that awaits her on the surface of the red planet or the results of her encounter when she gets back to Earth.

This book is very entertaining. It will grab hold of you, and keep poking at you to finish it. I would recommend this story to science fiction readers that enjoy something a little different. This will not give you the highs of the shoot-em-up in outer space. It takes place on earth, for the most part. It could be a real story and has enough elements to be good fiction. I look forward to reading more by this author. – Charles Kravetz – Keeping Dreams

I loved the uniqueness of the story and the high-caliber action scenes. The adventure and the sense of awe kept me reading late into wee hours. – Laurie Jenkins – Laurie's Thoughts and Reviews

Wow. First off I'll start by saying the book was amazing. In the beginning I was a little iffy about the whole deal then the book got better, and better, and obviously better. I was surprised at the level of detail in the storytelling – Ezekiel Carsella – Books N Tech

DEMON STONES

It's been almost a hundred years since warlock meddling freed the demons from their underground domain. Their eventual capture has encased them in large stones across all the lands. They became known as the *demon stones*.

Over time, the truth of their imprisonment devolved into legend and tales to frighten children.

Now, the seven kingdoms are in upheaval. The demon stones are being opened and the vile creatures once more roam the land. War has broken open between realms as the fingers of accusation are pointed.

Caught in the middle is Gar Murdach, a farm boy who recently passed the age of ascension of sixteen marking him as a man, and his younger sister, Darlee, as they both struggle in their separate ways to escape the horrors wrought by the demons and the war that swarms round them.

Sometimes a trip into a fantasy world, filled with the magic of the mind is a good place to go, add the intense story line, the detailed world and a young hero who clearly started out WAY out of his league and it becomes clear that sometimes fantasy characters mirror reality. – Diane at Tome Tender (Amazon Top 500 Reviewer)

Die-hard fantasy fans, particularly those who like a bit of high fantasy, will adore this book just as I did. – Kyra – The Review List

I would recommend this book to those who enjoy a good fantasy which is well-written and easy to follow. Well done, Mr. Drakich! – S. A. Molteni – And So It Begins…

I AM

Genius, wealthy and life regenerated, Adam Spenceworth is living the dream aboard his custom spaceship run by Mum, his first designed AI, protected by Gort, his first robot, and occupied by Eve, his sexbot. With each regeneration he returns to start over as a twenty-five-year-old man ready to enjoy the pleasures of his success. What could go wrong? Except, maybe, planetary wars, territorial space battles, alien invasions, and the disturbing fact that each regeneration is taking exponentially longer than the one before bringing him into one galactic crisis after another. A frolicking space drama filled with references sure to strike home with any science fiction aficionado.

Michael Drakich's I Am is a brilliant space opera about one man's journey through eons of time in a futuristic world where worlds and galaxies collide in wat, join in peace, and may only survive through Artificial Intelligence that almost believes it is alive.
Diane @ Tome Tender Book Blog – Top 500 Amazon Reviewer

One of the top five independent author'd kooks of all time.
Lilyn @ sciFiandScary, Reviewing Both Independent and Traditionally Published Works

Everything I love about science fiction was in this book. The aliens, the robots, the advanced technology, and the humor make this book an enjoyable and engaging read from start to finish.
Tori@ Tori Lex, Judging Books Beyond The Cover

Overall, the story meets all my criteria for an excellent science fiction. It's epic scale, rich world, plausible futures, and focus on the people (both organic and not) make this one for the bookshelves, definitely worthy of reading over and over again. I'd highly recommend this to folks who love science fiction, hard, epic, space opera and otherwise.
Patricia @ Pure Textuality, Book Reviews, News & Everything In Between

ASSASSINS OF RIAZ

In Riaz, the profession of assassin is an honored one. Hired throughout the other eight realms, their use of powerful magic to complete assignments makes them a valuable commodity. When a regional trade negotiation is scheduled in their capital city of Lymos, the demand for the skills of the assassins is sure to change the dynamic of the meetings. Caught in the maelstrom of political intrigue is young Kero, the ward of the assassin lord. He's joined by Darlee, a girl from Sechland with her own magical powers, and Prince Brumaine of Morica, as each of them struggle to navigate the affair in their own way. Will old animosities prevail, or can new alliances alter the path toward all out war?

Michael Drakich writes for all ages and brings a tale to life that will entice any reader who looks for engaging storytelling, characters to admire or detest and a richly detailed plot that unfolds with mind-boggling energy! Easy to read, hard to put down, highly recommended reading that never lets up, page after page!
Diane @ Tome Tender Book Blog – Top 500 Amazon Reviewer

One of the things I liked about the story is that it feels bigger than it is. Feels like part of a greater story, even though it wraps up nicely in one volume. I got the impression of a greater world, an important aspect in any epic fantasy.
Trish @ Pure Textuality Book Reviews, News & Everything In Between

REQUIEM FOR A GENOCIDE

JAK037 is a warbot.

Built for the sole purpose of killing the enemies of Dalrea, he has survived longer than any other and is the last of his generation still in operation. Being the last JAK model, he is simply referred to as Jak, no unit number necessary. When word comes of a treaty with their nemesis, Carthia, Jak holds out hope his final days will be ones without war. It is with disappointment he learns the treaty is so a new front can be opened against a race of settlers from another world.

Humans.

In the coming conflict, can Jak and his comrades of aged warbots survive against an enemy with superior technology? In a mission to wipe out the settlers, will it succeed? Or will Jak's days finally be numbered. With the aid of a human child, a seven-year-old girl named Hannah, Jak hopes to end the war and save his people from what he believes is a looming disaster. It's a race where not only humans but Carthians, Dalreans, robotic laws, and his own failing body all conspire to stop him.

The book is certainly science fiction, but in the contemporary mode, where the emphasis is more on the characters and the situation, and less on the intricacies of the science. At a high level, the story is nicely structured, with a solid introduction, a rapidly paced and logically developing story, and a satisfying conclusion. The author has a straightforward writing style that makes the book a surprisingly fast read, particularly given the level of detail of some of the scenes. 5 STARS – Jack Kuhn, Author of the scifi Tomorrow's Wilderness series.

The first- "person" narrative gives us a chance to see into JAK's mind, and what I loved most about the book was his intelligent and down-to-earth philosophical musing about things like war, ethics, free will, and life in general. 5 STARS -Angie Boyter, Amazon Vine Voice ranked in the top 1000 of Amazon's ranked reviewers.